Two Wings to Hide My Face

Penny Mickelbury

Bywater
BOOKS

2023

Bywater Books

Copyright © 2023 Penny Mickelbury

Print ISBN: 978-1-61294-277-3

Bywater Books First Edition: December 2023

Printed in the United States of America on acid-free paper.

Cover design by TreeHouse Studio

Bywater Books
PO Box 3671
Ann Arbor MI 48106-3671

www.bywaterbooks.com

This book is dedicated to American women who lived—and occasionally died—in pursuit of freedom one hundred years *after* the women portrayed in this book lived and faced death in pursuit of their freedom.

The same freedom and some of the same songs.

For Sojourner Truth, Harriet Tubman, and Ida B. Wells:

"Wade in the water,
wade in the water children,
wade in the water,
God's gonna trouble the water."

For Ella Baker, Daisy Bates, Claudette Austin Colvin, Dorothy Foreman Cotton, Fannie Lou Hamer, Diane Nash, Rosa Parks, and Viola Liuzzo.

"We who believe in freedom will not rest until it comes."
—Ella Josephine Baker

CHAPTER ONE

Hezekiah English was neither afraid of nor discomfited by the dark. Not even in the middle of a cemetery on a moonless night, which, if the young doctors in the hospital could be believed, was unusual for those of his kind. They laughed and discussed him as if his ears could not hear their words or their loud laughter: *Niggers are more terrified of the dark than they are of us! This one now, he's lasted the longest! Only nigger I've ever seen didn't piss himself at the thought of going to the cemetery at midnight! Maybe because he's as tall as a tree and every bit as black as the night itself.* More than unafraid of the dark, Hezekiah felt one with it, for the dark of the night did not hate the dark of his skin. The silly young doctors were right about at least one thing.

Not only was he unafraid of the dark, he had no fear of dead people or their spirits, which he didn't believe existed but which others of his kind did—again according to the young doctors. *All of them fear ghosts and spirits, too! They call them haints, of all things, and I don't think they mean the Father, Son, and Holy Ghost!* The combination of the ways in which Hezekiah was unlike others of his kind made him well suited for the illegal—and many of his kind would say immoral—job he would perform this night: the theft of the newly buried body of the newly dead

1

Henry Goins from his newly dug grave.

The doctors at the medical school paid Hezekiah handsomely to bring them the undecomposed bodies of Black men, though Hezekiah had no way of knowing that what they paid him was much less than they would be required to pay to obtain fresh cadavers through legal means. He cared only that it was more than he could otherwise earn at any job available to a Black man in Philadelphia in the summer of 1859, especially a Black man who, despite his years in Philadelphia, retained many of the behaviors of the African, to say nothing of the demeanor and appearance of one.

Hezekiah had just begun to dig when he was hit from behind with such force that, dazed, he fell to his knees. Before he could gather his wits sufficiently to wonder what was happening to him, he was hit again and pounced upon whilst being yelled at and cursed. Instinct told him that it would be both foolish and dangerous to resist. Hands and feet tightly bound, he was hauled upright where he towered above his two captors. The light from the kerosene lantern held to his face blinded him. He squeezed his eyes tightly shut and let his body go limp so suddenly that the men holding him on either side almost dropped him. Angered, they tightened their grip, drawing him closer to them.

"Dear God, he stinks!" one of them exclaimed.

"Hold your breath then, until we can put him down!" the other one muttered, as they stumbled forward more quickly, dragging him the length of the cemetery and causing him pain as his long, thin body bumped and bounced against the gravestones along the way to the road, though he would never give them the satisfaction of acknowledging how much pain they caused him. Hezekiah knew they had reached the road when the dragging stopped but he was not prepared for the suddenness with which they lifted, swung, and tossed him into the back of a cart as if he weighed no more than a bag of flour. He landed hard.

"Ah! Ah! Ah!" Hezekiah exclaimed.

"I wish we could give you more pain!" one of the men shouted at him. "Do you know how much pain your filthy work has brought to good and decent people?"

"He'll not answer you," the other man said grimly. "He doesn't talk to the likes of us."

"Like him being born across the waters makes him better than we who're born here!"

"I still don't believe he was born over yonder. The white men stopped that slaving way long time ago."

"I know they were 'spozed to stop, but you know how they are." Disgust dripped from his words, tempered by what came next: "But he was just a boy when he come. His ma died on the crossing and he was left by hisself. And drive the horses faster if you please. Blow some of that stink away!"

Hezekiah went rigid. And he was so angry he almost spoke. How could they know these things about him? No one knew his truth. He had told no one. He was certain he didn't know these men and yet they knew the deepest within parts of himself. But how could they?

"I don't care a damn how he came here, or when. I just care that he steals the bodies of our dead men and I dearly want to know why!"

"Whatever the reason you can believe there's a white man behind it."

"But what reason could there be? They cause us plenty enough suffering when we're alive. What can they do to us when we're dead? Bring us back to life and kill us again?"

Hezekiah didn't hear the response because the cart now moved along the cobblestone road and the clip-clop of the horse hooves and the rattle of the metal wheels on the stones obliterated their voices. Though still unnerved by their knowledge of his past, Hezekiah's thoughts were not on his captors but on how he could continue this night's interrupted mission and earn the payment for its completion. Maybe if he could get free of them

3

quickly enough, he could return to the cemetery . . . surely they wouldn't expect that of him after being caught.

The perspiration pouring from Hezekiah was not all due to the heat from the blacksmith's furnace that he hung above by his shackled wrists: He was actually afraid. He expected righteous indignation and pious lectures from these men but not torture. Though he would never give them the satisfaction of showing fear—or even anger—he was deeply shocked and unnerved. These men believed in and prayed to a God they had no proof existed, and they forgave their enemies as taught by the black book they held so dear—the same book the white men held so dear. They didn't torture them.

"You will tell us why you desecrate the bodies of Black men, or you will tell the fire," the oldest of the men said quietly, tossing yet another handful of pipe tobacco into the flames of the forge.

Hezekiah did not respond, but he looked closely at the man. He was certain he did not know him yet there was the hint of some vague familiarity.

"Just drop him in, save the devil the trouble of having to burn him when he gets to hell," one of the men, a cripple, growled at him, as if a menacing tone of voice was frightening. Hezekiah stared into the eyes staring at him. Six pairs of them. Two were filled with hatred—those of the two men who brought him here. The eyes of the others reflected a mixture of confusion, wariness, disbelief, and some other thing Hezekiah didn't recognize but that he knew was not conciliatory. Then he averted his eyes and observed the faces without making eye contact. He didn't want them to realize that his orbs held nothing. No emotion or feeling at all. He knew they wouldn't understand. He sometimes didn't understand himself why he allowed his African-ness to keep him separate from people who were like him except for the place of their birth, or of his. Perhaps that one difference was sufficient to require their separation.

After the initial shock of his capture, and the surprise of the unexpected torture, he returned his internal self to its usual emotionless state. He had no feeling about the bodies he stole from their graves, nor did he have feelings about the white doctors who paid for his desecration of those graves, or about the research they conducted on the black corpses—whatever the research was and whatever its purpose. This inside nothingness kept him safe. Kept him alive. Kept him isolated and alone. He was different from them; they were different from him.

Hearing his captors discuss him, hearing their knowledge of his past, pulled emotion from deep within him and almost brought it to the surface. It made him realize how absolutely alone he was. How could they know things about him when he didn't know them and knew nothing about them? Though one man, the older one . . . yes, there was a familiarity . . . but no knowledge. Hezekiah did not know this man. "He seems unafraid of fire," a small man at the rear of the crowd said. "Perhaps it is water that he respects."

Hezekiah looked closely at this man, blinking sweat from his eyes to see clearly, and what he saw was a woman in men's clothing. That did not surprise him. Many women—Black ones as well as white ones—hid themselves in men's clothing when away from their homes, trying, hoping to provide some protection from the lawlessness that was more and more prevalent in the streets of Philadelphia, especially in the poor and working-class sections of the city, and most especially in the Colored sections. What did surprise Hezekiah, however, was the deference the men paid her. They all watched her and waited for her to speak further, and when she did, her words horrified him.

"Take him to the docks, bound and gagged and crated as cargo, for the journey to Liverpool—"

"NO!" Hezekiah screamed, suddenly freezing and shivering,

5

no matter that he was still dangling mere feet above the smithy's forge, almost gagging on the acrid smoke of the pipe tobacco the men continually fed into the fire, though having no understanding of the reason for their action.

"Then you will tell us why you steal the bodies of Colored men from their graves, or you will be in the hold of a packet ship before dawn breaks," said the man standing beside the woman who was dressed as a man, the one Hezekiah found familiar though he didn't know why or from where.

"Because they pay me!" Hezekiah screamed. "They pay me for each body I bring them!"

"Who pays you?"

"The doctors at the hospital."

That information silenced and stilled everyone for a moment. A brief one. "Why?" asked the woman disguised as a man.

"They study them, and do experiments—"

"Why!" thundered a muscular man who pushed his way to the front of the group. "And you'll answer or I'll bind and crate you and throw you into the hold of a Liverpool-bound packet ship myself." And Jack Juniper, former seaman, was more than capable of making good on the threat. Of making it a promise.

One look at this man and Hezekiah knew he spoke the truth, so he told his captors everything he knew, all of it overheard from the conversations the doctors and medical students had with each other, not because they shared information with him. They did not. They told him only when they wanted a body delivered to the back door of the medical college, and because he never knew when that would be, Hezekiah made it his business to know who died when, and where the body was laid to rest. And how did he know when a corpse was required? They sent a messenger to his rooming house, and that was another bit of knowledge about him that he didn't know how or why these strangers possessed.

"What do we do with him now?" Arthur, the crippled man,

growled, his voice further roughened by the acrid smoke.

"What do you mean?" William responded.

"Do you trust him not to be robbing graves tomorrow night is what I mean?" Arthur growled. And there was no response because no one trusted or believed that Hezekiah English had learned anything from this night's experience except that it was best to avoid getting caught. "Anyway," Arthur continued, "his landlady put his belongings out on the street when he left tonight to do his grave-robbing—"

Hezekiah shrieked and ended his silence. He could not stop talking. Words exploded from his mouth as if lit by an inner fire, but his audience may as well have been deaf for all they understood because Hezekiah spoke, moaned, shouted, and cried in the language of the Wolof people of his homeland, and it was the same three phrases over and over, representing everything he remembered of his native tongue. After all, he hadn't heard the language since he was eight years old and the three phrases he uttered repeatedly now were the ones his mother spoke, moaned, shouted and cried until breath left her and the ship's captain, Hezekiah Borders, had her thrown overboard. And though Hezekiah remembered the phrases, he did not remember—if he had ever known—their meaning.

"He did that when he first came to my mother," William said. "Repeated the same words over and over, but we never knew what they meant." He'd spoken quietly, though loud enough to be heard over Hezekiah's wailing, and Hezekiah heard him and immediately quieted. Now he knew who this man was. He'd been a very young man when Carrie Tillman took in the African child whose mother had died on the brutal journey across the Atlantic.

"You beat me!" Hezekiah accused William, as if the beating had occurred yesterday.

"I would have killed you if my mother hadn't stopped me," William replied in his usual matter-of-fact tone. "You struck her and she was merely trying to help you."

The two men regarded each other across the years of their memories and the circumstances of their lives. William Tillman, the freeborn son of a slave woman whose freeborn husband purchased her freedom, was a blacksmith who owned the place where they were gathered. The place where the Africa-born man, a son of the Wolof people of The Gambia, hung by his shackled wrists above the forge, a man who was not a slave because the slave ship's captain had changed his mind and his heart about slavery and had given the child his freedom when the ship reached the Port of Philadelphia those many years ago.

"Genie?" William asked. "What do you think?"

She looked hard at Hezekiah, who refused to meet her gaze. She shrugged. "Maybe putting him on a ship is the best—"

"No!" Hezekiah cried out in the language of the people whose name he'd taken, and the only language he knew how to speak. "Not that! Please!"

"Then what, Mr. English, in light of your disregard for us?" she replied calmly. Too calmly. And those who knew her recognized the danger sign: When she became still and silent, her formidable rage lurked just beneath the surface of her beautiful face. And she was beautiful, Hezekiah thought, as if she could be one of the Senegal tribeswomen.

Hezekiah shifted his gaze away from Genie and did not answer her.

"You refuse even the courtesy of a reply—"

Uncharacteristically, Arthur interrupted her. "Turn him over to one of them slave catchers you see everywhere you look these days."

"I never do be a slave!" Hezekiah cried.

Genie and Jack were the only ones of their group who had been slaves and it was not a fate they'd wish on anyone, not even on the likes of Hezekiah English.

"Maybe Jack could find a use for him?" William posed the

question and watched Jack Juniper's face as he considered the possibility, though only briefly.

He shook his head. "His smell would kill my business," he said with a grin that was more of a grimace, and that facial expression spread among the gathered. Except for Hezekiah.

"What mean you for my smell? And what for landlady? What is smell?"

"The smell of death, man." Arthur growled. "You smell like death."

Hezekiah twitched as if he'd been hit. Then a series of emotions roamed his countenance, each expression the result of a thought or a memory. He finally understood that people moved away from him or avoided him because he smelled like death, not because he was an African and as black as the night and as tall as a tree. He hung his head in shame.

"What do the doctors pay you for the stolen corpses?" Jack asked, and when Hezekiah told him eight dollars a month, Jack shook his head. "I won't pay you that, but I will give you a place to sleep and food to eat if you work right. And a place to bathe."

"Well, sir?" Genie looked up at Hezekiah. "What will you do?"

Hezekiah's head still hung, but he nodded and eventually looked up. "What be the work I do for this man?"

"I make shoes," Jack replied. "You will help me in my shop. You will do whatever needs doing."

Hezekiah inhaled deeply. "You make shoes for the Black peoples?" And when Jack nodded, he asked, "I learn how to make shoes?"

But it was William who spoke. "No more stealing the bodies of the dead, Mr. English. Not ever again. Do you understand?"

Hezekiah nodded. "I do. I do understand. Yes."

"Then I think we can let him down," William said as Arthur began working the pulleys that would swing Hezekiah away from the forge and down to the ground. Arthur held his breath as he unbound and released the newly contrite man. William gave instructions for "washing away the death stink" and Genie left to get clean clothes for him.

"And Arthur," William said, "don't burn his things. Put 'em in a flour sack with lots of river rocks and sink 'em. Including all the hair." Then he looked steadily at Hezekiah until the man met his eyes: "You are to shave all the hair from every part of your body, Mr. English. *All* the hair from *every* part. Do you understand?"

At Hezekiah's confused expression, William pointed and both men averted their eyes in embarrassment. William thanked the two men responsible for ending the grave desecrations and asked if they'd help Arthur manage Hezekiah's cleaning. They agreed, and William thanked them again, adding, "Dinner for you and your families at Joe Joseph's Family Restaurant as my guests."

Then William and Jack Juniper were alone in the forge room, but neither man could find words to express his feelings about the very unusual and unexpected event they had just witnessed, and both men hoped that "the African" could make a success of his new employment. "Maybe having someone teach him how to be—"

"He didn't just come off that ship from Africa last week, William."

"I know, Jack." William rubbed the stubble on his face. Neither man had had time to shave this morning. "But the man didn't know he stank of death, and he still doesn't talk easily. Those things tell me he doesn't have people close to him."

Jack nodded and rubbed the stubble on his own face, controlling the smile that threatened his composure as he thought how much his Margaret liked that stubble. William most certainly would not understand a smile at such a serious moment.

Genie's quick return from her place of business made further conversation unnecessary, and that was good since she said she hadn't the time to talk. She held several items of men's clothing, which she gave to William. "I have work this morning with Ezra and I'd like to get a bit more sleep before embarking."

Jack's scowl spoke volumes as his concern for his new and quickly cherished friend, Eugenia Oliver, replaced thoughts of his beloved Margaret. Jack liked Ezra MacKaye well enough but he liked his friend Eugenia Oliver much more. "I do hope Ezra will not be placing you in any danger, Genie."

She shook her head. "I assure you, Jack, that I am in no frame of mind for danger."

William harrumphed. He knew Genie longer and better than anyone. "Where you and Ezra are concerned, Eugenia, danger lurks, your frame of mind notwithstanding."

As quickly as the protest rose in her, Genie tamped it down. There was truth in his words. Ezra MacKaye, the former Pinkerton's agent and current Private Inquiry agent, and Eugenia Oliver, the runaway slave and current dress and hat shop owner, had joined forces on several occasions, and while they produced successful outcomes, the danger they faced was considerable. Once, Ezra had been beaten nearly to death while helping Genie protect a Harriet Tubman safe house, and once, Genie almost came face-to-face with a member of the family who'd owned her and her family on the Maryland plantation where she was born. Though she had escaped many years ago as a young girl, the memory of slavery and her escape from it remained ever-present in heart and in her memory. "I always endeavor to be careful, Jack," she said, "but even if I'd had a change of heart about today's work, which I have not had, I have no way to reach Ezra to tell him so."

"Should something untoward occur, just be certain that Margaret and Abigail know who is to blame," Jack said dourly.

Genie's heart and stomach cartwheeled at the sound of Abby's name but she controlled her reaction. She could not let them see how deeply the mere mention of Abigail Read's name affected her, though she suspected that Jack knew because his wife knew and Maggie was a dear and trusted friend. William did not know and almost certainly would never understand. Nor would his wife, Adelaide, Genie's business associate.

"If there is any hint of danger, I promise that—"

"It will be too late for you to forestall it," William interrupted, sounding cross.

"If I don't sleep, I won't have the wits or strength to forestall it," Genie replied, stifling a yawn and heading toward the back room of the forge for a brief nap. She stopped suddenly, remembering that Jack and Arthur were shaving and bathing Hezekiah English there. The yawn finally got its way and Genie bid her friends a quick good day and left them. She dearly wished she could return to the comfort of her own home. Instead, she walked briskly to her own place of business a few doors away where, in the back room, she could nap uninterrupted for the next two hours. And dream of Abby.

CHAPTER TWO

zra drove the horse cart slowly toward the train station, too slowly for Genie, but she understood and appreciated the need for caution. He sat on the bench and she sat on the floor in the rear of the wagon, as custom dictated: The white man rode in front, the Black one in the rear. But their configuration was more about caution than custom. Ezra could keep watch in front and Genie could keep eyes on who and what was behind them. Just as William and Jack were justified in their concern for her safety, she and Ezra were wise to be wary of the potential dangers lurking in every crowd, down every alleyway. Two or three men could overtake Ezra and control the cart as another clambered into the rear of the wagon to subdue and capture her. She smiled to herself, taking comfort in her weapons—the Deringer in her pocket and the new Colt revolver in her waistband. Ezra had two revolvers, and both he and Genie regularly practiced using them with speed and accuracy. They would not be taken by the ordinary hooligan who, fueled by whiskey and hatred, preyed on helpless and hapless Blacks who, once captured, could be sold down South with no questions asked.

"Who will we be looking for at the train station?" Genie asked, keeping her head forward and her eyes maintaining their side-to-side search for potential problems.

"Whoever is damaging Edward Cortlandt's trains," Ezra replied, maintaining a similar body posture. "And the degree of the vandalism seems to support Cortlandt's fear that someone is trying to put him out of the railroad business."

"No doubt because he is such a good, decent and honorable man," Genie responded with as much dry-witted sarcasm as she could manage. She would never forget nor forgive Cortlandt's cold, cruel comment that he didn't care who died in the very dangerous but ultimately successful effort to rescue young Arthur Cortlandt, his wastrel son, from a gang of kidnappers.

It was more than a year ago, but the memory was as fresh for Genie as if it had occurred yesterday. Ezra was nearly beaten to death, and the men whom Cortlandt didn't care lived or died saving his son were Black men hired by Genie to keep the boy safe. Young Edward Cortlandt, the only child of his wealthy parents, was a drunkard and a gambler, but they wanted him back alive no matter the risk or cost.

"I know what you're thinking, Eugenia," Ezra said.

"I'm sure you do, Ezra, but the past is just that and has no bearing on the task at hand—"

"Arthur is right! You truly have spoiled this horse, Genie!"

"What are you . . ." She was completely confused.

"The horse hears your voice and keeps looking around to find you instead of watching the road ahead!"

Genie stifled a giggle. "My sweet girl horse. Of course I spoil her—"

"Well, you must stop it. The horse isn't a pet; she's a working animal, but more importantly, she could compromise our charade."

Now Genie was even more confused. "Our what?"

"It's supposed to be my cart and horse, but if the horse wishes to listen only to you—"

Now Genie laughed, then quickly covered her mouth. She certainly would compromise their charade if she revealed herself to be a woman. "I'm glad you're my friend, Ezra, hopeless though you are. Now, please consider, Mr. MacKaye: you're the master and I'm the servant, so who do you think would care for the horse, and who would the horse respond to?"

Ezra was silent but Genie did not expect a response. The native-born Scotsman and former Pinkerton's agent didn't think about such things. He certainly never thought of himself as anyone's master, and he most certainly did not consider the half dozen or so Colored people he called his friends to be his servants. Eugenia, the closest of those friends, was a runaway slave and, as a result of the Dred Scott Supreme Court decision two years ago, could never be a citizen of the United States. She therefore could not afford *not* to think about such things. Her life literally depended upon it. Abby understood that . . . *no*! She could not, would not, think of Abby! She closed her mind to thoughts and images of Abigail Read. Abby was much too distracting, and Genie was, she reminded herself, about to follow Ezra MacKaye into danger where any distraction could cost her life—and Ezra's.

"What happened this morning to cause so much tension and anger among you?" Ezra asked, changing the subject, for which she was grateful, though she wondered how he knew about the tension and anger.

"I've known you long enough and well enough to know that predawn meetings in William Tillman's forge almost always leave you tense and angry," he said, answering the unasked question. Since she couldn't argue the point, and since she didn't want to think about danger—or Abby—she told him in great detail about the encounter with Hezekiah English.

"How did he come by such a name?" Ezra asked, leaving the issue of Hezekiah's behavior for a lengthier discussion.

"He named himself Hezekiah after the ship captain who decided not to sell him into slavery, and the surname English because every person he met who wasn't African was English."

15

"One could almost admire the man," Ezra said. He couldn't imagine what a Black person had to pull from deep within to survive in a strange world filled with people who hated his very existence.

"Almost," Genie replied drily. She knew exactly and intimately what a Black person had to pull from within to survive in a world filled with people who hated her very existence— who hated both her Blackness and her femaleness. What she didn't understand was stealing a person from his grave. That's when a thought struck her hard enough to make her head hurt. Hezekiah English had not experienced immersion in the tenets of the AME Church, or in any Christian religion, so he wouldn't know that a burial place was sacred. She would talk to Adelaide about this. She was a pillar of the Mother Bethel AME Church and belonged to several church and civic organizations, and Genie was certain she would want to know about Hezekiah. She was just as certain that William wouldn't tell her. His need to shield his wife from life's ugliness both annoyed and angered Genie. True, Adelaide very often, too often for Genie's comfort, was silly and naïve in both belief and behavior, but the woman was her business partner and Genie knew her well enough to know that she was neither stupid nor timid. Did William believe she was?

In the faint light of dawn, the wide, congested space behind the train station was replete with motion and movement. Much of it was both necessary and justified as it seemed the station was always under construction with new railroad companies arriving to compete for business. However, a significant amount of surreptitious and illegal commerce also transpired behind the station, but under cover of darkness. The arrival of a new day and legitimate commerce spurred the denizens of the darkness to scurry away, like so many rodents or other vermin.

Few people paid notice to Genie and Ezra as their cart joined many others clattering into the construction site, and the few who did notice were, in turn, noticed by Genie and Ezra— men who looked to be the kind to attempt to capture a lone Colored person for sale down South. No way would they know that as long as she was with Ezra MacKaye, Genie was not alone.

"To the right, Ezra, over there where the stacks of lumber and piles of bricks are," Genie said, and Ezra turned the cart in that direction. She'd just recently learned that this was the area where half a dozen young Black boys lived and worked, when work was available, and where the boys hid from the slave catchers.

"Are you sure they'll talk to me?" Ezra asked.

"I'm not even sure they'll talk to me, Ezra," Genie replied, "but we come strongly recommended and we bring food so . . ."

He stopped the wagon and she clambered down, walking slowly but deliberately into a shadowy and narrow space between stacks of lumber and bricks. Her hands were deep in her pockets, her right hand wrapped around the revolver, the left holding the Deringer. "My name is Eugenia Oliver and I'm looking for Daniel. Joe Joseph sent me." She spoke clearly and not too loudly and if the boys were there, they heard her.

After about ten seconds came a muffled reply: "Why is you got that white man with you?"

"He's the one who needs your help and he'll pay for the information you give him," said Genie.

After another ten seconds two boys edged into the clearing, keeping close to an escape route. One approached Genie. He was very cautious and clearly afraid, but he put his bravery on display. "Thank you for meeting us, Daniel," Genie said, freeing the revolver in her pocket and offering her hand to Daniel. He gave it a brief squeeze, then looked up at Ezra.

"Tell him to come down here with us."

"Ezra—" Genie began but Ezra quickly jumped down from the wagon and in two quick, long-legged strides faced Daniel with an outstretched hand.

"My name is Ezra MacKaye, Daniel, and I really appreciate your help."

"You brung us some food? Mr. Joe said you'd have food for us," Daniel challenged.

Ezra nodded, pointing to a box in the back of the wagon. Daniel grabbed the box, sniffed it, nodded, and emitted a shrill whistle. Four boys emerged from the shadows. Two were about Daniel's height and age, but the other two were much smaller, and one of them was little more than a toddler. "Who are those children?" Genie exclaimed.

Daniel shrugged. "We brung 'em with us 'cause they didn't have nowhere to be."

"Found them!?" Genie was ready to explode. Ezra's calming hand on her arm tamped down her anger. And her fear. Had slave catchers seen these children wandering about . . .

"Daniel, can you tell me what you know about men doing damage to train cars?" That was Ezra's priority. Daniel had his own. He reached into the box of food and withdrew one of Joe's famous bacon and egg biscuits, then gave the box to one of the larger boys. He returned to the shadows and the other boys followed. Daniel unwrapped his sandwich and took a big bite. Genie's empty stomach rumbled.

"Does that little one have teeth, Daniel? Can he eat food like this?" she asked.

Daniel halted mid-chew and frowned, then ran into the shadows, returning after a few seconds smiling. "He can eat eggs real good so we all give him the eggs off our biscuits."

"Thank you, Daniel," Genie said, and asked him about Ezra's concerns.

"It's English Jack's boys what tear up the trains."

"How do you know English Jack? Have you done work for him?" Ezra asked. The question was innocent but Genie heard a hint of surprise in Ezra's voice.

Daniel nodded. "We keep a look out for Irish Jack and his

boys, and we let English Jack know when they comin'."

The Irish and the English. Even on American soil they kept their mutual hatred and fight alive. Genie had even heard Abby make disparaging remarks about the Irish, and heaven knew Ezra's Scottish countryman and childhood friend, Donald Bruce, hated the Irish. Still, to enlist the aid of a destitute Black boy in their feud for a few pennies when either man would sell the boys to a slave catcher without hesitation if the opportunity presented itself—it was the worst kind of cruelty. Genie wished she could exact a suitable retribution, though she was glad that Ezra was Scottish, so she didn't have to include him in the punishment.

"Are you absolutely certain, Daniel?" Ezra's tone was almost sharp, and Genie realized she'd missed something important.

"I heard him clear as day, Mr. Ezra, 'cause he was talking real loud, to make sure his men could hear him. They was mad 'cause he didn't have their money, and he was making them listen to him. He said real loud, *I'm gon' see Mr. Purvis tonight and get all the money and pay you t'morra night.* He said this last night 'bout tonight, 'cept he won't be payin' 'em tonight." And Daniel gave a sly smile when he said this and waited for Ezra to ask the question.

"Why not, Daniel?"

Daniel's grin grew. "'Cause Eye-talian Tommy beat the snot out of him—"

"Ezra, really!" Genie had heard enough. "Please pay Daniel so we can go."

Daniel's eyes lit up and he exhaled deeply, and Genie realized the boy had been afraid that he wouldn't be paid. "Thank you, Miss Genie, Mr. Ezra."

"Daniel, those two little ones, I need to take them with me," Genie said gently and quietly, not meeting Ezra's eyes. "They're too young to live like this. You and the other boys can fight if necessary, and run away, but they can't. They're too small."

"Yes, ma'am, you right. And that baby boy, he's 'fraid of the dark. He cries almost all night long."

"He'll be well cared for, Daniel, I promise."

"You gon' take him to live with you, Miss Genie?"

Now it was Genie's turn to take a deep breath, not because she didn't want to care for two homeless boys, but because she didn't have the time or patience for it, and because as a runaway slave herself, she had to protect her own safety. "They will live at the Home for Destitute Boys—"

"The what kinda boys?" Daniel bristled.

"Poor boys, Daniel. Boys who don't have anywhere to live. It's on Darby Road. You can visit them—"

"We're poor, Miss Genie, all us boys. Can we live in that home, too? I'll give Mr. Ezra all this money back if we can live in that home, too."

Genie heard something in Daniel's voice that hadn't been there before: fear and desperation. He knew the danger lurking in every shadow, and while he may not have known slavery personally, he knew enough to fear it. Every Black person did.

Genie looked at Ezra. He met and held her steady gaze. He looked at their horse cart. He said, "It will be a tight fit, and possibly a dangerous one, but we'll take them. All of them."

"You leave me speechless, Eugenia." That's all Adelaide said, and for her, that constituted speechless, so Genie seized the opportunity to tell her that the boys were with her husband and Arthur, getting cleaned up and ready to present to the matron in charge of the Home for Destitute Children.

Adelaide had yet to speak so Genie again took advantage of the unusual opportunity. "There's another reason I asked if we could keep the shop closed today. I've had practically no sleep at all."

And Genie told her in full detail why she'd had so little sleep the previous night, from Hezekiah's grave robbing to the construction site visit where the children were rescued. She watched the expressions roam across the older woman's face, the shock, horror, sadness, disbelief, and finally anger. Hezekiah English's sacrilege, Genie thought, was the cause of the anger. She was wrong.

"Why does William treat me like this? Does he think I'm too stupid to understand the work all of you do? Does he think me disloyal? Or worse, unworthy?" Tears dripped down Adelaide's cheeks and Genie took her hand. She'd wanted for some time to speak with William about his treatment of his wife. She would do so today.

"None of that is true, Adelaide, and I think you know that—"

"What, then, am I to think, Genie?"

"He thinks he's protecting you—"

"Does he think I don't know the peril our people face every hour of every day? The fear? Especially since that evil Dred Scott ruling! Am I not supposed to know that slave catchers roam everywhere? I know that's why you brought those children here, Genie. So why is it all right for you to work to protect our people and not me? Why does my husband value you over me?"

Genie couldn't bear her friend's pain. "You know William's heart better than anyone, Adelaide, and you know that isn't true! I suspect he doesn't view me as a wife, and therefore not needing protection."

Adelaide gave a very unladylike snort. "You don't view yourself as a wife, Eugenia, though you could be one in an instant if you so wished, even despite your ever-advancing age. I know several most worthy men who'd be proud and honored to call you wife."

Genie groaned inwardly. She'd brought this conversation upon herself. She wished to be called Eugenia Oliver and only that, but no point in saying that to Adelaide. Instead, she asked,

"Do you think a generous donation to the destitute children's home would help ease the burden of having six boys deposited on their steps this morning?"

Adelaide nodded and grinned widely. "Especially if clothes, sheets, and blankets come with them." She was happily in her element now. Her work with the social service organizations of the AME church put her in direct contact with the issues confronting the Colored residents of Philadelphia. She further proved the point when she told Genie that the Home for Destitute Boys was a Quaker operation. "I know the woman who runs it. We've worked together on several issues."

How could William imagine that he was sheltering her? Genie would speak to him later today as soon as—a huge yawn stopped that thought in its tracks.

"I beg your pardon," she said to Adelaide as a second yawn followed the first.

"Go home, Genie. I'll take care of getting the boys settled in the Home."

"Are you quite certain, Adelaide? I don't want to place too heavy a bur—"

Adelaide stopped her with a quick hug. "It is no burden at all, Genie. In fact, it gives me something useful to do and I welcome it. Go home and rest."

After giving Adelaide all the money she had on her person and promising more, a grateful Genie hurried to the front door and exited their store. She heard Adelaide lock the door behind her and she was about to turn right, toward home, when she saw the two men coming toward her, both of them weaving and stumbling, as drunk as if it were still last night, and no doubt smelling like it. She knew they saw her and she turned left, walking quickly now. She passed the blacksmith shop and turned into the alley just beyond, emitting a loud whistle as she did. The signal was one she and Arthur shared. He immediately left the forge and stepped into the alley, spotting Genie and the two drunks following her.

"Bastards," Arthur muttered. "Too lazy and too drunk to work, so they take what little we have!" The white in his hair and beard marked Arthur an old man but the strength and power of his anger were those of a younger man, and that anger led Genie deeper into the alley, toward the docks.

Their pursuers, wearing twin evil grins, moved purposefully toward their prey, a young man and a crippled old one. This would be easy. They'd get no money for the cripple—unless he was a smithy—but a strong young man would fetch a handsome price. They were almost upon their quarry when they realized that the two Colored people stood still, facing them, waiting.

Emboldened by the whiskey, as drunks often were, they stumbled forward. One held a pistol pointed shakily in the direction of their prey. They knew niggers were scared of guns, which is why they were so easy to capture.

Genie and Arthur knew that whiskey made stupid white hooligans even stupider than usual, so they stood and waited, the wooden club each gripped ready to swing.

"Hey, you niggers!" the one with the revolver called out when they were close enough that Genie could smell their stench. That's when Arthur swung his club hard and fast. He hit the man's wrist with enough force to crack the bones and send the gun clattering to the ground. Genie swung her club at the other man's head before he fully understood what was happening and he crumpled to the ground as if his body held no bones.

Arthur knew it was a futile exercise, but he checked the revolver for bullets—none—and he threw it with all the strength of his powerful upper body toward the river. Men like this spent what little money they had on whiskey, not bullets, and they never had more than the few coins they were paid for turning over the Blacks they captured to the men who sold the stolen people down South into slavery for real money.

"Let's drag 'em closer to the docks, make it look like they

was fightin' with their own kind," Arthur whispered, a task easier said than done. While Arthur possessed enormous upper body strength, his crippled legs made movement difficult and slow, but Genie knew better than to help him. When they finished, the July sun was high in the sky and they were dripping sweat.

"Thank you, Arthur."

"You don't need to thank me, Miss Eugenie. You did what we talked about and practiced."

He was breathing hard as they walked back up the hill from the docks to the back door of the blacksmith shop, and his limp was more pronounced than usual. She did not know how old Arthur was, but he was not a young man. "I've got yams and beans cooked—"

"Where the devil have you been!" William yelled when they entered the forge. "And Eugenia! What are you doing here? What do you want?"

"Two of 'em followed her when she left her shop—" Arthur began, but William cut him off.

"So you brought them to my door!" William was furious. Genie had never seen him like this, and she didn't know how to respond.

"She did how we planned, William, if one of us got in trouble."

"One of us will always be in trouble as long as we're Colored. Nothing we can do about it," William said sourly. "Now if you don't mind, Eugenia, Arthur needs to get back to work."

Genie gave her old friend a long, sad look. "Arthur may well have saved my life this morning, William, and for that I am grateful, and I do not apologize, but I will not take him from his work again. Nor will I be returned to slavery. I will be shot dead in the street before I allow that to happen. Good day to you both." She left the blacksmith shop the way she'd entered with Arthur and up the path to the rear of her own shop where her knock startled and frightened Adelaide.

24

"Adelaide!" she called out. "It's Genie, and it's only me!"

Adelaide opened the door a tiny fraction and, satisfied that it was, in fact, Genie, she opened the door. "I thought you were long gone!"

Once inside with the door locked behind them, Genie told Adelaide what had happened and Arthur's part in the events. "He's braver than men half his age and twice his size," Genie said, adding, "but I'm worried about him. His anger may be becoming too large." And before she'd finished explaining her thoughts Adelaide was rapidly nodding her head.

"I've tried to tell William that Arthur wasn't himself, but he won't hear of it! He insists that Arthur is as he's always been, but you're right—he isn't!"

Neither is William, Genie thought, but she could never, would never, speak those words to Adelaide. The woman revered her husband. Jack Juniper was the only other person who would have some insight into the change in William's behavior and she was too tired and, truthfully, too frightened to journey to his shoe shop now. Home was but a short distance away and that's where she'd go, as fast as her legs would take her. And dressed as Eugene Oliver, that could be fast.

"I intended to give you this earlier, Genie," Adelaide said as she followed her to the front door. She placed a cloth-wrapped parcel in her hands. Genie could smell the fresh-baked bread. She put the parcel to her face and inhaled deeply. Her stomach rumbled and Adelaide laughed, shooed her out, and locked the door behind her.

Genie stood as still as a statue for several seconds, looking both ways up the busy main street. There were no white men in sight. She hurried up the block, crossed the street in front of a horse-drawn streetcar, and hurried into Thatcher Lane, a residential street composed totally of Colored people. It was all but empty, as it should be late morning on a day of work. She walked swiftly then suddenly stopped, turned sideways, and slid into a narrow space between two houses. A space that would go unnoticed unless one knew it was there.

She emerged on The Back Street, mere steps from her house, and exhaled with gratitude and pleasure as she stepped up onto the porch with its wide railing, installed by Jack Juniper. She lifted the heavy iron latch and opened the heavy new door, also compliments of Jack and Maggie Juniper—their thanks for Genie's decision to let the Juniper family live in her house while Jack recovered and recuperated from life-threatening injuries. Genie had never regretted the decision, especially since the family had never had a home of their own. Jack was at sea most months of the year, and Maggie and their daughter lived with Abigail. When Jack came home the three of them lived in a boarding house until he left again, and Maggie returned to Abby's. Genie was glad to be back in her home, and glad the Junipers now had a home of their own, where Genie would visit them after she ate and slept.

CHAPTER THREE

The Cortlandts' butler, Ezra's hat in hand, was leading him to the master's sitting room when Mrs. Cortlandt crossed the wide hallway. Both men halted and faced her, the butler frozen in place like a statue. Ezra dipped his head.

"Good morning, Mrs. Cortlandt, and I apologize for my early arrival, but I wanted to see Mr. Cortlandt before he left for his office."

"Good morning, Mr. MacKaye, and no apology is necessary. Your early arrival suggests that whatever you've come to say is important, and it's either very good news or . . . not." She studied him, giving him the opportunity to study her. She was not a beautiful woman, but even in a dressing gown, with her hair unpinned and falling to her shoulders, she was an elegant one. "And since you obviously shaved in a hurry, you most likely have not breakfasted. George, please bring Mr. MacKaye tea and scones while he waits for Arthur. Unless you'd prefer coffee?"

Ezra inclined his head again. "Tea is perfect, Mrs. Cortlandt. Thank you most kindly." He rubbed his face and the whiskers that had evaded his razor bristled and scratched. "And I do apologize for the . . . ah . . . oversight."

She smiled and continued on her way. Ezra followed George into Arthur Cortlandt's sitting room where the curtains already were drawn, several small coals burned in the grate to combat the chill in the room, and a fully stocked sideboard waited. George poured tea from the silver server, and gave the cup and saucer to Ezra, followed by a plate with two scones. He instructed Ezra to help himself to butter and jam and left to be ready to greet his master in the hallway.

Ezra had finished half a scone and half a cup of tea when Cortlandt appeared, and he was glad he wasn't chewing. The man didn't look happy to see him, but Edith Cortlandt arrived before he could direct the displeasure at Ezra. He made the mistake of turning it on his wife. "If I require your presence, Edith, I'll send for you."

"If I require your permission to be here, Arthur, I'll ask for it." She faced Ezra. "You have information regarding the train vandalism?"

"Yes, ma'am, and you were correct: it is both good news and not so good—"

"Get on with it, man!" Cortlandt barked.

"The vandals are in the employ of William Smythe."

Cortlandt bristled and puffed up like one of the feral felines that frequented the dockside, and though he didn't hiss, he did growl. "That's ridiculous. Absurd! The man is my partner."

Ezra inhaled. "Yes, sir. I know who he is. And he's who hired a man known as English Jack who, in turn, hired the men who destroy your train cars."

"But it makes no sense," a clearly confused Cortlandt said.

"It makes perfect sense, Arthur. He inherits total and sole ownership of the train line if you are insolvent," Edith said, and her husband looked at her as if she were some mythical being. And perhaps to him she was. It never ceased to amaze Ezra how often men discounted the intelligence and competence of women. He thought of all the women he knew, and every one of them was his intellectual superior. Like his new bookkeeper, Ada Lawrence, to whom he had gladly turned over his financial affairs, and whose advice he followed assiduously.

"Well, it would seem that Smythe has the upper hand," Cortlandt said sourly.

"Not at all, sir," Ezra replied.

"Explain, please, Mr. MacKaye," Edith said.

"I have paid the chief of police twice what Mr. Smythe paid him, and he will see to it that all of the vandals are arrested tonight." He looked at Mrs. Cortlandt. "These men will say that Smythe paid them to destroy the Cortlandt trains, which is illegal, and because he has a voting interest in that enterprise—"

"He loses it, and total control reverts to Arthur," Edith said. Ezra nodded. "Well done, Mr. MacKaye," she said.

Cortlandt's face went white, then red, then almost purple. Ezra didn't know why he'd be angry, but he did know that it was time to take his leave. He stepped forward to submit his bill, but Cortlandt turned away. Ezra's jaw locked in anger. The man was refusing to pay him. Edith pulled the cord that summoned her maid, and the woman appeared immediately. She was right outside the door waiting to be needed. Edith whispered to the maid and she hurried out. Edith looked daggers at her husband, then offered Ezra more tea and scones.

"Thank you, Mrs. Cortlandt, but—"

"He's not here for you to entertain him, Edith," Cortlandt snarled at his wife.

"No, Arthur, he came here to save your business and to be paid for his services, but since you seem unable to complete that transaction, and unwilling to face the man as honor dictates, I will—"

The maid entered, hurrying to give Mrs. Cortlandt a silk pouch. She opened it and withdrew a hand full of coins, which she offered to Ezra without looking at the invoice, though she took it in hand. "Good day to you, Mr. MacKaye."

Ezra practically ran from the Cortlandt mansion, hurrying down the landscaped walkway to the waiting brougham owned by his wealthy friend Abigail Read and driven by his childhood friend, Donald Bruce. He threw himself into the too-opulent-for-the-likes-of-him coach, and Donnie had the carriage swiftly underway. Once safely clear of the Cortlandt residence, Donnie stopped the carriage and waited for Ezra's instructions.

Ezra still clutched the coins given him by Edith Cortlandt. He opened his fist and gasped at the handful of pound sterling and gold eagle coins. Not only was he greatly overpaid, but his bookkeeper had recently advised that he accept only these coins in payment for his work, especially from Arthur Cortlandt, due to what she called "dangerous economic uncertainty" in England and the United States. Especially in banking, railroads, and insurance, three of Cortlandt's businesses. If she were a man, Ada Frances Lawrence would lead her own financial empire. He knocked on the window and Donnie opened it.

"I'll go to Ada's please, Donnie," and he blanched at the look his friend gave him. "Is something wrong?"

"I don't think you'll want to be romancing the lovely Mistress Lawrence when Abigail has likely tied herself into knots waiting to hear what Eugenia got up to this morning. As I am myself."

Ezra's insides sagged. He did not often feel shame, perhaps had never felt it, and he did not like the feeling, but of course Donnie was right. "Let's us go home then, Donnie, if you please," he said. Abigail Read's exquisite Society Hill mansion, where he rented a suite of elegant rooms on the first floor, was more of a home than he'd ever had. His preferred habit of exiting the coach when it was in the mews behind the mansion, where the stables were, allowed him to enter the house via the scullery door. The welcome looks on the faces of Abby, Maggie and Eli when he entered the kitchen shamed him for the second time this morning. How could he seriously have thought to come anywhere else but here? This was his home, where those he cared the most for lived, Ada Lawrence notwithstanding, and he had not examined or defined his feelings for the woman who also was his accountant.

Ezra wanted to hug them all but settled for a bone-crushing embrace from Eli as the boy threw himself forward the moment he entered the scullery door. Ezra barely succeeded at catching him. When had this child become near a man? Keeping Eli close with one arm, he entered the kitchen and touched Maggie and Abby on the shoulder, in turn, as both had stood up to greet him. Anyway, hugging either of them would be inappropriate— Maggie because she was a married woman, Abby because she was well above his station economically and socially, though she'd never have imposed this stricture.

"Can I go help Mr. Donald put the horse and carriage away?" Eli asked, hopping from foot to foot. He was out the door the instant both Abby and Maggie nodded approval.

"You really must stop feeding him," Ezra said to Maggie, massaging his bruised bones. "He doesn't need to get any stronger."

"Then perhaps Donald can stop teaching him to fight," Abby said drily. It was a sore point between them. Ezra was of the belief that since Eli was the only person in the house with her at all times, day and night, the boy should be able to defend her if necessary. Not only was he learning to fight with his fists and his feet, but he was becoming proficient with a knife and a revolver. Abby didn't know about that, and Ezra didn't intend to tell her. She'd have his guts for garters. He rid himself of his hat and suit jacket, hoping to change the subject. Maggie, bless her, did that for him:

"Speaking of eating, Ezra," Maggie said, "have you had food this morning?"

"Half a cup of tea and half a scone, courtesy of Mrs. Cortlandt."

Abby looked perplexed. "Why only half, Ezra? And why didn't the man himself offer you sustenance?"

Ezra looked pained as he recalled and repeated for them Arthur Cortlandt's behavior and his words: *He's not here for you*

31

to entertain him. "Nor, apparently, was I there for him to pay me. That, too, fell to Mrs. Cortlandt."

"How appallingly rude!" Abby exclaimed, the shock on her face verifying her words.

Maggie gave a dignified harumph and exchanged a look with Abby. "Me thinks the gentleman is broke and the woman refuses what most certainly would be yet another contribution from her fortune to keep him in business."

Abby nodded, then suddenly looked very sad. Her own mother had had to hide her inherited fortune from her husband—Abby's father—or he'd have spent that, too, having already depleted his own fortune. They had fled England for America, her father's reputation barely intact, his once immense fortune decimated. He had made more money in America and then lost it all as well. Only perishing at sea in a violent storm had saved his honor, but not her mother's shame, which was Abby's to bear for years after. "I wonder if I shall live to see the day when the ownership of people is forbidden, whether it is the ownership of slaves or the ownership of women—"

"Ownership of women!" Ezra exclaimed. "Whatever do you mean, Abby?"

"Why do you think I haven't married, Ezra?"

"Because there's been no worthy suitor—"

Abby gave a gentle laugh and touched his hand. "You truly are a good man, Ezra MacKaye, and the world would be a better place if there were more like you in it."

Then all the softness left her face. Her dark blue eyes flashed and her lips compressed into a thin line. Had Ezra not known this was his dear friend, the transformation would have frightened him. As it was, he was unnerved by the abrupt change, especially since he didn't understand it, but she elaborated before he could ask.

"If I had a husband, you'd most certainly not be renting a suite of rooms in my house, Ezra, because it no longer would be my house. And I most certainly would not be sitting in the kitchen eating and talking with all of you because my husband would forbid it—my sitting in the kitchen as well as my having all of you as friends." Ezra let the truth of the words sink in. They were, without a doubt, an unusual and unlikely, by any measurement, group of friends. Though Abby and Maggie had been friends since childhood, Abby was white and wealthy. Maggie was Black and not wealthy. He, the tall, blond Scotsman and the beautiful, Black Maggie were friends because he had rescued her young daughter from slave catchers. Genie, though absent, was the dearest of friends to Maggie and much more than that to Abby, though how much more was not discussed because Abby was a wealthy white woman and Genie a runaway slave. Eli had been brought to this house to help Ezra recover from life-threatening injuries and retained because all of them— Abby, Maggie, Genie and Ezra—had fallen in love with the boy. Ezra recalled clearly what he'd witnessed just a short time ago: Cortlandt's wife understood more about the man's business than he did, and she was able to pay Ezra when Cortlandt could not, yet he surely would never allow that elegant woman to eat in the kitchen with the help. "I never thought . . . I never realized . . ."

"Of course you didn't," Abby said softly. Then added, "But you will think of these things when you decide to wed, Ezra."

"I assure you I will not!" Ezra exclaimed. "The woman I marry will know that she is not owned."

He had jumped to his feet to emphasize his point when Eli burst in, followed by Donnie who was trying unsuccessfully to restrain him.

"Ma Maggie! I forgot to take a carrot or a apple to Gerald! Mr. Donnie said he won't be mad at me 'cause horses don't get mad at people, but Miss Eugenie said to always remember to take 'em something so the horse don't forget you—"

"I told Eugenia just this morning that she must stop spoiling that horse—" Ezra began.

"You saw Miss Eugenie this morning?" Eli shouted.

The mention of Genie Oliver was the only thing that could turn Eli's attention away from horses. What Maggie said next was the other thing. "Eli, you and Donnie sit down, please, so we can eat."

After a six-word grace, which Donnie always insisted on, breakfast was underway, and as usual, Eli ate more than the grown men at the table. When Genie had first brought him to them, a half-starved street boy who'd never had enough to eat, Maggie had let him eat his fill of bread, butter, jam, rice, potatoes, and gravy—a habit that continued. He ate the bacon because Donnie and Ezra ate it, and the boy did whatever the men did. But then he had more bread, butter and jam, and more eggs and potatoes and gravy.

"Thank you, Ma Maggie. That was most delicious." He stood and took his scraped clean plate to the sink in the scullery, missing the smiles of love and pride on the faces of the adults. He was very special to each of them, though for very different reasons.

"Why don't you take Gerald an apple, Eli?" Abigail called out, and Eli poked his head back into the kitchen, a wide grin creasing his face.

"Thank you, Miss Abigail! I'll tell him you sent it. And maybe a carrot, too?"

"A carrot, too, Eli," Abby said, the grin on her face matching Eli's wide, toothy one.

"That boy!" Maggie said.

"Yes," Ezra heartily agreed. "You and Abby have spoiled him completely."

"And you certainly haven't contributed to that at all," Donnie said.

Ignoring his good friend, Ezra told them about his morning with Genie and the rescue of the five boys, including the two very young ones, from the train yard. Silence reigned for several long seconds. No one needed to be reminded that Genie had rescued a starving, skinny, filthy Eli from the streets not three years ago, and that was after she'd been feeding him and several other boys for a couple of years. But what concerned them most, as it had concerned Genie, was the fact that the two youngest boys she brought to safety that morning were "found" by the older boys, wandering about on their own.

"Found where?" Maggie asked, clearly distressed.

"I don't know," Ezra replied, "but I'm sure Genie and Adelaide Tillman will try to find out so they can search for the parents."

Maggie shook her head sadly and tears leaked from her eyes. She had a daughter and she mothered Eli, thought of him as a son. "I cannot imagine. It is too much to contemplate."

Abby held her hand tightly. The two women had been friends since they were children, when Abby's father had hired Maggie to be his daughter's companion. Maggie was not to be a servant—that was made clear by her parents. Yes, they were poor, but not so destitute that they would sell a child, not even a Black one to a wealthy English family. The two little girls did everything together. They became inseparable, from the school room to the church pew, and when the Reads decided to leave London and move to Philadelphia in America, they asked Maggie's parents for permission to take the now thirteen-year-old, who wanted to go if Abby was going. Her parents sadly agreed, envisioning and hoping for their young daughter there would be opportunities that did not exist for her in London.

"Do you think there's any way to find the parents of those children, Ezra?" Abby asked.

He shrugged, and then shook his head. "Not if they don't want to be found. And who would look for them, and where would they look?"

"Well, Philadelphia has a police department now—" Abby began. Ezra and Maggie scoffed as one. Though it was barely five years old, it was well known and accepted that the Philadelphia police department was controlled by the political establishment and the wealthy men who controlled the politicians. And there was something Ezra knew that he hadn't shared with the women in his life: There existed a cadre of former New York City policemen recently come to Philadelphia, ostensibly to help train the new Philadelphia cops. What they really came for, however, was to take advantage of the large number of Blacks in Philadelphia they could ensnare and sell South into slavery—an offshoot of a group of New York cops engaged in the same heinous though very lucrative practice. So not only were the Philadelphia cops poorly organized and ill-trained, they most certainly would not be inclined to help locate the Black parents of homeless Black boys, themselves people who may already have been sold South into slavery.

"We should leave the safety of those boys to Genie and Adelaide," Maggie said. "They couldn't be in better hands."

"That home for destitute boys," Abby said to Ezra. "Will you ask Genie how I can make a donation?"

"You can ask her yourself in a few days," Ezra replied, and explained that Genie and Adelaide were considering closing their shop for a couple of weeks since it was so hot and there were so few customers. Ezra said Genie planned to spend the time here. Abby's breath caught in her chest and her heart leapt with joy. She didn't understand how both things could be happening simultaneously, yet they were.

Maggie shared her friend's joy. Even though she didn't fully understand the nature of it, she knew that Abby and Genie loved each other and that being apart was torture. It was ever more difficult and dangerous, though, for Genie to make the journey from Black Philadelphia to Abby's Society Hill neighborhood.

In fact, Maggie and Eli soon would need to stop visiting Abby as well. Only the fact of their secret transport in Abby's beautiful brougham, driven by an almost-livery clad Donnie made their journey possible. But Jack Juniper constantly was pressing Maggie to put a stop to it, and she knew she must. No law in America protected her and Eli from capture and sale into Southern slavery.

CHAPTER FOUR

Well rested and fed, Genie set off for Jack and Maggie's. The sun had not yet set and it still was hot; she soon was perspiring heavily, though the fact that she was too heavily clothed was the main reason. She was dressed as Eugene Oliver, attire that included shirt, jacket and vest, as much to conceal her womanhood as to conceal the several weapons she carried.

She walked rapidly. Her eyes constantly scanned both sides of the street. She suddenly stopped walking from time to time and, with her back against a storefront, studied who was walking with her, who and what was behind her, on the sidewalk and on the street. There were so many people out and about these days—on foot or on horseback, on the omnibus or in a horse cart. Some hurried, others moved casually, and none of the white men she observed looked like drunken hooligans intent on grabbing Colored people to be sold South into slavery.

As she stood still and observant, Genie realized that her ears also were working and that she heard more accents and languages than she ever had. Not just the English and Scottish and Irish speech patterns with which she was most familiar, but others she'd never heard before.

Arriving at her destination, she asked Jack and Maggie, "Who are all these people and where did they come from? And when?"

"From everywhere," Jack said.

"And almost every day it seems," Maggie said, adding that she heard Abby's friend, Florence Mallory, say that the population of Philadelphia was over half a million people and most of that increase had occurred in the past ten years.

"But where do they come from," Genie asked again, "and why do they come here?"

"Many of them come from Germany and Italy," Jack said, "and they come because there are jobs in the banks and railroads in the city, and at the port, on and off the boats."

Genie recalled the location of Italy and Germany on the maps she'd studied in the schoolroom with the daughter of the plantation owner at the house where she lived. The girl, hated by her mother, refused to learn, but Genie learned. The mother also hated the slave girl assigned to be the daughter's companion and so ignored Genie completely, making it possible for her to study and learn for several hours every day. The slave girl had absorbed every syllable that emanated from the German tutor's mouth, including the suggestion that she run to freedom in a place called Philadelphia if ever the opportunity presented itself.

Genie pulled herself back to the present to find Jack eyeing her intently. He, too, was a runaway slave, and like her, no matter how satisfying the new life one so carefully constructed, the ugly past was never completely past. She took a deep breath, pushed the memories back into their dark closet, and told them the reason for her unexpected though warmly welcomed visit. She told them of her worries and fears about William and was surprised at the response.

"Jack's been telling me for a while now that something was wrong with William," Maggie exclaimed.

Genie looked at Jack, and the big man's broad shoulders slumped. William was a new friend, and Jack admired and respected the older man and his wife, not least because William and Adelaide Tillman were so admired and respected by Genie. He looked at his wife, then at Genie. "He's afraid," he said gently, and Genie was rendered speechless. William was one of the bravest men she knew, second only to Arthur, and he was fearless.

"Afraid of what?" Maggie finally managed.

"Everything and everyone, it seems," Jack said, with a sad, helpless look at Genie. William changed after the 1857 Dred Scott Supreme Court decision, Jack said. "He could not believe that not only did the Court declare that we were but three-fifths of a person, but that we would never be citizens of the United States." Jack sighed deeply "He couldn't see how that was possible. He was born right here in Philadelphia. Of course he was a citizen!"

Genie knew part of the story. She'd heard from Adelaide how William consulted with the ministers and lawyers in the city; then he wrote to lawyers in Washington, DC, and New York, and received the same answer from all of them—that only the Supreme Court itself could overturn one of its decisions.

"He talked over and over about what a good citizen he was and how he was of value to America. How he was good and hard-working and productive. How he owned his own business, and so did his wife—I'm sorry, Genie but that's what he says."

Genie shrugged. She didn't care about that. Yes, *Miss Adelaide's Dress and Hat Shop* was painted on the storefront glass of the building and business Genie owned but if it would make the Tillmans happy, if it would ease William's pain, they could have it. What Genie knew for certain and what caused her pain was the knowledge that nothing Colored people did could or would be right enough or good enough for those at the top of the government—or the bottom. If the United States didn't want William Tillman, it certainly would never want Jack Juniper and Eugenia Oliver. Even though they, too, were born in America—both in Maryland—they were runaway slaves who to this day bore a bounty on their heads.

Their names weren't even their names. Jack and Eugenia—

and Eli—were the names the runaway slaves gave to themselves when they believed themselves to be free, or at least when they freed themselves from the places of their enslavement. But according to the Supreme Court, not even those born into freedom, if they were Black, were good enough to be whole people and citizens in the place called The United States of America.

"It helps explain a bit his anger at Arthur and me—" Genie stopped herself. She was about to give voice to something she'd only thought—that Arthur was a runaway, too. She had no knowledge of the man's history and that certainly wasn't a question one Black person asked of another. But given what she'd seen and learned of Arthur, she could easily believe that he, too, had freed himself. If anyone knew the truth it would be William. But why, then, would he demean and humiliate that good and gentle man in the way that Genie witnessed earlier that day?

How were they to help their friend? William was older than all of them, perhaps even older than Arthur, so they certainly couldn't tell him what to do. Trying would only make him angrier, but because they all cared so much for him, they also couldn't allow him to walk around feeling empty and angry because white people didn't see his value. Any Colored person fool enough to pin his hopes and dreams on what white people thought about him was destined to a life of disappointment at best. At worst it could cost him his life. And there was not, in Genie's mind, any good reason for one of them to treat another the way William treated Arthur, treated her, that morning.

Her thoughts were tangled in her brain like the threads in her sewing basket after she dropped it. She usually ended up throwing away a colorful mass of thread because it would take too much time to untangle it if it were even possible to do so. Too bad she couldn't toss away the tangled thoughts in her brain.

41

"What would account for the angry mood within Arthur, then?" she asked, and was surprised when Jack laughed.

"Arthur looks at things the other way 'round from William: He's mad and gets madder every day. He never had any love for white people to begin with, but he hates them now."

Genie thought about the changes she'd seen in Arthur and nodded slowly. Yes, Jack's assessment was true, but it also was dangerous. "It is that," Jack agreed, "but I don't think he cares," he added. "I think he thinks and feels that he'd rather be dead than ever be enslaved again, and if I didn't have my wife and daughter to love, I'd think and feel the same way."

"I want to see Auntie Genie!" It was ten-year-old Elizabeth Juniper streaking into the room and throwing herself at Genie. She was a beautiful child and growing as fast as Eli was. The children considered themselves sister and brother, and Maggie and Jack thought of them as such and treated them as such.

Genie and Elizabeth hugged each other tightly for several long seconds. These people, along with Adelaide and William, were the family she claimed for herself, and the fear of being snatched off the street and sold into slavery kept them apart. This was especially true of this child that Genie held.

Before he knew any of them, Ezra MacKaye had snatched Elizabeth out of the grasp of two slave catchers on a busy thoroughfare at the start of the workday one morning. The street was full of people, yet no one came to the aid of a child screaming at the top of her lungs that she was not a runaway slave. And Elizabeth possessed a prodigious set of lungs.

Ezra fought the men, then paid them what they'd have earned for selling the child. He met Maggie and Abby that day and asked to rent a suite of rooms in Abby's mansion, where he came to know and respect them both. At that time, Maggie and Elizabeth lived there because Jack was at sea for months at a time. But after the near loss of her daughter, Maggie had Elizabeth live with friends near her school and visited on weekends. Keeping her safe was more important than keeping her close.

"You are growing up much too fast, Mistress Elizabeth," Genie said, still hugging the girl tightly. "And as beautiful as your mother."

"I agree," Jack boomed, "on both counts," and he beamed with pride.

"But not as beautiful as you, Auntie Genie," the girl said, causing Genie to suddenly release her hold on the child, giving her a surprised look. "Mama and Auntie Abigail say you're the most beautiful woman they've ever seen!"

A speechless Genie looked at Maggie who muttered that the child still talked too much.

"Off to bed with you," Jack said to his daughter. When she began to protest, he added, "now, please," and she climbed down off Genie's lap. Her father's permanent presence had had a dramatic and positive effect on the girl's behavior.

"Will you come again soon, Auntie Genie?"

"Yes, I will. I promise."

"Go on to your room. I'm coming," Maggie said, before turning to Genie. "Will you really come again soon?"

"Perhaps I should wait until I'm invited?"

Maggie emitted a very unladylike snort, and Jack harrumphed and they all laughed and hugged like the family they had become. "I'll walk with you, Genie."

"No, Jack," Genie said emphatically. "You mustn't leave Maggie and Elizabeth alone. I can find my way. I know this area, the side streets and alleyways, the shortcuts. I'll be fine, and I'll be hurrying."

Maggie walked her to the door. "Abigail misses you terribly," she said when they were alone.

"Please tell her I'll be with her soon," Genie replied, and left, walking quickly toward the Back Street and home.

A year ago, Jack Juniper had bought a fully equipped

shoemaker's business from an old man whose hands, after more than thirty years of making and repairing shoes, no longer could do the work. He taught Jack everything he knew, largely because Jack paid what the man asked without question or argument. Jack had seized the opportunity to learn a trade practiced on dry land, which included a home for his family: Most shops and stores contained living quarters for the proprietors and their families.

Born a slave on a coastal Maryland plantation, Jack had been put to work on the master's fishing vessels as a boy of seven or eight, work he performed until at age fifteen he returned home after several months at sea to find that his parents had been sold South. Heartbroken and furious, he took his revenge, sinking all but one of the master's fishing and sailing boats and destroying the nets and traps. The one vessel Jack did not destroy was the master's prizewinning racing sloop. This Jack used for his escape North, selling it at the docks when he reached Philadelphia. The sea was the only skill he knew, and he quickly found work sailing regularly between Philadelphia and Liverpool, England. His work at sea had ended three years ago when he got wind that the ship's captain planned to bypass the Port of Philadelphia and sail for Charleston where he planned sell all the Black crewmen into slavery, netting a healthy profit.

Jack and his mates had killed their captain, taken all of his money, and abandoned ship in the middle of a storm as it approached Philadelphia. No one believed they could have survived.

Genie relived the story as she made her way home, picturing how it was Ezra and Arthur who had driven a horse cart along the icy and snowy Philadelphia coastal roads and byways looking for traces of Black seamen who might have washed ashore. They had finally found Jack Juniper, battered and nearly drowned but rescued by a Quaker farmer. They got him back to Philadelphia—and to Genie's house—where William and Arthur cleaned and bandaged his wounds, shaved him and cut his hair, fed him soup and tea with brandy. When he finally resembled a human being, Ezra had gone to Abby's to get Maggie. And when he explained why Jack wasn't coming for her himself, she had fainted dead away at the thought of her beloved husband being returned to slavery in South Carolina.

And that's how the Juniper family came to live in Eugenia Oliver's house. Now they were in their own home, for which they all were grateful, but they saw each other so much less often because visiting loved ones was too dangerous.

CHAPTER FIVE

enie woke to the sound of her horse's whinny. She lay still. Was she dreaming? Sweet Girl Horse whinnied again, and Genie jumped up and ran to the door. "Arthur?" she whispered.

"It's me," came the whispered reply. Arthur here at midnight in the horse cart—it could only be trouble. She dressed rapidly, pocketed her weapons, grabbed a carrot for the horse, and opened the door.

Arthur was already on the seat, the reins in his hands. She climbed aboard and when they were moving faster than she'd ever seen Arthur drive, he explained. Two hooligans had tried to rob the Joe Joseph Family Restaurant after closing time. Husband and wife fought back, steadfastly refusing to relinquish the cash. Joe was shot with his own gun, which one of the would-be robbers took from him because Joe didn't shoot fast enough, and Mrs. Joseph was badly beaten.

The commotion alerted the busboys and general helpers, Absalom and Richard, who were cleaning up in the back of the building. They came running, and when they saw what was happening, they attacked the thieves. Richard managed to get Joe's gun away from the thief and shot him with it, killing him. The other busboy beat the second thief with a broom handle until it broke, then smashed a chair over his head, and kept smashing until the man stopped moving. Then, seeing the condition the

46

Josephs were in, the boys ran to get Arthur.

"I went to Joe's to see what was what. I gave one boy a horse and sent him for the doctor, and I came for you. We got to get them dead white men outta there before the doctor comes," Arthur said.

That much was certainly true, Genie thought. But how to explain the injuries to the Josephs? "We'll tell the doctor the fight woke the boys and they came to the rescue, chasing the thieves away, and the Josephs took such a beating because they refused to give up their money, which is true. But you're right, Arthur. We must get rid of the thieves, and quickly." Then she had another thought: "Are we certain they're both dead?"

The door to the restaurant opened when Genie and Arthur arrived. They couldn't see who opened the door so they both entered with revolvers at the ready. They relaxed when they saw Richard, the busboy, and their first query was the state of the would-be robbers: Were they both dead?

Richard said that one definitely was and the other almost was. In the dim candlelight inside they saw Mrs. Joseph sitting on the floor, her husband's head in her lap. She held several blood-soaked cloths on his shoulder. Thank goodness it wasn't a stomach, chest, or head wound, Genie thought as she considered the amount of blood.

"Thank you for coming, both of you," Aurelia Joseph said.

Genie nodded acknowledgment of the thanks, but her focus was elsewhere. "We've got to get them out of here before the doctor arrives," Genie said, pointing to the dead thief and the almost dead one. She knew the doctor only slightly from her very infrequent visits to the AME church with Adelaide—a pleasant enough man, but was he one who would overlook the killing of white men even if they were thieves and would-be murderers? Maybe he would, maybe he wouldn't. The uncertainty meant it was best not to take a chance.

She knew the busboy-waiters much better and trusted them

much more, just as they trusted her. She had gotten Richard and Absalom their jobs when they were still living on the street.

"You did well, especially to go for Arthur," she told them. "And you saved the lives of the Josephs. All of us are grateful for that." She looked at the couple splayed on the floor, Joe barely conscious, Aurelia still terrified. She told them what she and Arthur were about to do. And she told Aurelia to tell the doctor that the thieves tried to rob them and they beat and shot them when they refused to give up their money, and they ran off when Richard and Absalom came to their rescue.

"Can you boys get these two into the cart?" Genie asked Richard and Absalom. She didn't want Arthur having to lift the dead weight of grown men. The two young men made quick and easy work of the task. Then Genie pointed to the blood puddles where the thieves had lain and the boys nodded their understanding. "Put the bloody rags in the burn barrel," she said, "and wrap up that gun in something and give it to me." Before she and Arthur could get out the door, one of the boys made a noise that sounded a lot like a sob.

Genie turned to look at them—tall and strong, yes, but still closer to being boys than men. "Miss Eugenie, will y'all hurry up and come back?"

"I promise we'll be as fast as we can," Genie said. "I promise."

"Where can we take them?" Genie asked when they were underway. "And what should we do with the one who may be still alive?"

"Pray he's dead by the time we get into the forest—" Arthur began but Genie cut him off.

"I'm sorry, Arthur, but we don't have time to bury them. Those boys are terrified. I don't know how much bravery they have left in them."

Arthur nodded but was quiet. He clicked the reins and Sweet Girl Horse picked up her pace. "There's a place on the river where the current runs hard and fast. We tie some rocks on 'em and drop 'em in, they'll be way far gone before sunup."

Arthur turned the cart toward the river, and they could only hope and pray not to be seen before their work was done. Genie didn't know this part of the river, but she could hear the rush and roar of the fast-moving current. The riverbank was steep and rocky. She clambered down, found big rocks she could roll uphill far enough so that Arthur could lift them. They worked quietly and quickly and soon were ready to dispose of the bodies—both of them now dead.

Arthur drove the cart a short distance farther down the riverbank to a place that dropped directly down into the river. They rolled the bodies to the edge and over. Genie listened for a splash but the roar of the water was too loud. "Don't worry, Miss Eugenie, they gone," he said, as if reading her thoughts. And perhaps he was: They knew each other that well.

He turned the horse and cart back the way they came, back toward the Josephs' restaurant. Genie wanted to wash the blood from the cart bed before it dried. Among the tools kept in the cart was a bucket. A short ride away, at a place with relatively easy access to the river below, Genie dunked the bucket in, then handed it up to Arthur half a dozen times. They could not see in the dark and they dared not light the new kerosene lantern. They had to hope and trust that no trace of blood remained.

Back at Joe Joseph's Family Dining, Richard opened the door as soon as the cart rattled into the yard. He looked terrified, which made him look even more like the child he was instead of the man he was called upon to be. Genie squeezed his arm until his face relaxed. Arthur greeted both boys with a firm handshake and a simultaneous shoulder grip, gestures that spoke more loudly than words ever could of his pride in them.

Aurelia Joseph was sitting, barely upright, in a chair at one of the tables. One side of her face was heavily bandaged and her left arm was in a sling. Joe was nowhere to be seen and Genie's heart sank at the same moment she heard Arthur gasp. Aurelia roused, saw them, tried to stand, then dropped heavily into the chair.

"Joe—" Arthur managed.

"In the bed," she said. "The doctor gave him a heavy dose of laudanum. Tried to give me some, but I wanted to stay awake to see y'all, to thank you." She began to weep, shaking her head from side to side.

"You should be in bed, too. We'll come back tomorrow; we can talk then. But your thanks belong to these two," Genie said, pointing to Richard and Absalom. "They'd done the hard work by the time we arrived."

Aurelia Joseph nodded. "I don't know what we'd do without them. They are a godsend, Genie," and she beamed at the boys—as much beaming as she could do with her damaged and bandaged face.

"Something I want you and Joe to think about before we talk," Genie said: "Hiring a guard." And she and Arthur left, but stood at the door until they heard it lock and saw the lamps extinguished.

"We need to hire guards, too," Genie said to Arthur when they were back in the cart headed home. "You cannot continue to be the person everyone seeks out when there's danger. Even I do it, Arthur, and it's not fair to you. I'm so sorry that I caused you difficulty with William the other day."

"You don't owe me no apology, Miss Eugenie."

"Yes, I do, Arthur. I know we promised to look after each other, but not if it interferes with your other duties."

"You got other duties, too."

"Yes, I do, but there's no one to cause trouble for me if I put those duties aside for a moment."

Arthur was quiet for a moment. Then he said, "I wish I knew what was worrying and troubling William. He don't act like the same man I been knowin' for so long a time."

Genie told him what Jack had told her and his reaction

surprised her. Sounding both sad and angry at the same time he said that he believed Jack was correct in his assessment, and that there was nothing any of them could do about it. "If any man—or woman—can turn against their own 'cause of what white people think or do, then there ain't no hope for 'em. We got to take care of ourselves and each other, like you and me did that other day."

"I always thought that's what William believed," Genie said. "All his work with the Underground Railroad—"

"He hates slavery 'cause of his ma, and he looks out for us what was slaves. 'Least he used to. Jack is right about how that Court thing took William's mind—he ain't been in his right mind since. I shoulda knowed that's what was troubling him."

Arthur had spoken more words at one time than Genie had heard in all the years she'd known him. "He's our friend, Arthur. How do we help him?"

"We can't, Miss Eugenie, not if he don't want our help, and we can't make him take it," Arthur said with a helpless shrug.

"But he has helped me so much over the years, and I know he has helped you. I can't just ignore him," Genie said, and her shoulders sagged and remained down.

Arthur was quiet, then, "Maybe you can talk to Miss Adelaide."

CHAPTER SIX

The mixed emotions churning within Abby Read made it impossible to eat, but she was on her third cup of tea. Eli happily devoured the bacon and biscuits she pushed aside without sharing a single morsel with Donnie Bruce, who didn't even notice because he was too busy getting caught up on the news brought by Ezra and Maggie to think about the extra bacon and biscuits. Everyone knew the Josephs and Richard and Absalom, and Abby knew of them. Unsettling as this news was, it was Maggie's announcement that caused Abby's upset. Jack was very close to deciding that Maggie no longer could make the daily round-trip journey to Abby's. It wasn't safe. No Colored people were safe, especially not one riding back and forth across town in a fancy brougham driven by a liveried white man. Abby not only understood, but agreed with Jack. She couldn't bear it if anything ever happened to Maggie yet she couldn't imagine a life without her. But Maggie also told her that Genie would come in a week's time, which almost mitigated the loss of daily contact with her oldest and dearest friend.

"What about Eli?" A discussion of Eli and she'd missed it!

"If Donnie's not driving Maggie back and forth every day with Eli as passenger, will he wish to remain here or with Maggie and Jack?" Ezra asked, and Abby's stomach sank.

"I think we must ask that question of Eli himself and not speculate on a decision for him," Maggie said like the wise mother she was. She'd be heartbroken not to see him every day; she and Jack thought of him as a son. However, the boy was old enough, and wise enough, to decide for himself what he wanted to do.

"Of course you're right, Maggie," Abby said. She knew it was the truth, but she couldn't deny the desire deep within to run screaming from the room. What did it mean that those dearest to her, with the exception of Ezra, were Colored? She could and would easily relinquish contact with every white person she knew, even Ezra, if she didn't have to relinquish contact with Genie, Maggie, and Eli. What did that mean? What did it say about her? She needed to ask Genie. If there were an answer, Genie would have it, and if Genie gave her an answer, she would trust it. She also needed to know why she didn't have the answer for herself and she knew that only deeply honest looks within would reveal such insight.

"I think, Abby, that Eli and I are very fortunate to have you care so much for us," was Genie's response.

"But you don't find it the least bit odd that I, a white woman, don't harbor similar deep feelings of love and respect for those of my own kind?"

"Who among your associates and friends shares your hatred of the Dred Scott decision as we do? Would your parents? Does your friend Florence Mallory? And if no one does, do you understand why?"

Abby shook her head back and forth as tears leaked from her eyes. Then she wept and Genie held her tightly. She did not, could not, understand how decent, intelligent people could embrace such a judicial travesty. So did that mean that perhaps there weren't very many decent, intelligent people who looked like her? Her mind gave the equivalent of a shrug. Their loss, she thought, as she felt Eugenia Oliver's strong arms tighten around her. And my gain, she thought the next morning at a breakfast shared with Genie and Maggie and Eli and Ezra and Donnie. Perhaps one of their last together.

Everyone at the table read a broadsheet or newspaper. Genie had brought dozens with her, from every corner of the nation, many of them out of date, but every one of them telling of the increasing and intensifying danger confronting Blacks in every part of the country.

Most horrifying, though, was the open talk of war. Not a war against a foreign nation but a war within the United States, a war between the pro- and anti-slavery factions. But what galvanized the group at the table were the stories in the Philadelphia broadsheets about the late-night grave robbing in Colored cemeteries.

"What manner of heathen depravity is that then!" Donnie roared, pounding the table so hard the plates and cutlery danced, which Eli found most amusing.

"I thought that had stopped," Ezra said, looking from Genie to Maggie. Both shook their heads.

"A delegation from all the denominations visited the police chief who said there was nothing he could do. Then the Catholic bishop weighed in," Maggie said with a grin, "and the Irish police chief said perhaps he could look into the matter after all."

Donnie muttered darkly, and while no one but Ezra, the other Scotsman at the table, understood what he said, everyone understood the intent of the words.

Almost as if obeying an order from on high, everyone closed what they'd been reading at the same moment. Then they all laughed and ate and talked.

"I was listening to you read out loud to Donnie and Ezra," Maggie said to Eli, "and I was most impressed. Mistress

Elizabeth will have to study hard to catch up."

Eli beamed and said Mr. Donnie had been helping him a lot with his reading. Then he opened the paper he held and read aloud—in perfect imitation of Donnie Bruce's heavy Scots brogue, and the laughter rang out, Donnie laughing louder and longer than anyone.

Early one morning several days later as Genie and Abby lay tangled together, Genie said it was time she left. Abby knew this day was coming and she had promised she'd accept it graciously. She almost made it.

"Oh, how I shall miss you, Dearest Genie!"

"And I you, Abby. And how I long for the day when our separation no longer will be necessary."

Abby sat up straight, her hair the tangled mess that Genie loved. "Do you believe there will come such a time, my love?"

Genie nodded, her gaze so serious that Abby almost smiled. "I do think so, yes. I do not know when or where, but I do think that it will." And that expression of hope, strong enough to be a belief, strengthened them.

CHAPTER SEVEN

Fall's arrival in Philadelphia felt and behaved more like winter. Though the unseasonal weather didn't last long—just three days—a cold, driving rain kept people inside and close to the fire if they didn't have to be out in it. On the third day of the foul weather Jack tried to convince Maggie to remain at home, but Eli and Donnie were outside waiting in the carriage, and there was no way to tell Abby that she wouldn't be coming. She wished they hadn't come for her. She'd have understood if they didn't want to sit outside in the cold rain. Gerald, the horse, probably would rather have stayed home, too. Maggie tightened her scarf, hugged her husband and daughter, telling them she'd see them at dinner, and stepped out into the cold rain and ran to the carriage.

Donnie turned the brougham onto the wide avenue that led to the street Abby lived in. There was an omnibus in the middle of the street going in the same direction, and a horse train on the opposite side, but there was nobody on horseback, there were none of the small horse carts, and there was no foot traffic.

Until suddenly there was—two of them, one on either side of the carriage. Donnie reacted quickly and knocked the one who'd grabbed him to the ground. Eli reacted more slowly but just as forcefully, surprising the one who'd grabbed his arm. The boy brought all of his fight training to bear. He hit his attacker hard, blow after blow. Surprised, the man released his hold on Eli, which is when Eli kicked him in the face and when Donnie slapped the reins hard on Gerald's back.

Unaccustomed to such treatment, Gerald reared and took off at a gallop. Even if they'd been so inclined, the slave catchers never could have caught up. And they were not inclined as both were hurt and bleeding, not to mention shocked.

Donnie turned into the mews behind Abby's mansion and stopped. He opened the back door and helped Maggie down, then he grabbed Eli from the bench and told him to get Maggie inside. "Now, boy. Go! Don't try to help me, just get Mrs. Maggie and go!"

Eli grabbed Maggie's hand and pulled her up the flooded garden path to the scullery door, which Ezra opened.

"I heard yelling! Is something wrong?"

"Someone tried to take Eli—" Maggie began, but Abby, who'd also heard the raised voices, was there, right behind him, and she grabbed them both.

"Are you all right, both of you?"

"We just fine, Miss Abigail. Me and Mr. Donald took care of things. We wouldn't let no harm come to Ma Maggie. I made that promise to Papa Jack." Eli looked so serious the adults didn't know whether to laugh or cry.

"You did just as you were taught, Eli, and I'm proud of you," Ezra said.

"Yessir, I did just like Mr. Donnie taught me. I hit him as hard as I could but he wouldn't let go, so I kicked him till his teeth rattled."

Ezra guffawed, Maggie giggled, and Abby sniffed, said something about finding dry clothes for everyone, and hurried away.

"Can I go help Mr. Donald—"

"No," Maggie and Ezra said in unison. "Go find Abby and

get yourself into the dry clothes she has for you," Maggie said, and they watched until he was out of sight.

"You think they were after him?" Ezra asked.

"Sure of it," Maggie replied. She knew how much a strong young boy like Eli would bring on the slave market. From her vantage point in the rear of the coach she had seen the slave catcher grab Eli, heard him yell *I gotcha!* as Eli lashed out with his fists, and then with his feet. Yes, they definitely were after Eli. She'd have to get home this evening, but she knew this was her last journey between her home and Abby's. And now Eli must decide where he would live because this was his final journey as well.

"Why do I have to decide?"

They were dry and calmer and seated at the table.

"You're the only one who can," Maggie said in her calm, reasonable tone, but it was lost on Eli who was growing more stubborn and mule-like every second.

"I just want to do like I do every day—"

"Maggie won't be coming here every day, Eli," Ezra said. "It is too dangerous—for both of you."

Eli's face said he was struggling to understand. His tightly hunched body said he was resisting mightily.

"If they had captured you this morning, Eli, you'd be on your way South, back into slavery, maybe even back to Virginia," Maggie said.

The reactions of Abby and Ezra to those words showed they'd forgotten that Eli had freed himself from slavery as a child by swimming across a river, then making his way, alone, to Philadelphia. And Eli's reaction showed that perhaps he'd forgotten as well, though more likely he'd buried the memory very deeply with the hope that he'd never have to resurrect it.

He began to cry and shake. Maggie pulled him onto her lap. She held him tightly and rocked and whispered to him until he was calm. When he made no move to change his position, Abby and Donnie saw to the breakfast preparations

"Can I ask Miss Eugenie?"

"Ask her what, Eli?" Abby said.

"Where I should live," Eli replied.

"You know Eugenia longer and better than anyone, Eli, so you know what she'll most likely tell you, don't you?" Maggie still held him tightly and he made no attempt to leave the comfort and safety of her lap and her arms. Her words were not a rebuke and he knew it.

"She would tell me to decide for myself," Eli said with an exaggerated sigh.

"And so you must, and whatever you decide, Eli, you have our full support," Abby said.

"Then I decide to stay here with you and Mr. Ezra 'cause you need me. Ma Maggie, you have Papa Jack and Hezekiah to take care of you and Elizabeth, but when Mr. Ezra and Mr. Donald are gone, Miss Abigail don't have nobody but me to take care of her." He climbed down from Maggie's lap and stood tall and straight as he said the words.

Donald Bruce jumped to his feet and saluted Eli. "Hear, hear!" he shouted. "Jolly good man!" Ezra followed suit, adding a hearty clap on the back.

Abby and Maggie collapsed in tears and hugged each other. Ezra and Donnie first looked startled, then confused, then helpless. So did Eli, as if following a play script. He might not yet be a man, but his behavior left no doubt that he belonged to the same species.

The following morning Ezra met Ada Lawrence, his accountant, in her office while Donnie went shopping for Abby. With Maggie gone, the cooking now was down to Abby and Donnie until a proper cook could be hired. They could hold their own at a stove—no one would starve—but they were by no means proficient. And Ezra made it clear that he did not enjoy the cuisine of his homeland, which was all Donnie could cook. Florence Mallory, who'd promised to find Abby a cook as quickly as possible, would be urged to complete the task soonest.

Ada and Ezra welcomed each other as they always did, with warmth and appreciation. They genuinely liked and respected each other, and both believed more could be possible, but both were reluctant to explore the possibilities, for reasons they'd be surprised to learn were similar.

Ada's office was a wonderful blend of the comfortable and professional as she spent considerable time here. There was a bright fire in the grate as it still was cold, just without the hard, blowing rain. Ezra had all of his papers, which he gave to Ada once he'd removed his hat and coat and she'd hung them. She put the papers on her desk then joined him in front of the fire.

"Are you quite all right, Ezra? You look a bit . . . I'm not certain what. Bothered? Worried? Upset?"

How perceptive she was. He was all of those things and more. He'd left Eli and Abby alone in the huge house with instructions not to worry; they'd be fine. Eli was well armed, and Abby didn't voice a single objection. That alone was cause for concern. That the boy would give his life to protect Abigail there could be no doubt. But he didn't want the boy to die—for any reason.

"Ezra, whatever is the matter?"

How to tell her about Eli without telling her all of it? So that's what he did. He told her all of it, from the rescue of Elizabeth Juniper from slave catchers several years ago, to the attempt by slave catchers to capture Eli several days ago. He told her everything, relieved to share it yet worried how she would receive these self-truths. And when she said nothing, his heart sank. Abby, Maggie, and Donnie teased him about what was apparent to them: that he was enamored of Ada Lawrence. He did not deny it. He only wondered how honest he could or should be. Now it seemed he knew.

"It would appear that we both have made the mistake of not trusting each other with the beliefs that we hold dear," Ada said when at last she spoke.

Ezra stared at her as if she'd spoken a foreign language.

She rose and went to the hearth to stir the fire and to add more coals. The skirt of her dress was a deep emerald, which seemed to reflect the firelight. Donnie would laugh him out of the room for such a thought. He wanted to laugh at himself! He'd never before noticed a woman's dress except to find it pleasing . . .

"I understand why you didn't tell me the more . . . intimate details of your life, Ezra. It is for those same reasons that I have not shared similar facets of my own life."

He turned in his chair to face her. Her steady gaze met his own. Her eyes were gray. How had he not noticed that?

"You may have noticed aspects of home here in my office. That is due to the fact that I now live here, because I fear it is dangerous for me to return to my rooming house."

Ezra stood up, then quickly sat back down, his hands clenched in his lap. "Why is that, Ada?"

"Because I helped my Colored driver escape the clutches of some of those new police officers that I believe to be slave catchers, and because they're police they can learn where I live."

"Then you must live elsewhere."

Ada actually laughed, a lovely sound that was merged with a sigh of relief. "And where should I live?"

"At Abby's—and don't look at me like that! It's a huge mansion. I occupy the only first-floor suite with a private entrance. The other suites are two and three floors above. And

61

anyway, Abby would never countenance any untoward behavior, should there exist the likelihood of untoward behavior between us, and that does not exist. Does it?"

Now Ada was laughing at him, and he joined in the merriment, welcoming how good the feeling was. Then, when they sobered, he asked for the details of the event that had led to her taking up residence in her office.

"As good fortune would have it, we were driving away from home because I had a file to deliver to a client. Otherwise, I'd have taken them right to my door—and to poor Esther!"

Ada choked back a sob and explained that Esther Lane was her elderly landlady whose ill health likely would have been made worse by violence inflicted on a member of her household staff, and she thought of Daniel as part of her household even though he was Ada's employee.

"We'd discussed what we'd do if an attempt was made on him, how he'd run, collect Josie, his wife, and go to my house in the country—"

"You have a house in the country?" Ezra exclaimed, surprised.

"Am I not allowed to have a house in the country, Mr. MacKaye?"

Ezra colored crimson as he recalled the conversation with Abby and Maggie about women, and men's treatment of them. This most certainly was a woman who never would be owned or controlled by a man. "Most assuredly you are, Mistress Lawrence. You are a free woman, free to do as you wish, when you wish."

"You are to be commended for your enlightened thinking, Mr. MacKaye, and I do commend you. As much as I also look forward to meeting Mistress Read and Mrs. Juniper, for I am sure I have them to thank for it."

CHAPTER EIGHT

Both Josephs were recovering from their injuries, though slowly. They were not young people, but they also had not taken the necessary rest to recover from their injuries. They could not afford to close their place of business, and they didn't have anyone to do the cooking if they couldn't. So they did what they could, which meant fewer menu items. Several women came when they could to help Aurelia Joseph in the kitchen, Richard and Absalom helped Joe run things in the dining room and tend the grills in the back, and armed men took turns standing guard front and back. People were upset, frightened, and angered by the attack on the Josephs. They were a fixture and a staple of the Colored community in South Philadelphia where both had lived all their lives.

Both Josephs rushed to greet them as fast as was possible when Genie and Arthur entered the dining room two weeks after the attack. They'd told everyone that Genie and Arthur had saved their lives though it was Richard and Absalom who had done that. What Genie and Arthur had done was get rid of the corpses of the attackers though they'd never said that to anyone, and apparently neither had the Josephs because no one asked them about it. Thankfully.

"How are you, Genie? Arthur?" Joe asked.

"How are the two of you?" Genie asked in answer to his question. She scrutinized them. "To tell the truth, you look weak and tired, both of you. Aren't you resting?"

"We can't rest—we can't afford to," Joe said, sounding as weary as he looked.

"We have people to pay—the men who tend the fires for cooking the meat, and especially the boys—and there's quite a few people who take their meals here every day. Where would they eat if we didn't cook?"

Genie didn't bother mentioning that there were other restaurants since this is where she ate if she didn't eat at home. She sighed, feeling a bit weary herself. "I hate to come to you with bad news, but some other businesses have been robbed—"

"The lazy bastards!" Joe yelled, and everyone in the room turned to look at him. Several men stood, guns in their hands, ready for action should the situation warrant it. Arthur waved them back down and touched Joe on his good shoulder, hoping to calm him, to no avail. "Too damn lazy to work so they rob people who work most of the hours in every day."

"What are we supposed to do, Genie?" Mrs. Joseph stood close to her husband, as if to protect him. The mixture of anger and fear caused her to tremble so hard she almost lost her balance. Joe steadied her with his good arm, but he was none too steady himself. Rev. Richard saw their distress and hurried over with a chair for each of them, and one for Arthur.

"Nice to see you, Miss Eugenie," he said. "How Eli doing?"

"He's doing well, Richard. I'll tell him you asked."

"Can he come visit us? We miss him, me and Absalom."

Genie didn't want to tell him no, or tell him why, so she just said yes without saying when. He thanked her and walked away. Genie pulled another chair over so she could sit beside Arthur, facing the Josephs. "The men who're guarding this place—there must be more of them, and they need to be part of a formal militia. We need to have our own militia to protect ourselves and our businesses and our communities. We cannot rely on that new police force to protect us. Half of them are nothing but slave catchers in uniform."

"How do we do something like that, Genie? Make us a militia?"

"Call a meeting of all the shopkeepers and merchants you know. Offer to have the meeting here. Then first make certain that everyone agrees on the need to create your own militia, and then decide how much each business will contribute—"

"We'll have to pay them?"

Arthur snorted and Genie gave Joe Joseph a penetrating look. "Of course you'll have to pay them. It will be a job, and a dangerous one. They will be risking their lives. You can't expect that they'll work for free."

"But you and Arthur—"

"We did you a favor. A one-time-only favor. I have my own business to protect, as do Arthur and William."

Genie leaned forward to make her point: "You should form the militia sooner rather than later. Not only have other businesses been targeted, but there have been many more cases of people being grabbed off the street, day and night, especially young men and boys—"

"Eli!" Joe exclaimed. "Is Eli all right?"

Genie sighed. She hadn't intended to divulge Eli's near miss. Reluctantly she told them what had happened and asked them not to tell Richard and Absalom. She didn't want to frighten them or cause them to worry about their friend. She and Arthur stood at the same time.

"We must leave now so as not to be out too late and therefore vulnerable to attack," Genie said.

The Josephs gaped at them, as if they'd believed the attacks they'd just discussed were isolated incidents, but Genie didn't judge them. It was difficult to grasp how widespread and how routine the danger was. None of them wanted to believe that being Black was illegal, especially people like the Josephs and William Tillman who were born free in Philadelphia. If they and all like them were safe, Genie would almost be willing to accept her outlaw status. Almost. "Please take care of yourselves. We will see you again soon," and she and Arthur took their leave.

Once again in the horse cart and headed home, Arthur was driving and Genie was seated in the rear, eyes roving from side to side, a weapon in each hand. It was not terribly cold, though it was far from warm, and the rain had stopped, so they were dry. It seemed that they were alone in their part of the world. Colored people avoided being out unless it was absolutely necessary. They had to watch their surroundings, but the relatively short journey home gave the old friends a chance to talk.

Genie told Arthur what Jack said he believed was troubling William. A grunt from Arthur was his agreement with Jack's assessment. "Is he any better?" Genie asked.

"He done got worser," Arthur replied in his customary growl, but it sounded sad, plaintive, even, rather than impatient or angry as was his norm. "He talked so bad to Miss Adelaide the other day I almost took after him. But she took care of him her own self, told him he didn't have no right to talk to her like she was a fool or a child."

"Oh dear," Genie said. Adelaide must be at the end of her tether to call William on his behavior. "What did he say, Arthur?"

"Didn't say nothin' for a long while; then he said she was right and he was sorry, and all the years I been knowin' William Tillman I ain't never heard him 'pologize to any other body 'cept his mama."

This was a voluble Arthur. Genie didn't know what to make of it—behavior as unexpected as Adelaide asserting herself to William. It was indeed a strange and unprecedented time. "If Adelaide was owed an apology, then I'm glad she received it," Genie said, leaving unsaid her belief that an apology from William to his wife was long overdue. She would look forward to seeing Adelaide at work in the morning.

"You know people think I got crippled 'cause a hoss kicked me," Arthur said, leaving Genie too shocked to respond immediately. Not only was Arthur still talking, he was talking about himself.

"Yes, Arthur, that's what people think."

"Well, it ain't true. What happened is my master broke my legs 'cause I kept tryin' to run. I wouldn't stop tryin' to run no matter how many times or how hard he whipped me. I promised my Ma and my Pa, when they got sold away, that I would get myself to freedom and that's what I done. By ridin' a hoss since I couldn't run no more."

Genie was speechless and breathless. She searched for the right words, and then for enough breath to speak them. "Thank you for trusting me enough to tell me this, Arthur. It means a lot to me."

"I trust you more'n I trust anybody 'cept for William, Miss Eugenie."

"And I trust you, Arthur, and I value you as a friend."

Arthur remained silent for the remainder of the journey home, speaking again only to bid her a good night when she jumped down from the cart in front of her house and to say he'd see her in the morning.

He was equally taciturn the next morning. After his usual "morning, Miss Eugenie," he was silent on the quick walk to her shop. Their conversation of twelve hours ago might never have happened. Foot and vehicular traffic on the main street were dense and heavy and therefore slow-moving, and it seemed to grow heavier each day. There were a good number of white faces in the crowd and Genie wondered where they came from and where they were going. She knew that significant numbers of white people lived south and west of the Colored section, and worked there as well, or so she'd believed. So much was changing so fast in Philadelphia.

Adelaide opened the door for her, then locked it quickly behind her.

"Good morning, Adelaide."

"Good morning, Eugenia."

"I expect we should prepare to be quite busy today, even though it's not quite as cold as before," Genie said.

"I expect so," Adelaide replied, and said no more.

Genie sighed internally. It appeared that the conversation she hoped to have with Adelaide would be even more difficult than anticipated. Over the years the two women had discussed many topics, and not always with mutual agreement. They had never discussed Adelaide's marriage or her husband, and Genie didn't look forward to it, but Adelaide clearly was in distress. Worse, she looked wan and sallow, as if the light within her had been extinguished. How did one help a friend, knowing that any attempt to do so would not be welcomed? In fact, might well be rejected?

They were barely prepared when the first customers knocked, and a steady flow kept them busy until it seemed that everyone was ready for the midday meal. "A very productive morning," Adelaide said as Genie turned the sign in the door from OPEN to CLOSED.

"Yes, it was," Genie said, pleased to see that they'd sold more than they'd given away. It wasn't always so, but the burgeoning population brought more prosperous Colored people to the city of Philadelphia, living in households where all the adults worked, to the benefit of businesses like Joe Joseph's Family Dining and Miss Adelaide's Dress and Hat Shop.

As soon as they sat at the table in the back room they began to shiver, and they laughed at themselves. They'd been too busy to feel the cold until they stopped moving about. Genie put wood and coals in the stove and they soon had heat.

"You know that Arthur and I visited the Josephs yesterday evening," Genie said.

Adelaide nodded. "How are they?"

"Not well, I'm afraid. They both were badly injured, and they haven't taken the time to rest and heal. And they seem so lost."

"What exactly happened, Genie? I can't get William to tell me. It's as if he thinks by telling me, I somehow will fall victim to the same thing."

Genie told her everything.

"Those poor boys. Children should not have to engage in such violent behavior."

"I agree wholeheartedly," Genie said. "I even thought of taking them to the Boys Home, but they would miss the Josephs, who would miss them just as much if not more. They're a family now."

"But, Eugenia. They killed people, those boys did! Surely that's not a habit you wish for them to foster."

"Of course not." Then Genie told her about Eli and she crumpled.

"Oh Eugenia, I am so very sorry. I did not mean to suggest—I had forgotten that it was you who saved all those boys from the street. That you fed and clothed them, that you got them jobs in reputable places, with people who will help them become good men." Tears leaked from her eyes and rolled down her cheeks. Genie took her hands and held them tightly.

"It is a difficult time for us all, Adelaide. We don't know what to do, and the bitter truth is that it may not matter what we do—"

"What does that mean, that it may not matter what we do?" More than merely weeping, Adelaide now was on the verge of hysteria.

"You do everything exactly as you should, Adelaide. You take care of your home and your husband, you run your business, you attend the AME church every Sunday, and you do good works for your people every day. Yet the Supreme Court says you're no more than three-fifths of a person and you'll never be a citizen.

What should any of us do in the face of that? What can we do, when we cannot control what happens to our lives?"

Adelaide stared at her and Genie let her look. She hadn't really asked a question and Adelaide wasn't really looking for an answer, but she was looking for something. Perhaps for a place to plant her feet for, in truth, that's all any of them could do. Stand tall and strong, as they always had done, in the face of unspeakable hatred and cruelty for those who'd been slaves, and in the hope that they could believe in the promise of America for all for those who had been free born.

Adelaide sighed deeply. "That is quite a lot to contemplate, Genie. Perhaps too much." And when Genie didn't reply, she said, "Well, then, let us unlock the door and return to our work." Adelaide started toward the front door. Genie heard her take a strangled breath and call out. Hurrying to follow Adelaide to the front door, Genie saw three white women standing there. Genie unlocked and opened the door and stood there, blocking entry.

"Good day. How can I help you?"

"We came for the free clothes," one of them said, and tried to push her way in.

Genie was momentarily speechless. "I beg your pardon?" She finally managed to say, holding her ground and using all her strength and the force of her will to keep the woman out.

"The Father at the church said you ones here gave clothes free to the poor people, and we came for them," the woman said, still pushing forward.

Genie felt Adelaide close behind her, so she stepped— lunged—forward, out of the door, forcing the three women to backpedal. Adelaide slammed the door but Genie did not hear the lock engage so she knew that Adelaide remained close. "What church?" Genie asked.

"The church of the twins," one of the women answered.

"No one should have told you to come here for free

anything," Genie said, "and especially no one from a church. Every church in Philadelphia has its own donation program, and you should seek assistance from your own church." Genie wondered whether the women understood anything she said. She also wondered what the church of the twins was. A real place? A real church?

"Is you a nigger?" one of the women asked in a very thick accent, one unrecognizable to Genie.

"No, I most certainly am not," Genie replied, and turned away from the women toward the door, which Adelaide opened and quickly closed and locked.

"I am speechless," Adelaide said, her back to the door.

"I shall be visiting the newspaper office after work," Genie said. "This must go into the paper: that the head of a church sends his people to us for free clothes." She paused, then asked Adelaide, "Have you ever heard of a church of the twins?"

Adelaide allowed herself to smile broadly and explained that's what people—church-going people—called the Church of Saints John and James. "And I will visit Rev. Thomas and ask him to call a meeting of all the Colored ministers. They must organize a delegation to visit the white ministers and have them put a stop to this. Immediately!"

"Did you hear her ask me if I was a nigger? Just off the boat and dressed in filthy tatters and rags and the first word of English they learn is nigger."

CHAPTER NINE

Abby and Ada were introduced by Ezra and found themselves so comfortable with each other that by the time dinner was over they behaved like friends of long standing. It helped that Abby's new cook acquitted herself most admirably. Emily by name, she'd come highly recommended by Abby's good friend and neighbor Florence Mallory, and she was available for immediate employment due to the sudden death of her employer, Florence's friend Sarah Willis.

Emily was a young woman—too young to be a head cook in an elite household—and without enough years of service to have an extensive reference list. Florence knew her qualifications because she'd dined often at Sarah Willis's home, and readily agreed to give the girl a reference.

Now, after spending an evening talking with and listening to Ada Lawrence, and deciding that she would be a welcome addition to the household, Abby found herself needing to decide if one of the grooms from Ada's home might be employed as well since, with Ada in residence, a second carriage and driver would be necessary.

"Do you know the name of this groom?" Ezra asked Abby, and controlled his own smile as he watched Abby control hers. While there certainly was sufficient space in the carriage house behind Abby's mansion for a second carriage, and room in the stable for another horse, it was the living space above, where Donald Bruce currently resided, that was of concern. He lived there alone, and Abby would never think to impose a second occupant without Donnie's approval and acceptance.

"I believe Ada said his name was Stewart Campbell," Abby said, and Ezra smiled widely, relief written across his face. Another Scotsman. Donnie would be most pleased.

By Christmas, Ada was moved into Abby's home and her carriage, horse, and groom into their places under the watchful supervision of Donald Bruce.

Abby, Ada, and Ezra had Christmas dinner at Florence Mallory's, where Ezra and Ada announced their engagement. Emily prepared the holiday meal for the staff at Abby's: Donnie; Stewart; Anne, Ada's maid; and Caroline, Abby's new maid, and the five of them ate, laughed, and sang carols in the scullery kitchen because it was warmer than the formal dining room where Abby said they could eat if they wished. But it was bitterly cold and a howling wind rattled the windows. Despite the fact that the heavy draperies across the windows were pulled tightly together, cold air circulated freely. All staff except Emily, the cook, were tasked with keeping coal fires burning in all the upstairs grates, in place of Eli who was spending the Christmas and New Year holiday with the Junipers.

Donald and Stewart hauled the coal upstairs to Abby and Ada's rooms, and Anne and Caroline, new at the job, fed the grates in their suite of rooms. Because their mistresses were decent and compassionate women, the maids slept in the parlor rooms of the suites instead of in the always frigid servants' quarters at the top of the house, just as Eli occupied the sitting room of Ezra's suite in weather like this. It was doubtful that any household staff in any mansion on this street, except the kitchen staff, slept in a heated room on nights like this.

The new year—the new decade of 1860—was no warmer

than the old one and arrived on a Sunday with the promise of abundant snow. Eli returned later that day to a warm welcome from Abby and Donnie. Emily, Stewart, and Anne were cordial. Caroline was openly hostile and demanded an audience with Abby.

"He has no business in the kitchen with decent people," Caroline fumed, stalking about Abby's sitting room like some kind of animal.

"I beg your pardon?"

Because she did not yet know her mistress very well, Caroline missed the danger in the flashing dark blue eyes, a danger that rendered them obsidian. "The nigger doesn't belong in the kitchen with white women, and I won't be in the same room with him—"

"What does your minuscule and deficient brain imagine will happen if you're in the same room with him?"

"My mam says they're all heathens who will ravage any white woman in sight."

"What does ravage mean, Caroline?"

Perplexed confusion creased the girl's face; then she shrugged. "It's just what my mam said, Miss."

Abby stiffened and practically growled, "You should avoid listening to stupid people. It turns your brain to gruel. Please pack your belongings and leave my home immediately. Donnie will deliver you back to where you came from—"

"No, I canna go back there!" the girl screamed in terror.

Abby was momentarily taken aback. She had been assured of Caroline's good references, which she'd most certainly not have received had she been dismissed for cause, and if anyone could ferret out a dismissal for cause it was Florence Mallory. "Why can you not go back there?"

Tears streamed down the girl's face, and she wiped them with the back of her hand and looked down at the floor. "Because the Master . . . he . . ." She began to shake. Fury rose within Abby.

"Was your Master a Black man?"

Caroline's tears immediately ceased, and she looked at Abby as if she'd turned orange. "Of course he isn't!" She was offended by the idea.

"So, the white master can have his way with you, but the Black house servant—and a boy, not a grown man—who has never even spoken to you, is guilty of unspeakable things in your mind?" She wanted to pummel the girl but knew it would be wasted anger. She pulled the bell to summon Eli and turned to her writing desk where she penned a hurried note to Florence saying that Caroline was proving to be most unsuitable and a distracting presence, and could therefore not remain. Eli arrived within seconds.

"Yes'm, Miss Abigail?"

"Please have Donnie take you to Florence. Give her this note. No need to wait for an answer. Then return here immediately and have Donnie pick up Caroline at the scullery door and take her to Florence. And Eli? You know where to ride in the carriage, yes?"

"Yes'm, Miss Abigail," he said, hurriedly leaving without a glance at Caroline, though he was acutely aware of the hatred she glared at him.

Miss Eugenie had taught him to pay no mind to what stupid white people did and said, but to always be aware of how close one was standing and to know what was in their hands. Those things were second nature to him now, so he could ignore the stupid girl and focus his thoughts on how he'd immediately drop to the floor of the carriage, out of sight . . . He had forgotten to ask Abby whether he should enter the Mallory home via the scullery door or the front door, but Donnie would know what to do. And he did.

Donnie took the note to Florence Mallory's front door, entered, and was gone long enough for the woman of the house to read Abigail's note, then write a response. Eli lay out of sight on the floor, beneath a blanket that kept him warm as well as hidden.

"We're home, young Eli," Donnie called out a few moments later, and he was down on the ground with the carriage door open when Eli emerged to find it was snowing quite heavily. "Give this note from Mrs. Mallory to Miss Abigail," Donnie said, then shouted, "and tell the *lady* Caroline to hurry herself," as Eli was halfway up the garden path to the scullery door so fast it seemed the snow never touched him. He would not have understood the sarcasm in Donnie's voice referencing "the lady Caroline" even if he'd heard it.

Donnie knew he would say nothing to Caroline, and it wasn't necessary as she was out of the door before he reached it, running down the path, dragging her case behind her. He hurried upstairs with the note from Florence Mallory. Abby called out for Eli, and he knocked and entered. She was on the sofa in her sitting room, papers spread all around her. She read the note and muttered something, words Eli did not understand.

"Is you all right, Miss Abigail?"

"Are you, and yes I am, Eli, thank you." She stood up, shivered, and pulled her shawl more closely around her. Eli hurried to the grate, adding more coals, then crossed to the broad expanse of windows to make certain the draperies were doing their work. They were tightly closed but the blowing, frigid air seeped in, and there was nothing the draperies, despite their weight, could do to prevent it.

When he turned back, Abby was peering into the fire, apparently lost in thought. She turned to him. "It seems I must inform Emily that Mrs. Mallory will be joining us for dinner, though I've no idea what we're having."

"Chocolate chicken," Eli replied with alacrity. Abby halted mid-stride and gave him an odd look. "That's what she said, Miss Abigail, that she was cooking coco—"

Abby started to laugh. It began as a giggle that she tried to control, but the laugh had a life of its own and suddenly it was out and free. Eli had never heard her laugh like that, and it was a wonderful sound. He did not have the words to describe it, but he liked it. He followed her into the wide second-floor hallway, closing the door to her suite to keep the heat in. She put her hand on the door handle to Miss Eugenie's suite—she did this every time she passed it—but she didn't stop until she reached the staircase.

"I think what Emily most likely said was coq au vin—"

"Yes'm. That's exactly what she said when she was cutting up the chickens. That's not chocolate chicken?"

Abby hugged him so tightly he squirmed trying to free himself. "It's French, Eli, and it's a delicious chicken dish."

"*Coq* means chicken in French?" Eli asked.

Abby shook her head. "It means rooster, but all the cooks I know of use chicken because the rooster is a tough bird no matter how long it is cooked. And I think chicken tastes better anyway. I'll ask Emily to serve it with potatoes because I know you miss Maggie's potatoes."

"I miss everything about Ma Maggie, and she misses you. So does Miss Eugenie."

What? she thought. Abby was halfway down the grand staircase and had to grab the wide banister with both hands to keep her balance. "How do you know that, Eli? That Genie misses me?"

"'Cause she told Ma Maggie and she was crying about it."

Abby wanted to cry, too. Life without Maggie and Genie was unbearable. She tried, and she thought succeeded more often than not, in concealing that feeling, but Ezra knew it, and so did Eli. She took the boy's hand and they continued down the staircase, across the wide foyer, down the hall, and into the kitchen.

Emily assured her that there would be sufficient food should Florence Mallory join them for dinner. "The house where I worked before had men—a father and two sons—and the sons had friends who often dined with the family, and I learned how always to make more than enough food, and to always have rice or potatoes and lots and lots of bread and butter."

"Excellent lessons, Emily, and I hope you will follow them in this house, as Eli eats more than the grown men."

"Yes, Ma'am, Mistress Abigail. I did notice that."

"What do we have for dessert? Florence has a notorious sweet tooth."

"Egg pudding with caramel sauce or a pound cake with caramel sauce?"

"Let's have the egg pudding, please Emily, and thank you," Abigail said, leaving the kitchen thinking she'd much prefer a good cook to a surly maid any day.

Eli, in muffler and scarf, came up from the cellar lugging two coal scuttles. He continued up the backstairs where he would leave them so they'd be on hand when needed. The other scuttles he would bring up closer to the time to light the fires in the parlor, dining room, and Ezra's suite. He knew that Abby's grate was full, so he checked with Emily to see how the kitchen stoves were and she surprised him with a thick piece of bread, butter and jam. She wasn't Ma Maggie, he thought, but maybe she'd be all right. And when she told him a little while later to look how hard the wind was blowing and how high the snow was drifting and maybe, she said, he wanted to light the downstairs grates now, he knew she'd be all right.

He had cleared the snow off the front walk, steps and porch just as Florence Mallory's carriage arrived, and he hurried down the walkway with an umbrella to meet her.

"'Evening, Mrs. Mallory."

"Good evening, Eli," she said, holding tightly to his arm. Though the walkway appeared to be clear, ice could form in an instant in such weather, and would likely be invisible until too late.

"Mr. Donnie is waitin' for you," he called out to Florence's driver before leading the woman to the front door.

"And it is so wonderfully nice and warm in here!" she exclaimed when they entered the front hall.

Eli was taking her hat and coat when Abby came down the stairs. "Good evening, Auntie Florence. I see that Eli has you well in hand."

"Indeed he does, Abigail," she said, following her hostess into the parlor where a roaring fire crackled and popped. "He has grown into a most worthy young man. You have done a fine job."

"Not without assistance from Maggie, Genie, and Ezra. He reveres them and they love him as much as I do."

"I daresay not another woman in Philadelphia can say as much about a houseboy."

"And yet Caroline called him a nigger heathen who would ravage her the moment the opportunity presented itself."

Florence Mallory's mouth gaped and she clutched at her chest. She looked at Abby in total disbelief. She tried twice to speak and failed. The third time she managed to say in a choked voice, "Whatever would lead her to say such things?"

"Her mother, it seems."

"I didn't know . . . I couldn't imagine . . ." A totally flustered Florence gave up the search for words.

"I realize that I owe you an apology for having her deposited on your doorstep, but I simply could not allow her to remain here, not only because of her ignorance, but because of the way she spoke to me. The overwhelming insolence of the girl." Abby stopped short of revealing that she had wanted to throttle Caroline, but although her anger still burned hot, she admitted there also was that small measure of pity for the girl.

"Pity? Why, Abigail? Based on what?"

"Because of her treatment at the hands of her master."

"What on earth are you talking about? What treatment?"

"The man was having his way with her," Abby snapped. "And my Eli is a heathen? She's lucky I didn't give in to the urge to throttle her. Why are you looking at me like that, Auntie Florence?"

"I was told she left the employ of her house because of the behavior of the eldest son, not the master of the house," Florence replied.

Abby looked stricken. She'd been totally convinced that Caroline feared returning to her previous employer for the reason she stated. Was the girl a liar as well? If so, she was a good one, and Abby acknowledged she had been totally taken in, though in truth it mattered not a bit whether it was the father or the son taking liberties with the girl. It was unforgivable that she should have to work in such conditions.

"Well, it falls to me to determine the truth, for without it I cannot refer her to anyone else." She looked steadily at Abby. "I certainly can learn whether a house employs Blacks, and if so, I'll not refer Caroline there. But I cannot, in good conscience, refer someone with a weak relationship to the truth."

"But Auntie Florence, what difference does it make whether it is the father or the son who takes liberties with the girl, no matter how unpleasant or stupid she is?"

Ezra knocked on the door of Miss Adelaide's Hat and Dress Shop and grinned at the look of wide-eyed surprise on Genie Oliver's face when she opened it.

"Ezra! Is everything all right?"

"Everything is fine, Eugenia. Or it will be if you'll let us in out of the cold."

"Of course," Genie apologized, opening the door wide for Ezra and Ada.

"Good day, Mrs. Tillman," Ezra said to Adelaide who

hovered in the background.

"Good day, Mr. MacKaye, and a Happy New Year to you . . . and your friend."

Genie pushed past Adelaide since she offered no welcome, and led Ezra and Ada in toward the cast-iron stove in the middle of the long room and away from the chill of the front door.

"I know you're both very busy, and we won't stay, but I want to introduce you to Ada Lawrence and to tell you that we are engaged to be married."

"Oh, Ezra!" Genie exclaimed and hugged him. She could feel Adelaide's disapproval at her back. "How very wonderful." And then she hugged Ada. "I am so very happy for you both."

"My congratulations," Adelaide said, locating her good manners and extending her hand to Ezra and Ada before returning to the cutting-and-fitting tables at the other end of the room.

"I can make some tea," Genie began, but Ezra was shaking his head and waving away the offer. No need to irritate Adelaide Tillman further.

"We will celebrate properly another time. I just wanted you to know, and for you to meet Ada, and to tell you that Ada now occupies a suite of rooms at Abby's. Upstairs, on the top floor." And he smirked, for he'd let her know not only would there be no late-night visits between him and Ada, but her visits to Abby on the second floor would be undisturbed as well. "I look forward to getting to know you, Ada," Genie said. "I think Maggie and I knew you were the one before Ezra did."

"You most certainly did not. Do not listen to them."

"I think I'll always listen to them, Ezra my dear," Ada said with a wide smile. "Ezra has told me so much about both of you and of his respect and admiration for you both."

"Have you told Maggie and Jack?"

"We will go there when we leave here," Ezra said.

"I do hope we can all be together again soon," Genie said,

"to properly celebrate your engagement. Please give Abby and Eli my love."

Maggie reacted as Genie had—hugging him first, and then hugging Ada. "Come, let's tell Jack," she said, leading them through to the shop where Jack was kneeling before a customer, taking measurements of the man's feet. He glanced up, surprised, but did not halt his work. Ada and Ezra watched, fascinated, as Hezekiah English, a short distance away, methodically and expertly continued the process of building a new pair of boots.

"I should get another pair myself," Ezra mused as Jack's customer stood, donned his soon-to-be-old boots, and exited with a polite nod and a tip of his hat to Ezra and Ada.

"To what do I owe the pleasure?" Jack said with a slight bow to Ada and shaking Ezra's outstretched hand.

"I am pleased to introduce Miss Ada Lawrence, soon to be Mrs. Ezra MacKaye."

"Well!" Jack exclaimed, beaming. "What wonderful news. My hearty congratulations to you both." He clapped Ezra on the back and gave Ada a more formal bow. "You look to be a very lucky man, Ezra my friend."

"I believe that to be true, Jack, and I will be looking to you and your magnificent wife to give me husband lessons."

Maggie sniffed. "Until I met Mistress Ada, I'd have said you were hopeless," and Ezra beamed as if she'd bestowed a medal on him.

"Genie mentioned that you've designed a way to prevent snow and water from seeping into boots by lining them with wool or some warm fabric to prevent frostbite of one's feet. I'll come in a few days to be measured for as many pairs as I can afford," Ezra told Jack.

"When will you create something similar for women, Mr. Juniper? It's not as if we can remain inside safe and dry whenever it rains or snows," Ada said, sounding wistful, her frozen toes curled inside her shoes.

"My Margaret has said the very same thing, and when two such noble women speak the same words, a wise man listens and heeds," Jack said, hugging his wife and bowing again to Ada, tipping an imaginary hat.

The bell over the shop door signaled the arrival of another customer, and Ezra and Ada took their leave, Ezra promising to return in a few days' time to be measured for new boots. Maggie walked with them to the front door and thanked them for coming. "We miss you Maggie," Ezra said. "The house is a bit lonely without you. Please give my regards to Mistress Elizabeth."

Donnie jumped down from the carriage seat to open the door for Ezra and Ada; then he ran to hug Maggie. "You are sorely missed, Mrs. Maggie!" He ran back to the carriage, helped arrange the heavy blankets around his passengers, then closed the door and climbed to his seat. He arranged heavy blankets around himself, wrapped his feet in an animal skin, and got underway. He was grateful that Ezra and Ada now lived in the same location so that on days like this, when it was frigid and spitting snow, he didn't need to first drive her to her residence, and then drive to Abby's home.

"What wonderful friends you have, Ezra—" Ada's words were interrupted by the sudden halt of the carriage and a voice calling to Ezra, a voice he'd know anywhere. Elizabeth!

Ezra jumped from the carriage and ran back toward the cobbler shop to see young Elizabeth Juniper running toward him, followed closely by the long-legged and loose-limbed Hezekiah English, with Maggie running behind him. He was terrified.

"Uncle Ezra! Uncle Ezra!" the girl screamed.

Ezra scooped her up, the memory of his initial encounter with the girl some three years earlier fresh in his memory. It would never dim or fade—the young girl running from two slave catchers and screaming at the top of her lungs that she was no runaway. "Why are you out alone, Elizabeth? Surely you know better?"

"I just wanted to see you."

Hezekiah was upon them then, and so too was Jack, running faster than Ezra had ever seen anyone run. He grabbed his daughter from Ezra's arms and shook her like a rag doll. Terror, anger, and tears marred his handsome visage. "I have had quite enough of your disobedience, my girl, truly I have," he thundered, then thrust the now weeping and wailing child into her mother's arms, where she found little comfort.

She was too tall and too heavy for Maggie to carry so she put the girl down but kept a tight grip on her arm. "Thank you, Hezekiah," she said, and hurried back toward home, dragging her still weeping and wailing daughter along.

Jack clutched Hezekiah's shoulder with one hand and Ezra's with the other. He spoke no words, but none were needed. He released them and followed his wife and daughter home. Hezekiah English had come to America on a slave ship and Jack Juniper was a runaway slave. Both men knew the depravity, damage and danger awaiting a young Black girl should she be caught and sold. Donnie, Ezra and Ada didn't want to think about such things. The carriage ride resumed in silence. But there would be little silence in the Juniper home for hours to come.

CHAPTER TEN

The two newspapers serving Philadelphia's Black population—the National Anti-Slavery Standard and the Christian Recorder of the African Methodist Episcopal Church—were very clear in their thoughts about events threatening their community: the grave robbing at the behest of the Medical College, the robbing of Colored businesses, the snatching of Black people off the street to be sold into slavery, and the practice of white churches sending their poor to the Colored community for handouts. The newspapers, widely circulated in the Colored community, made their way with remarkable speed into the white community where they were read with a mixture of skepticism, disbelief, and amazement. The more well-meaning and enlightened of the white readers sent messages to their Black counterparts asking for clarification: could these claims possibly be true? And when assured that they were, they took action.

Letters of outrage went to Mayor Alexander Henry and Police Chief Samuel Ruggles. The mayor shared the outrage, the police chief did not. But enough of the wealthiest and most influential citizens were outraged that the medical college was inundated with complaints, many from prominent physicians. Under that level of scrutiny, the practice of paying to rob the graves of recently deceased Blacks halted.

Since the police chief was pro-slavery, with many of his cops actively involved in the grabbing and selling of Blacks into slavery and the robbing of Black businesses, no protections would be offered to the victims of these abuses. And since they weren't citizens anyway, they had no right to expect protection. And though slightly embarrassed by the idea of poor white immigrants seeking assistance from poor Black organizations, the white churches and organizations would not promise to halt the practice of sending their own to seek assistance from those least likely to have it to give.

So the Blacks were on their own, a circumstance so commonplace that it was expected. What still surprised them, however, were the whites who were angered when they were turned away from the Colored churches, and occasionally chased away from the Colored homes where they sought handouts. They did not expect this behavior from the dark people and they did not know what to do about it, though there must be something they could do. After all, at the largest of those AME churches they could see through the glass in the front doors the tables of clothes being given away and the bowls of hot, steaming food being handed out. Why could these dark people have something they could not?

Under these circumstances, the most pressing concern for the dark people was to formalize the establishment of some mechanism of self-protection. Though warned by most of the church ministers to avoid any behavior that would upset the police, as well as business and property owners, they proceeded to form a protection committee, agreeing with Jack Juniper that "The fact that we draw breath upsets the police and since they won't protect us, we must protect ourselves." Unexpected validation of their position came from some of the wealthiest residents of Philadelphia, now embroiled in open disputes with the police department. This had all become a matter of public interest and concern, as well as raising public discussion in the broadsheets.

Despite the cold, dozens of poor people, many of them homeless, roamed the streets where the wealthy resided, knocking on doors and asking for money, food, clothes, or permission to sleep in their carriage houses. They had varying degrees of success. One was killed by a footman at one of the mansions when he walked into the scullery without knocking and frightened the cook so badly that she threw a pot of boiling water at the beggar. The water missed him and scalded a parlor maid instead, whose screams brought the footman at a run. He grabbed a carving knife and buried it in the chest of the intruder.

With no trust in or regard for the City's police, the wealthy hired Pinkertons or other private security to patrol their streets twenty-four hours a day. The police chief complained to the mayor, who ignored him. He had no intention of doing or saying anything likely to upset his wealthy citizens. He was quoted in the newspapers as saying that the city didn't have enough police officers to keep every resident safe, to keep every home and business secure, nor was there enough money to hire more officers. However, he said, not only did he understand the need for residents to hire protection for themselves, but he supported it.

"He didn't say citizens, he said residents, and we're residents." And the Black residents went about the business of arming and training a militia under the direction of former Pinkerton agent Donald Bruce. All business and property owners who expected protection were charged a fee and no one resisted. As it happened the militia's first job was at the far end of the street where Genie lived. It was called The Back Street by the few who knew of its existence. It did not exist on any map of Philadelphia City because it was not really a street. It was a wide alleyway running behind Thatcher Lane, accessible from a main thoroughfare at only one end—Eighth Avenue. The other end, the one nearest Genie's home, was blocked by an eight-foot-tall brick wall at Main Street, one of the centers of Black commerce in Philadelphia.

There were five houses on The Back Street, all of them occupied by people who wished to remain out of the public eye. Were they all runaway slaves like Eugenia Oliver? No one knew for certain, and no one dared ask, including Genie who had little knowledge of her neighbors or their backgrounds. Four of the houses were solid and well-built, like Genie's. The fifth was little more than a shack, once occupied by Eli and Richard and Absalom and other homeless boys whom Genie fed. She eventually found work and permanent living arrangements for the boys, but in winter the unheated and raggedy structure provided no protection from the elements, and not even homeless boys lived there in winter, so no one expected the shack to be occupied.

The late-night knock at Genie's door was the agreed-upon signal for militia members: three quick knocks, a beat, two quick knocks, a beat, a final knock. Genie was up and dressed and at her door in a matter of seconds. She opened it just wide enough to see Eddie James, son of the baker on Eighth Avenue.

"Trouble, Eddie?" she asked, stepping onto her porch and noticing it was snowing again.

"Yes'm. Squatters in the shack and they done lit a fire in there."

Genie didn't waste seconds getting a coat. She was off the porch and running toward the shack, close on Eddie's heels. An out-of-control fire would destroy every house in the Back Street, as all of them were one-story wooden structures of varying degrees of professional proficiency, but only one could be considered a shack. And at the moment half a dozen militia members fronted the shack, weapons at hand. The largest of them, a man Genie did not know, kicked in the flimsy door while yelling for the inhabitants to "come on outta there and do it quick-like!"

Eight barely awake men stumbled out of the shack, and half

a dozen Thatcher Lane residents carrying buckets of water ran in behind them to extinguish the fire, a pile of sticks and leaves atop the packed earth floor. If the fire had blazed and spread, half the men in the shack would have been burned alive before they knew what was happening to them.

"You people can't stay here. You must leave now! Do you understand?" William Tillman spoke clearly, but it did not seem that any of the men understood him. They did understand, however, when men with sledgehammers, post mauls, and axes began demolishing the shack. They unleashed a torrent of words and looked so bereft that Genie wondered how long they'd used the shack as their refuge. They might well have gone unnoticed for some time had they not lit a fire.

Genie wasn't the only one who felt a pang of mercy for the now shelterless men on a cold and snowy night. A man named Bert spoke up. "If somebody can figure out how to make 'em understand what you're tellin' 'em, you can send 'em to the Mariners Mission down on Dock Street. They'll take 'em in and feed 'em, at least for tonight."

"That's a good idea, Bert," William said. "Since seamen come from all over the world, someone there is bound to be able to speak whatever language they understand."

"*Sprechen Sie Deutsch?*" Genie said, and the startled squatters stepped quickly away from her without answering and hurried away. Genie shrugged. She knew the men were German. She'd heard them chattering when the shack was demolished, but if they chose not to respond, well, then they could wander around all night in the cold, she thought.

After the squatters fled, she watched the militia complete the demolition of the shack. The militia guard would be posted for the rest of the night, the shack remnants cleared away in the morning, and work begun on a more permanent wall at this end of The Back Street. Genie said she'd take first watch after she went home for a coat, scarf, and gloves.

—ᴍ— —ᴍ— —ᴍ—

"I didn't know you spoke German, Genie," was Adelaide's greeting the following morning.

"The tutor in the house where I lived was German. She taught me. Latin and French as well."

"The . . . people . . . didn't mind?"

"My owners? They didn't care what I did as long as I learned everything there was to learn about sewing, which I did."

"Indeed you did!" Adelaide said, admiringly. "You are, without a doubt, the finest seamstress in all of Philadelphia!"

Genie wasn't interested in Adelaide's praise. She was more concerned about how they would manage to secure the Eighth Avenue end of The Back Street now that the shack was demolished. It was not a wide space—a bit under four feet. During the previous night's militia shift Genie learned that the man who'd built it intended for it to be a house until he realized it wasn't sufficiently wide, so he abandoned the effort. Genie was amazed. Hadn't he measured the space before he began to build? Their laughter at the long-forgotten man's expense warmed them for a brief time. Then they returned their thoughts to ways to close the space until it was warm enough for bricks and mortar to make a permanent closure.

"William told me you had a very good idea for how to construct a temporary wall," Adelaide said a bit too enthusiastically.

Genie gave her an almost angry look. "Please tell William he may not use you as a vehicle for his apology." Even if William himself did apologize, Genie could not promise forgiveness. William had ordered her to stay away from his property, and he had threatened Arthur, who'd left his job to protect Genie from slave catchers who were pursuing her.

"But he is very sorry for the way he behaved toward you, Genie."

"As well he should be, Adelaide, and for his treatment of Arthur. But he can and should apologize himself, not use you to bathe me in platitudes."

It now was Adelaide's turn to bestow the shrewd look. "As William has changed, Genie, so have you."

"And how have I changed, Adelaide?"

"You're not as kind as you once were."

"I'm not as hopeful as I once was. Or as naïve." And they both were grateful for the arrival of customers.

Abby and Ada very quickly became good and strong friends. Both relished having a friend the same age with whom to share thoughts, beliefs, ideas, and hopes for the future. Ada quickly put aside her concern that Abigail Read's wealth and social status would put her out of reach of such a friendship. Ada had never met a woman of such great wealth who was so unconcerned about that status. Nor had she met one who had so successfully separated things and possessions from money when determining what mattered.

Certainly, Abby knew money was both important and necessary, but she also knew that her mansion, the things in it, her jewels and gowns, were no measure of her value as a woman or as a friend. She also knew that those beliefs most decidedly were not sentiments shared by her friend Florence Mallory, who had made it clear on more than one occasion that she tolerated Ada because she was Abby's friend, not because she was worthy of the friendship of Florence Mallory. To her credit, when Abby became aware of Florence's treatment of Ada, not only did she never again place the two women in each other's company, but she also limited her own association with the older woman to when Ada was away.

Much of Abby and Ada's conversation had to do with Genie

and Maggie specifically, and with Blacks in general—and the way they were treated not only in Philadelphia but throughout the country.

"I confess that I do not understand how people who have no power, who have never had power, have come to be so reviled," Ada exclaimed, "and while I am glad to have been able to meet your friends and Ezra's, I am most pained by the circumstances of their existence, as well as by the fact that I perhaps contribute to it." Ada was, by turns, angry, confused, sad, and angry again.

"I understand your feeling—"

"Does it ever stop? I am so sorry for interrupting you, Abby, but these feelings occasionally overtake me, and I find myself wondering how they can tolerate us after all that they have endured at our hands."

Abby often wondered the same thing and said as much. "I do believe that this, however, is true—the one true thing that those who hate the Colored are so fond of saying: They're not like us. And that most certainly is true, for if they were as venal, as dissolute, as evil as they are portrayed to be, surely they would have dispatched us long ago."

"So, if they won't dispatch us—the Junipers and Eli and Genie—what will they do? Surely they cannot continue to endure and suffer."

"They can leave," Abby said. "They will leave."

"And go where?"

Abby hoped she hadn't said too much but she couldn't stop now. "Canada." And at the expression on Ada's face, she began to wish she hadn't spoken.

"You do know that I'm Canadian?" Ada said.

"I had no idea! Ezra never told me that. Do you return often?"

"Unfortunately, almost never. It is a very difficult journey, but my parents and my siblings are there, and I miss them. I came here for schooling and remained," Ada said sadly. Abby had never missed London, but then she'd come to America as a child—she'd been brought by her parents—so there was no one for her to miss in her native country. No one that she remembered, and she remembered nothing of London.

"Where in Canada do you call home, Ada?"

"Toronto."

Toronto was a place she had heard Jack mention, along with Nova Scotia, but he had no firsthand knowledge of either city. They were just places talked about by Black sailors, places where, it seemed, Black people lived in peace. "Would you be willing to discuss Toronto with Genie and the Junipers? What might it be like for them to live there, to raise and educate children there? And how would they get there? And where would they live?" Abby heard herself and apologized profusely. "I am so very sorry, Ada. I was so excited to learn of your connection to Toronto that I got carried away."

Ada took her hand. "Am I correct in thinking that you will be calling Toronto home as well if Genie and the others really do leave?"

"Yes," Abby replied. "Which is why I would like for you to arrange to sell this house and everything in it for the most amount of money you deem to be possible. And the jewels and the gowns. I realize that such an undertaking will not happen overnight." Abby reassured a stunned Ada. "You and Ezra will not be homeless in the near future, I promise."

Ada was still and silent for a long moment. When she finally spoke, her tone was cautious and slightly wary. "It will take months to arrange a sale of such magnitude," she said, disconcerted at the thought. "Perhaps you would do better to consult an auctioneer—"

"I trust that you can manage, Ada. Unless you'd rather not?"

"Of course I will, Abby. It's just that I've never undertaken such a ... I only hope I don't disappoint."

"I have no fear of that," Abby said. "Anyway, I would so

much rather pay the commission to you than to some unknown auctioneer."

Ada threw back her head and emitted a most surprising cackle. "And believe me I most certainly would rather have it." Then she sobered, though only slightly. "If I may make a suggestion?"

And when Abby nodded, she said, "Do not sell your linen, silver, and crystal. It is European and of superior quality. Wealthy members of Toronto high society pay dearly for such quality—and they currently must send to Europe to obtain it. If it could be purchased in downtown Toronto in a shop owned by women who look like you and Genie Oliver—" Now she offered a sly grin. "There would be no end to the speculation."

"You do seem to be enjoying yourself, Miss Lawrence," Abby said to her friend, aware of the potential for speculation and the likelihood of its nature. She rather enjoyed the thought herself.

"I only wish I could wave a magician's wand and have it all come to fruition overnight, to save all of you from further worry!" Ada said.

"Oh how wonderful that would be," Abby enthused, "but I will happily save that magic and use it instead to produce a time and place for you to meet with Genie and Maggie and Jack to discuss Toronto, and ways to get there safely." Abby's lovely face suddenly clouded and something that resembled hopelessness took over. "Travel that already is difficult and dangerous is made more so by the fact that they travel with two young children."

"I may have a solution to that dilemma, but first, if you don't mind, one more question: What about citizenship, which is such a frightening topic for the Colored people here? Abby, you and the Junipers are British. Canada is a British colony so all of you have a right to Canada, as do the Juniper children—"

"And Genie?" Abby interrupted to ask.

"Genie is whatever you say she is," Ada replied.

CHAPTER ELEVEN

A da did indeed have a solution and it was a wonderful one: They all convened at her house in the country, a spacious, rambling structure three miles west of Philadelphia and out of view of any eyes interested in a gathering of friends who were not all the same color. Daniel Roberts, Ada's stable hand who'd been living at the country house with his wife, Josie, since escaping would-be slave catchers five months ago, was pleased to have company. They walked around smiling at and greeting and welcoming people over and over.

Daniel, Jack and Ezra took Eli hunting and fishing and taught him to clean and dress whatever it was they'd be eating at the next meal. Eli didn't really enjoy hunting, and he most certainly could have done without the cleaning and dressing aspect of the activity, but he'd never admit it because he relished every moment spent with Jack and Ezra. If he had to kill, clean, and gut to be with them, so be it. Josie brought in food from the garden and the women cooked and cooked, and they all ate and ate. More than once, more than one of them wished that they already were in Toronto, for surely this is what life would be like—all of them able to be together without fear. And it would be all of them, for Ezra and Ada had announced that they'd be taking up residence in Toronto as well.

Being out of Philadelphia, in a secluded location, meant that Genie and Abby could spend time alone, a need understood and respected by everyone except Eli and Elizabeth. The children left them alone at night, but during the day constantly inquired as to their whereabouts. Genie and Abby had little choice but to appear and turn themselves over to the children, whose obvious delight in their presence almost compensated for the women's loss of their privacy.

And while both children were quite fond of Abby, it was Genie they adored. With Eli holding one hand and Elizabeth the other, the three went for long walks and talks. Though she was assured that they were alone and quite safe, Genie was armed. She would kill, or die trying, to protect these children. Maggie and Abby took advantage of the opportunity to spend time together as well. They had not ever been separated for so long a time, and they had sorely missed each other. "Admittedly my mind has little free time to mourn your absence," Maggie said, "but my heart feels it acutely."

"I still look for you in the house. I turn a corner and expect to see you, and more than once I've almost asked Eli to give some message to you," Abby said.

"I am glad that Ada has proved to be such an agreeable companion, for you as well as Ezra. I think it is so much better that you have someone closer to your own age to share with than always having to rely on Florence Mallory," Maggie said, adding in her inimitable dry, flat tone, "who is your mother's age."

Abby barely managed to control a sly grin and Maggie prepared herself for what might be coming. "I don't need to tell you, I'm sure, what Florence thinks of my referring to Ada as a friend." Maggie snorted but did not reply verbally, so Abby continued. "I now see Florence only when Ada is otherwise occupied, either at her office or with Ezra. And do you know that Florence has not once asked about her? As if she doesn't exist. Never existed!"

"And for Florence, she didn't exist, Abby—a woman with no title, no lineage, no money—"

"Ada Lawrence has more money than Florence can imagine. Perhaps more even than I have." And when Maggie gave her a raised eyebrow Abby collapsed into giggles. "Perhaps I may exaggerate a bit."

"Just a bit," Maggie said laughing, then quickly sobering at the look on Abby's face, which, devoid of levity, left it full of sadness. "What is it, Abby?"

"I don't know what kind of people my parents were, what they thought and believed. There is so much about them that I either don't remember or I never knew." She paused, thinking, trying to remember . . . "My mother belonged to that Abolitionist group with Auntie Florence. Did they really oppose slavery, Maggie, or was that merely a society thing? Or perhaps my mother belonged just to spite my father."

With a wry grin Maggie allowed that Gerald Read most certainly was infuriated by his wife's anti-slavery views, but it was her refusal to give him the money he needed to buy an interest in a transatlantic slave ship that really enraged him.

Abby was appalled. "He really wanted to—" She could not manage to say the words. She began to weep, and Maggie held her, wishing that she could retract the words that had caused such pain. Surely at this stage Abby did not need to know that only the lack of money prevented her father's participation in the slave trade.

"I always wondered how she was able to hide her fortune from him for so long," Abby said through her tears. "She always promised that I would be a wealthy woman one day, but some part of me never believed it because every time she went out, he turned her rooms upside down and inside out, looking for her money and jewels. And my mother's maid, Elspeth, helped him!"

Abby's tears halted and dried as she pushed herself out of Maggie's arms. "I just this moment remember Elspeth helping

97

him search her rooms, and him telling her to search my rooms, too." The horror came back to her in a flood of memories long forgotten. "Or long suppressed?" Abby wondered aloud.

"Probably a bit of both," Maggie said.

"Then why do you remember more than I do?" Abby asked.

"Because it doesn't matter what I remember," Maggie said, and something in her tone prompted Abby to ask what she remembered, which in turn prompted a look of pure discomfort on Maggie's face.

"You know it cannot matter now what you tell me," Abby said.

Tears welled in Maggie's eyes surprising them both. "Your mother hid her things in my room, in my closets and cabinets and drawers, and your father never, not once, searched my things because it never, not once, occurred to him that what he sought would be in the possession of a darkie. That's what he called me, a darkie."

Abby finally grasped why she had suppressed all memory of her father and was grateful she had. But was her mother like him? Did Abby really want to know? It was time she did. "Did my mother love me?" she asked Maggie, because in truth, that really was all she wanted to know.

"She adored you, Abby, and . . . and she loved me. She told me that. She said she had to love me because my mother was on the other side of the ocean, so she had to be my mother, too, taking care of two beautiful, perfect little girls."

"Those words I do remember!" Abby exclaimed. *My two beautiful, perfect little girls.*

"And I am so fortunate to have two beautiful, perfect children. I think of your mother whenever I look at them and I think she would agree with me."

"Those children are fortunate to have you as their mother."

"And to have you as the other person who will always think of them as beautiful and perfect," Maggie said, thinking of Elizabeth and Eli, and glancing around. "And there's only one possible reason we can quietly discuss and have not been besieged by their perfect and beautiful selves."

Abby laughed, her good humor restored, knowing that only Genie could distract Eli and Elizabeth so thoroughly for so long.

"One other thing," Abby said. "I must now see and think of Auntie Florence in a different light," she told Maggie. "She was shielding me from the truth."

"If anyone knew the truths and secrets your mother kept it would be Florence."

"Was her husband as . . . awful as my father?"

"They were cut from the same cloth," Maggie replied sadly, "though I never heard him refer to me as a darkie." Abby shuddered and Maggie, with a complete change of tone, said, "And she can be so very welcoming of me. Why is that, do you think? I've wondered."

"Because you, Margaret my dear, are as British as the queen, as Florence has always wished to be. I think that's why she so revered my mother. And because you always bake her favorite sweets."

"How will she respond to your intention to move yourself to Canada?" Maggie asked.

"It is a British territory, and therefore it is British, and therefore Florence will find it acceptable," and even Maggie had to smile at the truth of that observation.

"One more question, Maggie, please? And I promise, just the one: was my father having an affair with Elspeth?" The expression on Maggie's face provided all the answer Abby needed.

"How will we get there and when will we go?" Genie asked.

There were days when she thought and felt she could not tolerate another moment in the country of her birth, for despite the bondage she was born into, she was an American born in the state of Maryland. And yet there were multitudes who wished her away, and she wished she could say to every one of them that she shared their wish—more than shared it.

"There really is no easy way to reach Toronto from here, which is why I don't visit more often," Ada said. "And for a large group?" She surveyed the group before her. "On the water, in a boat, may be the best, if not the only, way."

Jack rubbed his hands together gleefully. "Music to my ears, Mistress Lawrence. If necessary, I will pilot the craft myself—" He paused mid-sentence, his gleeful expression changing to dismay. "I've forgotten to mention that I feel obligated to take Hezekiah with us."

Genie groaned. Of those present, only she and Jack had witnessed Hezekiah English's reaction to the threat of being bound and shipped to England. Jack had certainly told Maggie about it, but Genie had told no one, not even Abby. Now she told everyone.

"Oh, that poor man!" exclaimed Josie. "Chained in the bottom of that boat all the way across the Atlantic Ocean, and he was but a boy then and not the man he is now. And he probably saw his Mama die. No wonder he don't want to be in a boat on the water."

"But I cannot leave him behind," Jack said, misery heavy in his voice. "He knows not another soul but us. Margaret is teaching him his letters and numbers, and how to talk to people, but if we leave him behind—"

"No, we can't leave him. That wouldn't be right," said Daniel. "I'll drive him and me in a cart overland if it comes to that."

"That would not be safe. In fact, it would be both foolhardy and dangerous," Jack said, and everyone agreed. Ezra and Ada were the only ones who had traveled outside of Philadelphia. Yes, Genie had arrived from Baltimore by train many years ago—but she no longer remembered how many, nor any details of the trip—and Abby and Maggie had arrived as children, again many years ago, and neither had any memory of the details of the journey.

Abby only remembered that during the journey across the Atlantic from London, in a first-class stateroom and not chained below decks, she was nauseated and sick and miserable from beginning to end. She shared Hezekiah English's dread of a large body of water no matter the size of the boat. However, her knowledge of geography left her satisfied that even if they journeyed to Toronto via waterways, they might do it without sailing on the Atlantic. But neither she nor anyone else, excepting Ada, had any real idea of how to get to Toronto, and Ada had said there was no easy way to accomplish the journey. For the first time since their arrival at this country home, a reprieve from Philadelphia, excitement turned to dejection among the would-be emigres.

"I'll visit the docks and see what I can learn about reaching Toronto on the water," Jack said.

"I'm acquainted with a few railroad experts. I'll make inquiries about getting from Philadelphia to upstate New York," Ezra said.

"I know other Canadians," Ada added, "and I'll ask about ways to get there."

They all knew that as fine a time as they all enjoyed, as soothing to their spirits as the last three days had been, they could not justify staying longer. Abby and Genie cherished the time they'd had alone. They knew it could be the last until Toronto, but the certain knowledge that Toronto was real would sustain them.

As helpless and hopeless as Daniel and Josie felt in the countryside alone, they were buoyed that they now had friends who would become more to them when they all were in Toronto together. They also were relieved to know with certainty that Ada Lawrence had not abandoned them.

Their last meal together was a joyous affair, especially after Ada shared the citizenship information, including the fact that those who were not British could obtain Canadian citizenship. No Canadian court had ruled that Blacks were but three-fifths of a person and therefore not eligible for citizenship.

Eli stood up, gazing all around. Silence descended. All eyes were trained on the boy. "Can I say what my Canada name is?" he asked, voice quavering.

"Of course you may, Eli," Maggie said.

He cleared his throat and said, "ELI OLIVER READ JUNIPER" in a loud, clear voice that, after a moment of silence, brought a sustained cheer. Ezra clapped him on the shoulder, and Jack hoisted him onto his broad shoulders. Eugenia Oliver, Abigail Read, and Margaret Juniper wiped away happy tears. They all loved this boy and were so proud of him. How thankful they were to know that he loved them, too.

"You need not wait until Canada, son," Jack said. "You are Eli Oliver Read Juniper right now."

"I want a Canada name, too!" Elizabeth shouted, hopping from foot to foot, and Maggie and Jack knew there would be no rest until a Canada name was created for her.

CHAPTER TWELVE

Genie lost count of the number of times Adelaide asked if she knew yet when she was departing for Canada, and she was losing all patience. Every time Adelaide asked, Genie said she would tell her the moment she knew. More than once, Genie explained the logistical challenges facing them as the reason they could not simply depart. After one such explanation Adelaide blurted out, "Then why are you making such an effort to do something so seemingly impossible?" Genie had not bothered to reply. This morning, Adelaide asked again when Genie thought she'd be leaving, and Genie did not reply, which annoyed Adelaide. "You're not the only one with important decisions to make, Eugenia. My life will change, too, when you leave, and I'd like some idea what the future holds for me here in Philadelphia since I can't run off to Canada."

"Why can't you, Adelaide?" Although Genie hadn't really expected an answer, neither had she expected the hatred and fury that suffused Adelaide's face. The woman's mouth opened and closed but no words came out. As Genie watched her, she realized she was not surprised by Adelaide's reaction.

"Can't think of anything to say? No matter. When I leave, this shop will become entirely and solely yours, Adelaide. If, however, you are worried for your future, I will go this very moment to the lawyer and have the papers signed. Then I shall go to Joseph's Family Dining and enjoy a huge meal, followed by dessert. Then I shall go home and read until I fall asleep. And home is where I shall remain until I do the impossible and run off to Canada."

Now Adelaide was wide-eyed and speechless, apologizing profusely. Genie remained silent and unsympathetic. She was weary of the woman's attempts to make her feel guilty for her decision to leave. She had told Adelaide of her thoughts, feelings, and fears in great detail, and she had done so more than once. Enough.

Ada, assisted by her young apprentice, took a complete inventory of the contents of Abby's mansion. This, after a master builder supplied her with a comprehensive assessment of the building's structure and the materials used in its construction. "These are expensive undertakings, I know, Abby," Ada told her, "but they are costs that we will add to the sale price. This information also will serve to justify the sale price, which I assure you will be too steep for the frivolous to even contemplate."

"But not so steep that there will be no buyer," Abby exclaimed.

"Fear not, Mistress Read. Among those who survived the collapse of the Bank of Philadelphia will surely be someone who will wish to show how solvent he is, and what better way than to purchase the Read Mansion."

Ada had predicted the failure of the bank and had advised all of her clients to withdraw their money and liquidate their stocks. Most ignored her—the men. Her few women clients had heeded the advice and now were completely solvent. They also were pariahs in the eyes of their male relatives. How dare these *women* still have capital when fathers, brothers, cousins, and in some cases fiancés and husbands, were practically paupers?

Well before the bank failed, Ada had advised her clients to use only silver and gold coins and to avoid the notes issued by private banks, because if the banks failed the notes would be worthless. So much fury was directed at Ada that one could almost think she alone was responsible for the bank's failure.

When Ada and her apprentice completed the inventory of Abby's silver, crystal, and linen, she gave a satisfied smile and nod, blonde hair askew and pencils protruding from several places. "If you were not already a wealthy woman, Abigail, you soon would be from the proceeds you'll garner in your Toronto shop. Your mother certainly had exquisite taste; some of these items are priceless. Are you certain you will wish to sell them?"

Abby called up an image of her mother, a stunningly beautiful woman who had surrounded herself with beautiful things. Yes, many of the items Abby had inherited no doubt were priceless, but Abby neither wanted nor needed them.

Entertaining noble and royal guests was her mother's favorite pastime, and though Abby wished she could know and understand why, she also knew and understood that it could not possibly matter now. Perhaps it was as simple and uncomplicated as the fact that she loved festive occasions. She recalled some of the art her mother cherished, especially the art of the Orient, artifacts her father had sold without her mother's knowledge, and certainly without her permission. Those things Abby would have kept because even as a child she thought them beautiful. Silver, linen, and crystal? Yes, she would happily sell it all for as much as wealthy Toronto residents were willing to pay.

The area around the docks was as familiar to Jack Juniper as the inside of his own home, and that included not just the docks at the Port of Philadelphia but the docks of Liverpool and any of the other places the ships he worked on sailed into. That familiarity perhaps no longer was a welcome one, but still a recognizable one. He promised his Margaret that his days as a seaman were over and that promise he intended to keep. Except, perhaps, for one last journey on a ship he would captain, a journey taking the people he cared most about to a place of safety. A place where his beautiful, impulsive daughter could run outside without fear of being stolen and sold into depravity.

He still knew men at the Philadelphia port, and many still knew him, willingly answering his questions about who might have a vessel available to take passengers and cargo to Toronto at some time in the next few months. And while no one asked him why he was interested, he could see and feel the question as if it actually had been posed, but he was here seeking information, not imparting it.

"Jock Juniper!" He heard his name shouted out and looked around to see who called him. It would be one of the men from Africa or the Caribbean, men who would pronounce Jack as "Jock." He spied him coming from the dockmaster's office, a bandy-legged Jamaican who courted trouble the way a normal man would court a woman, and who in addition to trouble also had, or had access to, many different kinds of useful information.

"Hearty greetings, Kingston!" Jack hollered back, calling the man by the name he used—the capital city of Jamaica—because no one knew any other name for him. Perhaps he didn't have one . . . or perhaps, like Jack, he'd given himself another name. Jack Juniper no longer recalled the name he'd had before he escaped slavery in Maryland and made a new life for himself, a life that included a new name.

"What brings you here, Mon? I thot you was done wit' de water," Kingston said, shaking Jack's hand.

"Done with sailing for men who would sell me into slavery, Kingston."

The merriment left the Jamaican's broad face. Every Black sailor had heard the story of the ship's captain who had bypassed the Port of Philadelphia to sail down to Charleston where he planned to sell his Colored crew to the highest bidder. Unfortunately for the captain, his crew learned of the plan and jumped ship when they saw it sailing past Philadelphia.

Unfortunately for Jack and his mates, it was in the middle of a brutal storm and most people feared they'd all perished. They all did perish. All except Jack Juniper. Those who knew him said if anyone could survive, he could, and he had. "I'm looking to find a ship to take passengers and cargo to Toronto. Can you suggest a captain?"

"How soon, Jock?"

"Soon, Kingston, before the hard winter sets in and ice collects on the water and puts a halt to sailing for all but the largest craft."

The Jamaican studied the horizon, as if an answer was writ there, and to a man of the sea perhaps there was, for he said, "The ship you want docks in perhaps six weeks. Captain is named Addams, coming back here from Canada and then sailing down to deliver cargo to Delaware and Baltimore." He studied Jack as he'd eyed the sky before. "How many passengers and how much cargo, Jock?"

"Not too much cargo, Kingston—household items—and ten, maybe twelve, passengers."

Kingston shook his head negatively before Jack completed his sentence. "Too many people. It's a good boat but it is not a big one. If any of the passengers are men . . ." He looked Jack up and down. "Your size? No, Jock." And he shook his wide head again, harder this time.

Jack himself, Ezra, Hezekiah—three big men—and two smaller ones. But to wait for a larger ship was not wise. The unrest in Philadelphia was growing like an ugly disease that, bit by bit, takes over a body and eventually kills it. An idea was taking shape in Jack's mind. "What kind of captain is this Addams?"

"I've sailed with him and would do so again."

"What kind of man is he?"

Kingston's eyes narrowed. "What you askin' me, Jock?"

"My wife and daughter, and two good friends who are like sisters to me, are some of the passengers. If I can't travel with them—"

Kingston chuckled, a low rumble in his throat. "He knows you'd kill him very dead if any harm came to your women and children."

"And how does he know that?"

"Ev'rybody who knows you, Jock, or knows about you, knows that."

"It is a true fact and I'm glad everybody knows it," Jack said quietly though he hoped not to have to kill anyone ever again. He extended his hand to Kingston. "I owe you my thanks."

"Worth a new pair of boots?"

"As soon as you come to have those huge feet measured," Jack said, looking down at Kingston's boots to see toes poking out. The man definitely needed a new pair, and Jack knew that Kingston would let Captain Addams know the moment he docked that a well-paying customer was waiting to hire him.

Ezra danced a little jig at the news, pumped Jack's hand, and hugged Maggie and Elizabeth. He hadn't realized how knotted his insides were until he felt himself relax. If he was this fearful and on edge, he truly was grateful that he didn't have to feel what Jack and Maggie and Genie felt. How they always felt.

Philadelphia was becoming a more dangerous place to live every day. Numerous fires in almost every part of the city not only resulted in the loss of life and property, but made the populace wary and nervous because it was impossible to predict where or when the next blaze would erupt. Then there were eruptions of violence. Native Philadelphians brawled with the new immigrants crowding into a city without enough housing or jobs to accommodate them. Very quickly what had merely been rundown neighborhoods became severely overcrowded germ-infested and filth-ridden slums. One positive aspect arising from this situation was that white men were so intent on battling each other that the Blacks enjoyed a period of relative peace, especially once it became known that they would guard and secure their neighborhoods and homes with force if necessary.

"Ada and Abby will be most relieved to get this news," Ezra said, "as will Eugenia. I'll go tell her when I leave here."

"Oh yes," Maggie said. "Please see to her. We hear from Arthur that she is having a most difficult time with Adelaide who, it seems, bitterly resents her leaving, and I cannot be a comfort to her because I cannot get to her."

That knowledge affected them all somberly, for Genie was everyone's favorite.

"There likely is one big obstacle," Jack said, and related what Kingston had told him about the size of the ship. "Certainly the women and children must go—"

"Not without you, Jack," Maggie exclaimed, clutching his arm.

"We cannot risk losing this opportunity, Margaret. We can have a hard freeze any time once winter sets in, and only the largest vessels can break up the ice and continue to sail through it." He took a deep breath. He hated the idea of sending his wife and children away without him, but at least they would have each other. "Ada knows Toronto, and she has family and friends there to help everyone get settled. And if it's all right with you, Donnie Bruce will accompany the women and children, and should it become necessary, Eli and Genie can help him with their defense and protection."

"It would be an honor and a pleasure," Donnie said, after receiving a nod of acceptance from Ezra.

"How long before we can join them, Jack?" Ezra asked.

"I'll make the arrangement with Captain Addams that when he unloads our people and cargo in Toronto, he comes directly back for us. Not only will we pay him handsomely, but I'll work on his crew for free. He's not likely to have a hand with my amount of experience at his disposal." He looked at his wife, searching for her acceptance and approval, and when he found it, his breathing returned to normal.

Ezra saw the displeasure in Adelaide Tillman's face and heard it in her voice when she opened the door to him. "Good day, Mr. MacKaye," but the words did not hold the warmth of welcome.

"And a very good day to you, Mrs. Tillman. It is always a pleasure to see you."

She harrumphed and stood aside. He walked toward the back where he knew Genie would be.

"Ezra!" she called out when she saw him, and there was enough warmth in her greeting to compensate for the lack in Adelaide's. "Would you care for tea?"

He shook his head and began speaking quickly, almost in a whisper. Her breathing quickened and she gripped his arm. "Can it really be so soon, Ezra?"

"Jack thinks it's possible if the weather cooperates."

Tears leaked from her eyes, and it required all of Ezra's strength not to embrace her. He'd never seen Genie cry—he didn't think anyone had—but he knew that Adelaide was watching them, he could feel her disapproving stare, and any perceived intimacy between him and Genie, no matter how erroneous the perception, would surely mean trouble. For both of them. "Thank you, Ezra."

"I think it best that Jack comes to tell you directly when he has more news to report," Ezra whispered after a surreptitious squeeze of Genie's hand and without a good-bye to Adelaide.

Genie stood at the door getting her emotions under control before turning to face Adelaide. She would not allow the woman to ruin this moment for her—that in perhaps a month or five weeks' time she could be on her way out of Philadelphia forever.

"So, what did the great Ezra MacKaye have to say?"

"Let's return to our work, Adelaide."

"Why can't you tell me? You look very happy about whatever he said." Querulous, chiding, needling. Nothing in her tone made Genie want to answer Adelaide's question. Still . . .

"You've made it quite clear to me, Adelaide, that you don't really wish to hear about my plans to move to Canada—"

"What I really wish is that you would tell me what paradise you hope to find in Canada." Challenging, demanding. And as annoying as always.

"Not a paradise, Adelaide, just a place where I can be a whole person instead of three-fifths of one. A place where I can be a citizen, which I cannot be here in the country of my birth. I have told you these things, I have told you why I'm leaving, but you have chosen not to accept or embrace my words and my reasons, and that is your right. But I will not continue to repeat myself."

She withdrew a folded document from the pocket of her smock and gave it to Adelaide. "This transfers the ownership of this building and this business to you, completely and totally." She untied and removed her smock and placed it on the worktable. She went to the storeroom for her scarf, hat, shawl and gloves, wrapping herself to keep warm as she made her way to the front door. "I will come to see you and William before I leave for Toronto," she said, leaving Miss Adelaide's Hat and Dress Shop for the last time.

She walked quickly to Joseph's Family Dining, already imagining her enjoyment of the food there. She'd felt the same way the last time she left the shop early and hurried to the welcoming warmth of Aurelia and Joe Joseph's restaurant. The realization that she could go there whenever she chose now that her daylight hours were not owed to her business—the one that bore another's name—caused a lightness within her that she didn't think she'd ever felt. For the first time since she'd known the woman, she allowed herself to have the thought that maintaining a friendship with Adelaide was burdensome. For all her good qualities, and she had many, her tendency to judge and criticize and occasionally belittle what she didn't like or understand seemed to outweigh, and even negate, the impact of her generosity and kindness. And then there was the matter of William.

Genie respected and admired William Tillman primarily because she revered his mother, Carrie, who had taken the young runaway slave Genie in and given her the first real home she'd ever known and provided the young girl the first human kindness she'd ever experienced. During the years she had lived with Carrie Tillman, Genie learned how to cook, how to take care of a house, how to dress, how to shop for food, and perhaps most important of all, how to care for her own self. William was Carrie's son and always present, but he was not involved in his mother's activities, and he was actively courting Adelaide.

Genie did not really engage with William until she was on her own, in the house that Carrie had encouraged her to build, and into which she moved after Carrie's death. Carrie had known that she soon would leave them—she hadn't been in good health for quite a while—and she'd wanted Genie to be safe, secure and self-sufficient before that happened. And Genie had been. Until now. Genie no longer felt safe and secure, so leaving seemed the most logical thing to do. Much more logical than living in fear, living without hope.

Then Genie had another thought, one that quite literally stopped her feet from walking. And it was more than a thought; it was a realization: William and Adelaide Tillman were not her friends. Had never been her friends. What, then, were they?

She ran the short distance back to her former place of

business and hurried in. Adelaide was seated at the cutting table reading the deed transferring ownership of the property to her.

"We've never really been friends, have we, Adelaide?"

Adelaide was so shocked she dropped the deed. Scrambling to retrieve it and stuff it into her pocket would have been funny had Genie cared enough to laugh. "No, of course not!" the other woman huffed. "How could we be friends when you've always thought yourself more man than woman? Behaving more like a man than a woman, with your guns and men's clothes. And you whistle, Eugenia. Women do not whistle."

Her question answered, Genie turned and left, hurrying again to the familiar comfort of Joseph's Family dining.

"Look, it's Miss Eugenie!"

People she didn't know looked up at the announcement of her arrival, and those she did know hurried to meet her. Richard and Absalom reached her first and all but hugged the breath out of her. She walked forward to meet the Josephs, and though they certainly looked better than when last she'd seen them, they were far from hale and robust. But the hugs they gave her were tight and strong.

"I'm glad to see you two looking a bit better," Genie told them.

"We have you to thank for that," Joe said.

"We seem always to be thanking you, Genie," Aurelia said. "This time it's for sending us Robert and Josie. They are such wonderful people, and more helpful to us than they—or you—will ever know!"

"They truly are," Joe said. "I don't know what we'd do without them. They have quickly become like family."

"Not only are they wonderful people," Genie said, "but I know from personal experience that Josie holds her own in the kitchen."

"She most certainly does," Aurelia said. "I now am able to feel comfortable taking time away from the kitchen to rest."

"And Robert grills the meat as well as I do," Joe said. "'Relia told Rev. Turner last Sunday that they were a gift from God, and when I begged to differ, I thought the man would faint dead away. They're a gift from Eugenia Oliver, I told him, and he said a gift is a blessing no matter who gives it."

Genie said she could agree with that and followed Aurelia to a table. She ordered her food and said she'd be taking Arthur his favorite meal of fried chicken backs and necks and whole roasted sweet potatoes. Josie brought her a mug of hot cider and a napkin-wrapped set of utensils and promised to come sit and talk later.

While she waited for her favorite food—fried chicken, rice and gravy, collard greens, and cornbread—Genie used the time to read through the ever-present pile of newspapers and broadsheets. Many of them were so old she'd already read them, but a few were current and she devoured those, especially the ones from New York and Chicago. She read while she ate, asked for more hot cider, and was so relaxed and calm she wondered if she shouldn't have turned things over to Adelaide a long time ago.

"It's wonderful to see you, Genie," she heard, and looked up to see Robert, his hand out to shake hers. His hand was as warm as toast and he smelled of the smoke and wood and meat from the cook fires he tended.

"It is wonderful to see you both," Genie said. "I feel sometimes as if I abandoned you. I brought you here and left—"

"You did us as big a favor as you did for the Josephs," Robert said, waving off her apology, "and we are grateful."

"That's true," Josie said, joining them. "We have loved being here. They are wonderful people. They feel like the parents we no longer have, and Richard and Absalom feel like the brothers we've been without for so long that we barely remember them."

Genie knew better than to ask her people about missing family members. She still felt the pain of having her parents and siblings sold away when she was a child. Though she no longer remembered what any of them looked or sounded like, the hurt places inside of her left empty by their absence had never healed and most probably never would. "Joe and Aurelia are very special to me, so I'm very glad that you have felt so comfortable here with them."

"So comfortable, Genie, that we don't want to leave," Robert said.

"Until we spent time here, we thought that going to Canada would be the best thing for us to do," Josie said. "We couldn't think how we could keep living in Philadelphia and being scared all the time. But we feel safe here with the Josephs. We feel protected here."

"We feel like we're surrounded by family here," Robert added. "We told Joe and Aurelia what we had planned to do, and how, after being here with them, we had changed our minds, and they said they'd be happy to have us stay."

"You ain't mad about that, is you, Miss Eugenie?" Arthur asked. She'd taken him his food and was about to hurry away before William realized where Arthur was and what he was doing. She'd hate him to lash out at Arthur again, but she took just enough time to tell him about Robert and Josie.

"No, Arthur, of course I'm not. Surprised, but not angry. They're happy, the Josephs are happy, Richard and Absalom are happy, what more could I ask for?"

Arthur nodded and stole a look at the door. "I better get myself back inside."

"Yes, go. We'll talk soon."

"In the morning, Miss Eugenie, when I come to get you to walk to work."

She shook her head. "I no longer work there, Arthur—" And

the look on his face led her to assure him she'd meet him in the morning, just like always and explain.

And the following morning she stood shivering, despite being wrapped in her heavy robe, a scarf, and a hat, as she told Arthur what she'd done, and admitted that perhaps she should have done it sooner, given the sense of freedom she felt. Arthur nodded his understanding, then spoke his wisdom: "I think both of 'em wish they was goin' with y'all, William and Miss Adelaide do, but they think they too old to start over. That and bein' too proud to ask."

"You are a wise man, Arthur."

He shook his head but he smiled at her. "Just a old one, Miss Eugenie, and I can understand how they feel. If I wasn't so old and a cripple I'd be goin' with y'all. Ain't no reason to stay here. But just 'cause I can't go don't mean I oughta be mad 'cause you can go."

Genie took a folded document from the pocket of her robe, thinking this was the right time. "Arthur, this gives you my house free and clear when I leave, but I don't know your last name and to be legal the document must have your full name."

For a brief moment shock and disbelief creased the old man's weathered face. Then he grinned widely and happily, something Genie had never seen him do. "My whole name, what my Ma and Pa give to me, is Arthur Lee Green. My Ma was Mary Lee and my Pa was Arthur Green. But after they got sold off, I was just Arthur 'cause I didn't have my other parts. But if I'm gon' have a house, then I 'spect I better have my whole self. Arthur Lee Green is my name."

CHAPTER THIRTEEN

Ada correctly predicted how many of Philadelphia's well-heeled would be interested in purchasing a four-story Georgian mansion on Chestnut Street. She also correctly predicted how many would be able to afford Abby Read's place of residence. However, she protected Abby's identity as the seller at her request, even from her near neighbors—because Abby didn't want them to know. "They'll find out when they see the moving crates and the back of me, and that will be soon enough."

Abigail Read had inherited her mother's beauty and sharp intelligence, but not her love of society and socializing. Her decision, made some years earlier, to fill some of the mansion's suites with boarders had scandalized society and had the desired result of dropping Abby from every list of potential invitees to every social event. It also succeeded in dropping her from the list of desirable and eligible potential brides, which was Abby's true intention all along. She knew that her beauty and wealth would make her an eternal target of eligible Philadelphia bachelors unless something completely unforgivable saved her. Taking in boarders, all of them men, was that thing. No one believed for an instant that Abby needed the money, but neither did anyone think deeply enough to wonder at the behavior. Until, one by one, all the boarders departed, except for Ezra MacKaye, a tall, handsome Scotsman. And then the gossip and speculation reached a fevered pitch. None of which Abby cared about because with Ezra in the first-floor suite, Abby and Genie could rest safely and securely above. And now so could Ada Lawrence, Ezra's betrothed—and Abby's good friend, confidante, and worker of miracles.

"My dear Ada, you have just relieved me of a tremendous weight, and for a greater price than even you thought possible. Why don't you look happier? I am practically delirious with joy."

"And I am happy that I could bring you such happiness, dear friend. I just wish a better, more worthy person would be inhabiting these rooms." Ada let her gaze roam the elegant parlor that had become her home, a place she enjoyed not so much because of its richness but because she shared it with Ezra and Abigail. Now it would be inhabited by the vile and totally despicable Montague Wright, who had purchased not only the mansion but everything in it except what Abby was taking with her, though she so far hadn't yet told Abby the name of the buyer.

"My mother loved this house and everything in it, and as painful as it is to say, I am most relieved that she didn't live to see her life here ruined by my father's . . . I deplore having to use the word to describe him . . . stupidity."

Ada considered her next words very carefully. "Then I am most relieved that she will not have to see what's most likely coming to the house she loved all too soon."

"Whatever do you mean, Ada?" Abby said, jumping to her feet suddenly and almost knocking over her teacup. "What's coming?"

"I fear, my dear friend—worse, I strongly believe—that drastic and dramatic change is coming to Philadelphia, and to avoid the direst consequences of those changes, the wealthiest will move out of the city, leaving houses like this one to become multifamily residences—"

"Multifamily—please explain what you mean by that, Ada."

Ada took Abby's hands and held them tightly as her light gray eyes held the deep blue ones across from her. "Large, elegant rooms in large, elegant houses will see walls erected to create perhaps four smaller rooms in which entire families will live. So, a house like this one could house as many as . . . two dozen families. More, perhaps. It already has happened in other parts of the city. And in New York. And in Chicago, I think."

"But . . . but . . . who are these people? Where will they come from? And why?"

"From every European country, Abby. You must know that immigrants arrive here daily—and to Boston and New York and Chicago—and they come because centuries of monarchy and feudalism throughout the Continent have guaranteed that the poor have nothing to look forward to but continued and worsening poverty. They come because Europe—all the countries of their birth—are the Old World and this is the new one, where all things are possible. At least that's what they believe, what they hope and pray for."

"Unless one is dark-skinned and born here," Abby said, bitterness and sadness heavy in her voice as she thought of Genie and Eli and Jack, and the thousands like them. "I wish we could leave tomorrow."

"So does Dr. Wright. He wants to move in immediately. He didn't even want you to take the things you are—"

Abby looked horrified. "Not Montague Wright?"

"Surely you don't know him. You can't know someone like him!" Now Ada, too, looked stricken.

"Oh Ada, you do know, don't you, about the terrible beating that Ezra—" As Ada vigorously nodded her head, Abby continued, "The horrible Montague Wright was his doctor."

"Ezra told me it was Maggie, Eli and Arthur who saw him back to good health," Ada said.

"Oh, yes," Abby agreed with a wide Cheshire grin, "so they

did—once he was back here and in their care. But in the immediate aftermath of the beating, while he was still unconscious, Arthur Cortlandt had him taken to Dr. Wright, and that odious man visited him here once during his recuperation, marveling at his speedy recovery and even claiming credit for it, never once imagining that Arthur's horse liniment, administered by Eli as instructed by Arthur, and overseen by Maggie, and not his prescriptions, could be the reason."

"I am so glad that I refused to name the seller or give the exact location of the house." Ada gave a small, self-satisfied smile. "He was happy enough with the schematic and the mention of the words Society Hill." Now it was Ada's turn to affect a wise, smug grin. "Did I mention that the new owner managed to prevail as the result of a bidding war?"

"Ada Frances Lawrence, you know very well that you did not!"

Through grins, giggles, and the occasional unladylike guffaw, Ada explained that three bids exactly matched the asking price though she suspected that one of them would have difficulty managing the all-cash requirement, and especially that payment be made in pound sterling and gold eagle coins only, the exception being that the only acceptable bank notes would be those drawn on the Bank of England. The wily, savvy Ada Lawrence was proved correct when he withdrew his offer. When one of the two remaining aspirants, a recent arrival from London, realized there was a second offer, he increased his offer by two percent, which Ada duly reported to Dr. Wright, giving him the opportunity to best it or the house would be sold to the highest bidder. Though he complained mightily, he not only met the new demand but offered a bid of five percent above the original asking price, resulting in the withdrawal of the Londoner's bid. Consequently, Dr. Montague Wright became the presumptive owner of the Society Hill mansion.

"And you are certain that he can deliver?" Abby asked.

"Of course, I required proof of his ability to meet the terms of the contract that he signed, and his bank provided the necessary documentation, to wit, the sale of his residence here, the sale of a substantial property owned by him in Maryland, and as collateral his half ownership in the Philadelphia Medical College and City Hospital."

"You truly are the most amazing woman, Ada Lawrence," Abby enthused. "I want to begin packing right away, which will require that you choose the dishes, silver, linens, crystal, and whatever else you and Ezra will want in your new home."

"Have you decided what you and Genie will want?" Ada asked. "And do you know what Maggie will want for her home?"

"Genie thinks that she wants nothing though I'm hoping to change her mind, and I think I've known Maggie long enough and well enough to have a good idea of what she appreciates. In the meantime, Florence definitely wants the piano, and she is sending movers to collect it within a few days."

And now it was real: She really was leaving Philadelphia. Not only was she leaving but so was her childhood friend Maggie, and her husband and children, and the wonderful Genie Oliver, and her friend and protector Ezra MacKaye. All of them, leaving together, journeying together to a new life in Toronto, Canada, to live in a place where Genie and Maggie and Jack Juniper and Elizabeth Juniper and the marvelous young Eli no longer would have to live in fear of being stolen off the street and sold into slavery.

Jack Juniper looked up when the bell above his shop door signaled the arrival of a customer. He did not lock his shop door as did many merchants, especially the Colored ones, in the face of the increasing lawlessness plaguing Philadelphia. He thought, correctly, that the sight of him and Hezekiah—two very large

Colored men—were sufficient deterrents to anyone with more than new or repaired boots in mind. When he saw it was Genie, he dropped the leather he was cutting and stepped quickly away from the table and toward his friend, smiling widely, arms outstretched, welcoming the surprise of her visit. Then he saw her face and his heart thudded in his chest.

"Fetch Margaret," he said to Hezekiah as he embraced Genie, whispering gently. "What is it, dear friend?"

"I am all right, Jack, really I am," she sobbed into his chest, giving him no reason to believe her.

Maggie Juniper rushed in, wiping her hands on her apron, skidding to a stop at the sight and sound before her. She had never seen Genie weep and had never seen her husband look helpless, even at the worst of times. She gathered her wits, hurrying to comfort these two people she loved as much as she loved her two children, wrapping her arms around them and holding them tightly. She stood close enough to Genie to whisper in her ear.

"What is it, Genie? What has happened?"

Genie Oliver finally got herself under control. She didn't remember ever having cried, so once she started it seemed she could not stop. All of the long-buried emotion within her just kept rising to the surface, many years' worth, bringing tears with it. But stop she must because she was frightening her friends.

"Please believe me, both of you. I am all right, really I am. It's just that I think . . . I believe that for the first time in my life I am truly happy." She burst into tears again, and then the three of them were holding each other and weeping, all the while struggling to gain their composure, then finally starting to laugh through their tears. The huge fear that had begun to grow within Hezekiah at the sight of a weeping Jack Juniper began to shrink as he hurried to get damp cloths for them to wipe their faces and blow their noses. But first, to calm himself, he dunked his whole head in a bucket of water. However, because he didn't like water, he didn't know not to breathe and his piteous and loud coughing and sputtering brought Jack quickly to his rescue.

"No more crying, you?" Hezekiah said when he could speak again, and Jack, laughing instead of crying, gave Hezekiah a hearty slap on the back and said they should return to their work and leave Margaret to care for Eugenia.

In truth, they cared for each other in the way that good friends do when they realize they have neglected each other, no matter how unintentionally. The two women hugged and wept a bit more, and settled themselves at the kitchen table. As always, Maggie had a fresh-baked loaf of bread and a cake and Genie, not feeling the need to choose, first enjoyed a thick slice of bread with butter and jam with a cup of tea, followed by a slice of cake with a second cup of tea.

"I'm so sorry to have frightened you with my tearful arrival."

Maggie dismissed Genie's apology with a snort and a backward flip of her hand. "I'm sorry I didn't know that Adelaide wasn't a better friend, Genie—"

"How could you know if I didn't tell you?"

"Why didn't you tell me?"

Genie looked into Maggie's eyes. There was no anger there, no judgment, no accusation, no hurt feelings—none of the things that would have been present in Adelaide's gaze. The clear, dark eyes looking back held only love, and a little bit of sadness. "I didn't know that I could, or that I should." And after a moment she said, "I've never had a friend, Maggie."

Maggie sighed and the sadness in her eyes increased. "I was too much focused on myself and my family to see what you were feeling, Genie, and I promise it will not happen again, for you are part of my family. You are as important to me as my husband and children and I want you to know that, and to know that this family bond travels with us all the way to Toronto."

Now Genie smiled. "And that is why I'm happy though I didn't know what I was feeling, nor did I know what to call

123

what I was feeling, because I've never felt it, Maggie. Happiness. I've never had a friend and I've never been happy." She paused and her brow wrinkled as a thought presented itself. "Though if I had been able to speak those words, to explain myself—" She shook her head in dismay, imagining Adelaide's reaction to hearing such words from Genie. An even more furious Adelaide was not a calming prospect. Then her face changed dramatically.

"What, Genie? What are you thinking?"

"Arthur," Genie said and told Maggie all about Arthur Lee Green, using his full name and the significance of it.

"He more than compensates for Adelaide," Maggie said with great warmth.

"Yes, he does," Genie agreed. "Now if only he could cut my hair so that I look presentable when I go to Abby."

"I will cut your hair, though I'm certain that Abigail will not notice. At least not immediately," Maggie said with exaggerated innocence, before adding that if Arthur cut her hair she would surely look more like Eugene than Eugenia.

Eli answered the knock at the scullery door wielding an iron skillet like a weapon, a protection he wouldn't hesitate to use if it became necessary. "Miss Eugenie!" he shouted, dropping the skillet and hurling himself at her. She barely caught him in a one-armed embrace as the other hand held a Maggie-baked cake.

"Hello, my most wonderful boy. I am so glad to see you," Genie said, hugging him as tightly as she could without dropping the cake.

Startled by Eli's shout, Abby and Ada stopped counting and sorting linen napkins and hurried from the dining room. Crossing the foyer and running under the center staircase, they flew into the kitchen. Abby's heart thudded so loudly she was certain Ada could hear it. Genie was here.

"Look, Miss Abigail. Miss Eugenie is here!"

"I see that she is, Eli," Abby said, glad that the boy still held Genie because she didn't trust herself not to replace him. She saw that Genie still held Maggie's cake and asked Emily to please take it. Then Donnie burst in, his arms full of bags and parcels.

"Miss Eugenia took us shopping," Donnie explained with a wide, happy grin. "Wait till you see what all we have here, Miss Emily. Take some of these bags, Eli, if you please." And only then was Eli forced to release Genie, who stepped into Abby's arms. They stood holding each other for several seconds before stepping apart and joining the general merriment in the kitchen.

Emily was astounded at the amount, kind, and quality of the food Genie brought. "Oh, I don't know what to cook first," she said. Ada, eyeing all the cut-up chicken pieces, said she knew what Ezra would want. "As do I," Emily said darkly. "Chicken fricassee. Would that Mrs. Maggie had never introduced him to the dish. He would gladly eat it daily."

"I like chocolate chicken better," Eli said to loud laughter, and at Genie's look of confusion, Abby explained that coq au vin was Eli's chocolate chicken. Genie laughed so hard she choked, requiring Abby to clap her on the back until her breath normalized.

With Genie between them, Abby and Ada returned to the dining room, agreeing that duty could wait until later so they could spend time with Genie. Ada welcomed the opportunity to get to know her better, and it didn't take long to understand why Abby loved her so much—and Abby very clearly loved her.

Eli arrived with a tray containing a pot of tea, cups and saucers, and a plate of cake slices. "Mr. Donnie said to make sure you know there's another cake," he said happily.

"Thank you, Eli," Abby said.

"You're welcome, Miss Abigail," he replied. Then he looked

at Genie. "I'm very glad to see you, Miss Eugenie. I miss you."

"I miss you, too, Eli. I miss all of you so very much." Her eyes glistened as she looked at them, but she controlled the tears. She had gone her entire life without shedding a tear and now it seemed that her eyes wished to make amends at every opportunity. "And one day very soon we no longer will need to miss each other because we all will be together."

Cheered by the thought, Eli unloaded the tray, grinned at Genie, and left. Abby poured the tea, saying sadly, "When you leave, Genie, you must take Eli with you, take him home to Maggie and Jack, where he belongs." Tears leaked from her eyes. She swiped at them then smiled at Genie. "And how long will you stay, Genie?"

"For as long as you'll have me, Abby."

It took Abby a moment to fully understand what she'd just heard. "You're not rushing back to Adelaide and the shop? I am delighted. But why?"

And Genie explained the situation in great detail, beginning with all the times she had told Adelaide why she was leaving Philadelphia for Toronto, including the pain of the Dred Scott decision and the fatigue of living in constant fear of being returned to slavery to Adelaide's final insulting admission that she'd never considered her a friend because Genie considered herself more of a man than a woman. "And if you don't mind, dear friends, I'd really rather not ever have to speak of Adelaide Tillman again."

"You're well rid of her, my dear, and I'm no end of pleased," Abby said.

"I heartily concur," Ada said. "What a horrid person. But you're a better woman than I am because I'd have given my property to that girls school you already support."

Genie's eyes widened; then she shrugged and smiled. "I wish I'd thought of that, but too late now. I see evidence that you were packing. May I be of assistance?"

"Indeed you may," Abby said excitedly. "Ada already selected the china and silver she wishes to bring for herself and Ezra. You must decide which we'll bring for our home—" She stopped mid-sentence at the look of horror on Genie's face. "Whatever is the matter, Genie?"

"I can decide nothing of the sort because I know nothing of china and silver patterns."

"You have exquisite taste, Genie. I've seen evidence of that for myself," Abby said, hoping she sounded calm and reasonable and not panicky, which is how she felt. She had caused offense.

"I am a seamstress, Abby. I know fabric and material and how to create beauty with them," Genie said.

"That means you recognize beauty when you see it," Ada said. "China and silver and crystal and tablecloths—all the things that adorn tables—they are merely patterns, but ones cut from different kinds of materials. I daresay the most accomplished silversmith wouldn't know the difference between a day dress and an evening gown, but he most likely would be able to discern which was crafted from the finest silk."

Abby exhaled, took Genie's hand, and looked at Ada with gratitude. "I wish I were as wise as Ada is and half as accomplished as you are, Genie my dear, but all I know how to do is manage and run a house—"

"And you should manage and run the one we will live in," but Abby shook her head back and forth before Genie could complete her thought. "And why not?"

"If we live in it together, we will manage it together. We will hire the staff together—"

"What staff?!" Ada stifled a giggle. Abby wasn't as successful, and Genie chided her. "Why are the two of you laughing? What is so humorous?"

"There will be a cook and a cook's helper, a housekeeper and housemaids and personal maids, and someone to bring wood and coal and tend the hearths and grates—"

Genie was up and pacing. None of this had occurred to her as part of moving to Toronto. Being out of Philadelphia and being with Abby—those were her thoughts, not where or how she would live. She managed a wry grin of apology.

"Abby can teach you how to manage a house, Genie, and you can teach her how to be a successful shopkeeper," Ada said, adding, "and you quickly will be grateful that your home is being cared for while the two of you are fully occupied charming the wealthy, for they will not be able to resist you. You two will be hailed as the most beautiful women in Toronto."

"I fear you exaggerate greatly, Ada," Abby said.

"I assure you I do not. Genie, Abby tells me you speak fluent French. Are you able to speak English with a French accent?" Ada asked, and the serious look she wore gave serious weight to her words.

Genie thought for several moments, finally responding in English with the accent of one born in Paris. Or Quebec. Ada gave a satisfied nod then said to Abby, "You must take everything: every piece of silver, crystal, china, porcelain, and linen. And the rugs, of course, Turkish and Persian if I'm not mistaken. Leave nothing. If I do nothing but manage your shops—and there should be two of them—and Jack's, I'll be kept busy. Not to mention very well compensated." And she grinned, then laughed out loud.

"Jack's?" Genie asked. "Why Jack's?"

"Machine-made boots and shoes are available almost everywhere these days, and more cheaply than handmade ones, but wealthy men still prefer handmade boots and shoes, famously Italian and British crafted. And since Jack is British—"

"Then I hope Maggie is working on his accent," Abby said. "He still sounds more like a Liverpool stevedore than a London bootmaker."

"I have every confidence in the magnificent Maggie," Ada said, standing and picking up the tray, saying she'd bring more tea, as well as cake or scones.

"She really is quite wonderful," Genie said as she watched Ada disappear. "Ezra is a very fortunate man."

"He is indeed and believe me, he knows it," Abby said.

"She knows more about earning money than any man I know, but their ridiculous pride prevents them from considering that fact to say nothing of listening to her," Genie said angrily.

"Which is why you and I and Ezra and Jack—and Ada herself—will be wealthy and enjoying the fact," Abby replied smugly, adding that she never expected to hear herself speak of enjoying her wealth.

"I think perhaps it matters if you've earned it yourself rather than inherited it or realized profit from the labor of enslaved people whom you didn't feel obligated to pay because they weren't human," Genie said in a strangely atonal voice.

Abby hugged her tightly and closely for a long moment without speaking because, in truth, there was nothing to say. Then, releasing her, she complimented her hair style. "It is a new one and I like it very much, but I can't imagine that Adelaide is responsible."

"I'll be sure to tell Margaret the Magnificent you said so," Genie said, adding Maggie's assessment that Arthur could cut her hair, too, with a straight razor, as he cut Eli's and Jack's and William's. "However, Maggie said I most likely would end up truly resembling Eugene rather than Eugenia." And Genie laughed but Abby did not. Instead, she gave Genie a steady, piercing look that held a hint of . . . something Genie could not name.

"That could well be something worth seeing," was Abby's eventual response.

Ada returned to find them huddled on a sofa next to the fire and giggling like schoolgirls. She was followed by Eli who carried the tray, which he placed on the table, then bent to stoke the fire to life while Ada poured tea. Eli retreated with smiles for the three women.

Abby looked steadily at Genie and announced that she had important information to share that Genie might find disturbing, and that Ada would supply the details. "It has to do with who will own this house when we leave it."

"If I am to be disturbed," Genie said, "may I first seek Ada's assistance on a matter of some importance?"

"Of course," Abby and Ada replied in unison. Genie withdrew a heavy leather pouch that obviously was full . . . of something. Abby knew what. Ada did not, and she gasped when Genie emptied the contents onto the table in front of them.

"I would like for you to . . . dispose of . . . to sell . . . all of this," Genie said.

Ada looked at Genie, then down at the items on the table. She began sorting through it all, creating separate piles of coins, bills, and non-monetary items. Then she looked at each item, finally looking closely at Genie.

"Some of these coins are quite valuable, especially the gold ones, and they will fetch a good price, as will the men's rings and tie pins. But these other items, Genie, the pocket watch and this pen"—she held them gingerly in her hand—"are solid gold and extremely valuable. Are you certain you want to sell them?"

"Shall I tell you how I came to have them?" And without waiting for Ada to answer, Genie said, "You know that I was born a slave. When I was about eleven years old, and I'm not exactly certain how old I was because I don't know exactly when I was born, the man who owned me brought me to Washington, DC, to sell me. He left me in the hotel room and went out for a night of drinking and gambling. My new owner was scheduled to claim me the following morning."

Genie detailed her actions because she recalled them in great detail. She ate the food the master had sent up to her as she was, it seemed, always hungry. Then she unpacked and put away the master's clothes as he had instructed, and turned down his bed.

She noticed a map, and maps had always interested her, but she had never seen a map like this one: The Eastern United States. She found Maryland, where she was born, and Washington, where she presently was, and there was Philadelphia. *If ever you have the opportunity to escape, go to Philadelphia* the German tutor had told her. And there it was on the map, so very close to Washington, DC. And this hotel was so very close to the train station. Her mind would not be calmed or quieted. She could escape from this hotel. She could go to Philadelphia instead of being sold tomorrow morning. She burned the lines of the map into her brain.

When the waiter returned to retrieve the tray and plates from her meal, she had asked him how to get to the train station, and she etched the directions into her memory along with the map lines, being especially thankful for the man's instructions that she exit the hotel through the Colored staff door in the basement, then walk straight ahead and keep walking until the train station came into view.

These thoughts and map lines and exit instructions filled her mind, but there was space for one further thought. She was to prepare a glass of laudanum for the master to drink upon his return; he took a dose every night for some ailment or illness. She added three extra drops to the glass of water and when the master returned, obviously drunk and in pain, he drank the potion down, fell across the bed, and was snoring within seconds. Genie poked him several times but he did not rouse. He was deeply asleep. She opened his money pouch and gasped. It was stuffed full of money and jewelry. Even at her young age, even though she had never had access to money or valuables of any kind, she recognized that she was looking at power. She took all of it. Then she made her escape, exactly following the map and the directions etched in her memory.

"Once I felt safe in Philadelphia, I used much of the paper money to feed and clothe many of the homeless boys I encountered, and I funded training schools for girls. I supported the work of the Underground Railroad, and I built my house, and I purchased the building that houses the business I had with Adelaide. And I gave money to people who needed it."

Genie looked at Ada and shrugged, forcing the corners of her mouth up in a small grin. "Now it seems I need it to pay for my freedom once again."

"And there is more than enough for that," Ada assured her. "I will purchase the gold watch and pen myself as they have the unusual and most welcome benefit of not being engraved. As if their owner had not had sufficient time to have his name etched on them."

Abby emitted a low chuckle. "I think I know what Ezra MacKaye may expect as a wedding present. Unless his birthday occurs first?"

Ada smiled and nodded. "Indeed, that beautiful watch will bear an inscription to Ezra, but the pen will be mine. It is beautiful and will bear my initials as soon as possible." Then Ada held up the other pen—not solid gold but still a fine writing instrument. "I think you may want to reconsider getting rid of this, Genie. Surely you can make use of it."

"I once believed that to be the case, especially since there was no inscription on it, either. But when I visited a stationer's to purchase ink and paper, I was thrown out. The proprietor at first didn't believe that I could pay for my purchases, and then he doubted that I could read and write." Genie shrugged. The anger had long since ebbed away, but the empty feeling left by the experience caused an indifferent feeling about the pen.

Anger rose within Abby as it always did whenever she learned of any mistreatment of Genie. And, as always, the anger was quickly replaced by sadness and sorrow that her Genie—this wonderful, giving, caring, unselfish woman—had to endure such ugly treatment at the hands of people so singularly unworthy of even being in her presence. She didn't expect that they could or should love Genie as she did, but why could they not understand that they had no reason to hate her?

Ada felt the anger rise within her. "Oh, how I wish I could inflict something harmful or painful on that . . . that despicable cretin who intended to sell you South. Something much worse than merely losing possession of valuables. Would that he had lost everything in his card game instead of winning so much." Ada fumed.

"He cheated at cards," Genie said calmly, "which would explain his windfall. And he died of a laudanum overdose in that Washington, DC, hotel room, casting the entire Wright family of Maryland into dishonor and disarray."

Ada's face registered shock, disbelief, understanding, and finally recognition. "Surely you're not telling me that—" Unable to complete the sentence, she dissolved into the wild cackling laughter that made them all laugh.

CHAPTER FOURTEEN

E zra was more pleased than annoyed when the knock on his office door halted his work because, truth be told, he welcomed the interruption. He intensely disliked the process of accounting for every penny he'd spent the previous month, but Ada Lawrence insisted that he do precisely that and that he do it properly. He was to note not only what he spent but when, where and why, and she didn't accept that he didn't remember as a good reason for not keeping good records. A woman bookkeeper. He still wasn't over the rarity of it or the realization that he actually retained more of his money if he monitored his expenditures. Nor was he yet able to take for granted that she no longer was merely his bookkeeper, but was his fiancée. His irritation vanished, immediately replaced by admiration and pride and no small amount of gratitude, for her diligence and oversight had resulted in a significant increase in his monthly income.

"Come in," he called out, the smile at the thought of Ada present in his voice.

"Looks like leaving Pinkerton's was the right thing for you to do," his former Pinkerton's boss said as he entered. Still ramrod straight as benefited an ex-military man, he seemed unaware that a layer of snow was heavy on his coat and hat. So engrossed in his accounting was Ezra that he'd failed to notice the snow's arrival. Donnie, who'd been his eyes and ears down at the docks, said the sailors were predicting the arrival of a snowy Nor'easter.

"You bring the Nor'easter with you, Captain Pitcairn?" Ezra asked with a warm smile as he stood and, hand extended, crossed the room to greet and then relieve the man of his top hat, coat and walking stick. The affectations now were so much a part of the captain that Ezra no longer found them as annoying as he once did. Pitcairn was no more a second-son nobleman in the military than was Ezra himself, but Pitcairn had always made the deception look good. First sons of noblemen inherited the title, and second sons entered the military with a rank and title bought and paid for. "It's good to see you, Captain, if surprising. What brings you to Philadelphia?" Ezra said to this man who never went anywhere uninvited or without good reason.

"May I sit, and may I smoke? And it's Colonel."

"Of course," Ezra said, and after adding more coal to the fire, he took a dusty bottle and an even dustier glass from the cabinet and wiped them clean with his handkerchief. Pitcairn drew his chair closer to the fire and let it and the whiskey warm him, while Ezra used the time tending to social niceties to ponder the meaning of the man's announcement of his advanced rank. They'd left the Army at the same time to join Pinkerton's, so how, in the civilian world, did a captain become a colonel?

"Still don't drink much, I see, but you do look prosperous, Ezra."

"I like what I do, and I've built a good reputation, so I'm kept busy and gainfully employed."

"I can see that. Those look to be handmade boots on your feet."

"I require good shoes since I spend the majority of my time on my feet and not behind a desk. Had you knocked at my door yesterday or tomorrow you'd have received no answer until evening." He turned a baleful glare toward his desk. "I'm late completing last month's accounting."

"Judging from the piles of paper I'd say you're doing very well indeed. Wealthy men looking to control wandering wives and daughters don't generate such lengthy reports."

Ezra gave a small smile. "However, men looking to control railway and shipping lines generate massive amounts of paperwork."

Pitcairn gave him the shrewd, calculating look Ezra so well remembered. "Do you find it difficult to walk the fine line between your clients and their competing interests?"

Ezra's eyes narrowed, and he offered his own calculating look. "What competing interests are those?"

"What's boiling down to the interests of the North versus those of the South, divisions that have intensified since Abraham Lincoln was elected president three weeks ago."

"If I know a man supports the holding of slaves I won't work for him, though some of them keep their beliefs secret, and a few are waiting to see which way the wind will blow before declaring those beliefs publicly," Ezra said, watching Pitcairn for his reaction.

"I don't give a damn about slaves. It's the union of the American states that I care about, and Southern states are talking of seceding from the United States and calling themselves the Confederate States of America, and it's that treasonous foolishness I won't tolerate. The US military will not tolerate it."

"Are you saying that you're here in Philadelphia preparing for war? That you've been recommissioned in the Army in preparation for war?"

"And so should you be. It is all but inevitable," Pitcairn said, and Ezra knew he was right. But he had no intention of rejoining the Army. He also had no intention of telling that to the newly minted Colonel Pitcairn.

"What has Philadelphia to do with these things?" Ezra

asked the question though he wished he didn't have to hear the answer.

"The government is establishing a military command here. This is a critical location as it lies almost midpoint between Washington, the center of government, and New York, the center of commerce. And there are critical waterways and rail lines here. And," Pitcairn said, giving Ezra a steely, steady look, "you're here, and that is of great importance to me."

"Why is my being here of importance to you?" Ezra asked, already knowing the answer but dreading hearing it spoken out loud.

"I'm here to offer you a commission as a major in the United States Army and the position as my second in command of the Philadelphia Barracks." Pitcairn spoke with the calm authority of a man accustomed to giving orders disguised as offers, with the expectation that his generosity would be gratefully accepted. That he, Ezra MacKaye would ascend from lieutenant to major as easily as Pitcairn had risen from captain to colonel, and be grateful for the opportunity.

There was a time Ezra would have jumped at the chance, but that time had long passed. Ezra remained silent for a long moment. Then, despite his reluctance to do so, he said as much to Pitcairn, watching the man's eyes narrow and his thin lips tighten into a straight line. "What has changed for you, Ezra?"

"I'm to be married, Colonel, and my wife-to-be is Canadian by birth, and she wishes to return to Toronto, her home. It is my intention to join her there."

Pitcairn poured himself more whiskey, not bothering to offer any to Ezra, and placing the bottle on the floor beside his chair. "I must confess my surprise. I never imagined you a domesticated animal," he said, making no attempt to conceal his disdain.

Ezra took no offense. He smiled benignly at Pitcairn. Trying to explain a woman like Ada Lawrence to this man would be

137

wasted breath, never mind any attempt to explain Abigail Read and Eugenia Oliver.

"I know much about Philadelphia," Ezra continued, "and I will do all I can to help you until I leave. I know people who can be useful to you, and I can identify people you would do well to steer clear of. Then there is also a most disgusting man who attempted to pay me with a note bearing the insignia of the Confederate States of America—"

"The devil you say!" Pitcairn erupted. "I have heard of the existence of such notes but I have not seen them. Can you gain possession of some of these notes?"

"I'm almost certain that I can," Ezra said, knowing that Montague Wright was far too self-absorbed and self-important to wonder why Ezra would suddenly want to possess the Confederate money. Ezra learned where Pitcairn was staying and promised to contact him when he had possession of the Confederate notes, and the man donned his coat and hat and took his leave. Ezra's whiskey went with him.

Alone now, Ezra let his mind wander to matters of interest and concern to himself: Where the devil was Captain Addams and his ship? He should have returned by now. He and Jack were worried about the weather, which had been most unpredictable of late—days that were alternatively frigid and snowy, and then sunny and balmy, so no ice had yet formed on the river and the longer that was the case, the better, meaning smooth sailing for Captain Addams.

But more than the weather, Jack worried about the hostility and violence growing within the white residents of Philadelphia and across the country in the wake of the election of Abraham Lincoln to be the next US president. Blacks were more imperiled than ever before.

He recalled Jack's conversation about slaveholders fearing Mr. Lincoln would take away their slaves. Jack chuckled darkly. "That would mean they'll be forced to do their own work or pay people to do it for them. You ever seen white people do any kind of back-breaking, spirit-killing hard work?"

"Come now, Jack," Ezra chided. "I work hard. So does Ada, and so, too, do Donnie and young Stewart—"

"I didn't say white people didn't work hard, Ezra. I said I don't see many doing hard work—like planting their own crops and cutting their own lumber and catching and cooking their own food and tending to their own children. Slaves do that work and they earn no money for it."

There was no adequate response.

"I will be happy when we're away from here. All of us, Jack—myself included. I am ready to be away from a place where people I care about must live in fear, and I take no joy in knowing that I grow prosperous working for men who keep this system alive."

Ezra knew that if Jack had any relevant information about Captain Addams and the ship he would have informed Ezra immediately. He also knew he was allowing worry to become fear. What if they couldn't get out of the country before war erupted? He could, if necessary, ride a horse from Philadelphia to upstate New York and cross Lake Ontario by boat to get to Toronto. Jack could paddle a canoe—or swim—up the Delaware River and other waterways to get to Canada. Their women and children could not. Where in blazes was Captain Addams?

"If you don't pay me, in *real* money that I can spend, every cent that you owe me, I'll have the dockmaster seize this entire shipment!"

Captain Harry Addams was as angry as he had ever been. His red hair stood up all over his head. He was dirty, tired, and hungry, and he knew he had a well-paying customer ready and waiting to sail. And here was this braying mule of a fool trying to pay him with useless notes. Confederate States of America indeed! He summoned one of his crew. "Get the dockmaster and tell him to bring a cart—"

"All right, all right," Dr. Montague Wright said as he reached into a waistcoat pocket and extracted a wad of Bank of Toronto notes. Addams knew what the man held because it was from this same wad of notes that he'd paid Captain Addams the deposit he demanded before setting sail from the Port of Toronto three weeks earlier. Addams was a good judge of men and this noisy buffoon, whether or not he was the doctor he called himself, was not trustworthy, as he'd just proved. The Bank of the Confederate States of America. No such thing existed!

He hurried the unloading of Wright's cargo, wanting to be rid of the man and his belongings. The crates were heavy, and the men working for Wright were ill suited for the work. They were small-framed and looked as if the heaviest items they'd ever lifted were forks and wine glasses. Addams shouted at them to hurry when one man lost his grip on the end of the crate he carried and dropped it. The top flew off, and through his shouting for the men to hurry and reseal the crate, Addams saw the contents: Smith and Wesson revolvers, dozens of them. But why? For what purpose?

With his vessel rid of Montague Wright and his frightening cargo, Addams ordered the thorough cleaning of both the cargo hold and the passenger cabin. Scrubbed and polished it would be, and ready to set sail as soon as could be managed. He gave the order and left to have himself tended to in like fashion, which he would do nearby at the Seaman's Mission. After he'd made himself presentable, he would send word to his wife to please join him for dinner at one of the dockside restaurants. He passed the Jamaican, Kingston, en route to the Mission, told him where he was going, and continued on his journey. Stopping to converse with the voluble Jamaican would cost him at least half an hour. Kingston headed in the opposite direction to Jack Juniper's shoe shop with the news that Addams had docked. He hurried because he wanted Jack to be present when Addams returned.

Jack, in turn, hired a driver to deliver notes to Abigail and Ezra, notes that Maggie wrote in excited haste, telling them to prepare to leave. Then Jack hurried to the dock where *The River Dancer* was moored. He wanted to see the craft for himself and was pleased when he saw the boat receiving a thorough scrubbing—interior as well as exterior. This made him think well of the captain. A man who took such care of his craft would take equally good care of his cargo.

Though he could not board the craft without the captain's permission, he scrutinized as much of the exterior as was possible. *The River Dancer* was a gunboat no longer used to wage war, so it no longer was carrying cannons. It was two-masted, steam and propeller-powered. A dancer indeed. This boat would be fast, making it safe as it could outrun just about anything. And because it once had carried cannons, it certainly could withstand the weight of four women, two children—and one Donnie Bruce—as well as the crates of household goods. Captain Addams had paid dearly for his *River Dancer*. It is no wonder that he kept it working whenever the weather permitted, and Jack was grateful for the weather permitting the Delaware River to remain ice-free. So far.

"I'm pleased that you like what you see, Mr. Juniper."

Jack turned to find a tall, thin, red-haired man scrutinizing him. He saluted, then extended his hand. "I do indeed, Captain Addams, and it is a pleasure to make the acquaintance of a man who takes care of such a fine boat."

"I'll take you aboard when the cleaning is completed."

"I'm happy to wait, Captain. The fact of your presence and of such a craft have relieved me of my greatest worries."

"Will you tell me, Mr. Juniper, who and what will be traveling with me? Kingston did not have the details."

Jack nodded. "Gladly, sir. My wife and children and her

141

sister, and the wife and sister of my good friend Ezra MacKaye, and Mr. Donald Bruce, the guardian and protector of all, including the several crates of the goods of three households." Jack watched Addams for a reaction to the description and function of Donnie, but his countenance did not alter.

"I think you will find the passenger cabin and the cargo hold both adequate and acceptable."

"I've no doubt, Captain." Jack turned for another look at *The River Dancer*, nodding with satisfaction. But he was anxious to see inside. "Did you sail the *Dancer* when she was a gunboat?"

The captain gave a crooked grin, making him appear younger than he most likely was. "No, I didn't meet my *Dancer* until she was decommissioned, but I did crew on one of the 100-foot British gunboats in the Crimean War." That war reference proved Jack correct about the man's age. Captain Addams grew quiet, probably remembering what certainly would have been a horror. "I was trading on the old and respected Addams family name, so no one questioned my desire to sail beneath the Union Jack."

"Are you not British, then?" Jack asked, his curiosity piqued.

"I am a poor relation of the well-respected American branch of the well-respected British Addams clan. I am a native of this city and this is my home port, the Delaware River my home water." He sighed happily before shifting his gaze from the river to his newest client. "I believe you sailed beneath the Union Jack yourself?"

"Aye, that I did," Jack replied with caution. Though he claimed to be from Liverpool, only a true native could replicate the accent of that city. "Sailed the packet ships between Liverpool and Philadelphia for almost ten years until crossing the Atlantic became too dangerous."

Addams was silent for a long moment, then said, "I heard what happened to you and your mates. Dastardly."

"Indeed, it most certainly was," Jack said grimly, "but it

served a noble purpose: It got me off the water for good, allowing me to keep a promise to my most wonderful wife. I soon will be placing her in your care, along with my daughter and son."

Before Addams could reply, they were interrupted by shouts from the vicinity of the dock master's office. When they looked that way, Jack was surprised to see Ezra arguing with a slight man in a top hat. He was even more surprised to hear Addams exclaim, "That damnable Wright! He tried to cheat me."

Jack hurried to Ezra. If he was having an argument with a man Addams called a thief . . . "Ezra!" he called out loudly, making certain he was seen.

Ezra immediately turned, all anger gone from his face. "Have you met our captain and seen our ship?"

"I have and I think you'll be most pleased. Come."

Ezra followed him and he introduced the two men, but instead of speaking of their upcoming journey Addams surprised Ezra by saying, "What do you know of that scoundrel, Wright?"

"He'd have to have improved his character by a wide margin to be a scoundrel," Ezra replied darkly. "He is monstrous."

"He's also a cheat," Addams said. "His cargo was my return trip to the Port of Philadelphia, and he attempted to pay me with something called Confederate money—"

"Did he indeed!" Ezra exclaimed. "Is he in possession of that currency now?"

Addams nodded. "That's probably why he can't get his crates moved off the dock—because he's attempting to pay men with those false notes. That and the weight of the cargo."

"What manner of weighty cargo could Montague Wright possibly be shipping from Toronto to Philadelphia?" Ezra asked, genuinely puzzled.

"Smith and Wesson revolvers," said Addams.

"Please excuse me," Ezra said, turning back toward the dock. "I'll return as quickly as possible," and his long-legged stride had him halfway to the dock even as Jack and Captain Addams wondered at the reason for his sudden and intense interest in a man he considered monstrous.

"You'll not find a single working man here willing to accept false paper as legal bank notes. They're not slaves that you can cheat out of honest pay for honest work," Ezra called out as he drew close to Wright.

"How dare you!" Wright exclaimed, too surprised to be concerned about the sudden arrival of a man he intensely disliked.

"How dare I speak the truth?" Ezra said with a chuckle. "As easily as you lie, Wright."

"We'll see this country set right, and that's a promise, not a lie. That fool Lincoln can't take from us what's rightfully ours, and we are more than prepared to fight for our rights."

"If only you could afford it," Ezra said, "which you cannot," and watched Wright deflate. He withdrew a thin leather case from the inside pocket of his coat, and from it withdrew several Bank of Philadelphia notes, which soon would be as worthless as Wright's Confederate notes. He knew this because Ada had told him the bank that issued the notes was on the verge of collapse and he trusted her implicitly in all matters financial.

"I'll exchange these for some of yours," Ezra said to Wright, and the doctor wondered why, but he knew he could not ponder too long or the dock workers would walk away, leaving his precious cargo unattended, for they'd made it clear they would not accept the Confederate notes and some of them were looking with interest at the handful of Bank of Philadelphia notes in Ezra's hand.

"Why do you want them?" Wright demanded.

"Why do you care?" Ezra replied. "Do you want to do a trade or not?"

Wright knew he was bested and there was nothing he could do about it. He made the exchange with Ezra—Confederate States of America bank notes for Bank of Philadelphia notes.

He turned to the dock workers, paid them, and watched as his crates of revolvers were loaded onto wagons the dock workers would push out to the street and load onto flatbed wagons he had waiting. He looked around for Ezra, wanting to ask him again why he wanted the CSA bank notes, and saw him standing beside *The River Dancer* talking to the disgusting Captain Addams and a large Colored man. Then he dismissed the man from his mind and concentrated on getting the revolvers delivered to the basement door of the Medical College where they would be safe until they were needed.

Ezra noted *The River Dancer* and Jack Juniper's reaction. If Jack was satisfied, then so too would he be.

"This is a most seaworthy craft you have, Captain Addams, and you obviously take good care of her," said Jack.

"Thank you, Mr. Juniper. I'm proud of her, and proud that you and Mr. MacKaye trust your families to sail with me." He asked whether the cargo hold would accommodate the crates of household items the families were bringing, and Jack assured him that the space was sufficient. He would supervise the packing and seal the crates himself.

Addams allowed that while the passenger cabin was not that of a luxury liner, he deemed it sufficiently well-appointed and comfortable, Jack and Ezra agreeing. There were six bunks in two rows, three at either end of the cabin, leaving the center open. Built-in cabinets contained a table and chairs, and others were empty for the storage of passengers' belongings. "Passengers should bring their own bedding, as I'm sure you can understand the difficulty involved with keeping such materials clean and fresh."

"Oh dear Lord, yes," Jack said with a shudder as he recalled nights he had relied on the sweaters and long underwear Margaret sent with him rather than wrap himself in bug-infested, mildew-ridden, filthy blankets and sheets. He truly would rather have frozen to death than have them touch any part of his body.

Jack and Ezra followed Addams to the ship's galley. Tiny was the only word for it. All galleys were small; they were meant to be functional, not attractive. "Our cook can handle the basics—"

"How long is the trip to Toronto, Captain?" Ezra asked, trying—and failing—to imagine Ada and Abby and Maggie eating whatever was prepared here.

"You understand, do you not, that I do not sail directly into the Port of Toronto—"

Jack and Ezra exclaimed in alarm simultaneously:

"The devil you say!" Jack yelled.

"We understand nothing of the kind!" Ezra yelled.

Addams blanched but held his ground. After all, these were gentlemen, not drunken deck hands. "Come with me, please," he said, leading them onto the deck, along a narrow passageway toward the bow and into the surprisingly wide space that was the wheelhouse. He faced a tall table upon which maps were stacked. Without the need to search, he withdrew one of them and spread it out, and beckoned Jack and Ezra over to the map table. "This," he said, tracing a line with his finger, "is our Delaware River."

Ezra and Jack looked closely. Jack understood what he was looking at. Ezra did not. Jack touched his shoulder and nodded, then asked Addams to continue. The captain produced another map, placing it on top of the previous one, again using his finger to point. "This is our Delaware River in upstate New York—"

"Good God!" Jack exclaimed. "Is that . . . that's the Atlantic." He placed a finger on the map to the right of the Delaware, to a very large expanse of . . . something.

"It is," Addams replied, moving the large hand in the other direction, to the left—but we won't be going there."

"Are you saying, Captain, that we will not enter the Atlantic Ocean?" Ezra asked, sounding nothing like a Pinkerton Agent.

"Precisely," Addams replied, his finger moving on the map. "This is a point where several bodies of water converge, and we will sail on to Lake Ontario here, and tie up here for a day, before continuing on to Toronto."

"How long will that journey take?" Ezra asked.

"Six, seven, perhaps eight days, weather and other variables permitting," Addams answered, hastening to explain what he meant by "other variables," the most crucial and important one being the availability of pilot boats, Addams explained. Ezra looked blank. Jack looked confused. Addams grinned, running his hands through his wiry red hair, causing it to stand on end. "Not technically the kind of pilot boat you're familiar with, Mr. Juniper, but it's what we who sail the narrow rivers call them. They lead us, not the other way 'round, when we sail overnight."

And Addams explained that he usually tied up shore-side overnight because it was safer to do so. However, if favored by a good, strong wind he would never drop his sails and would then follow the lights of a pilot boat all night into the next day. Strong winds could have disturbed the vegetation on the river bottom, bringing it to the surface, as well as blowing debris and obstacles from shore into the water. The lead craft—the pilot boat, Addams explained, cleared the way for the larger, and in some ways, more delicate craft. "There's a reason the gunboat was so successful at war on the high seas," Addams said. "They were made for open and deep water."

Jack nodded his appreciation of the captain's understanding of and his skill at navigating the river, and though Ezra knew little of the water he had learned much from Ada about the nature of businessmen, especially the insecure ones. They don't like explaining themselves, she said, especially when they're not sure of themselves, and therefore they masked their ignorance with anger and hostility. Captain Addams had displayed neither and had seemed almost pleased to be able to share his knowledge with them.

"We often experience high winds this time of year, and while that may result in having your families reach their destination a day or two sooner, it may also mean a day or two with porridge for breakfast and beans and rice for supper since we won't be tying up for supplies." Addams shook his head wistfully and confided that he had more than once tried to design a more spacious galley to no avail.

"How many crew do you have?" Jack asked.

"Eight. Six of them have been with me for the last two years."

"How soon can you leave?" Ezra asked.

"I'd like to spend a couple of days with my wife and children. If you can have your cargo loaded in that time, we can sail then."

Ezra withdrew a leather pouch from his trouser pocket and gave it to Captain Addams, who untied the leather cords. Looking inside to find what seemed to him a small fortune in silver and gold coins, he was stunned. He returned the pouch to Ezra.

"You may give me half of what's here when we set sail and the remainder when we return and set sail again, with you as my passengers." Jack scanned the sky, his palms shading his eyes. "Let us have our cargo and passengers loaded and boarded in two days."

Jack and Hezekiah closed the shoe shop and spent the next two days helping the women pack and secure the crates, using the sailcloth that Jack had waterproofed by spreading a thin layer of tar on one side.

"Even if *The River Dancer* should capsize, every item in these crates will remain dry," he told Abby, expecting she would be pleased—until he looked at her face. She had turned a sickly white and was shaking like a leaf on a tree in a storm.

"Oh Jack," Maggie said gently, embracing Abby since Genie wasn't there to do it. He remembered too late Maggie telling him how terrified the child Abby was on the journey across the Atlantic from London to Philadelphia, how sick she was for the duration, how she never overcame her dislike and distrust of water. She surely was summoning every drop of courage she possessed to make the journey up the Delaware. And now he had resurrected all that fear, and neither Ezra nor Genie was present to help calm her.

Ezra had gone to move the last of his personal belongings from Abby's to his office, where he would live until time for the men to sail. Then he paid a crucial visit to Colonel James Pitcairn at his hotel.

"Dare I hope that you've come to tell me you've had a change of heart and mind and are prepared to rejoin the Army?"

Ezra handed over the Confederate notes he had obtained from Montague Wright and watched Pitcairin's face register a range of emotions, from disbelief to horror to full-bore rage. "I will see him hung," he roared. "The traitorous bastard!"

"I think you can cause him more pain than merely hanging him, which he most probably would consider an honorable death," Ezra said, "given the disregard in which he holds the Union of the American States."

"Tell me how?"

"You will require a headquarters from which to operate, will you not? And I know you may requisition any property you deem necessary." And he told Pitcairn about the mansion on Society Hill into which Montague Wright would be moving in the next day or so—with his crates of Smith and Wesson revolvers . . . and his slaves.

"Did you say *slaves?* In *Philadelphia?!*" Pitcairn turned purple with rage. He threw the glass he'd just drained of whiskey across the room, but it bounced off the wall of heavy drapes and thankfully did not shatter. Retrieving it, he poured himself more whiskey, then calmly asked Ezra to tell him everything he knew about the despicable Montague Wright.

Genie sat enjoying her last meal at Joe Joseph's Family Dining, an emotional event as she'd expected it would be. She cared very deeply about all of these people, and she would miss them. Joe and Aurelia could read, and she promised to write as soon as she was settled. She told Richard and Absalom that Eli was learning to read and write, and she made them promise to learn as well, so they could share their lives with each other.

Turning to Joe and Aurelia, she asked them to promise that Robert and Absalom would learn to read and write. She told Josie and Robert that she wished she could have gotten to know them better and promised she'd have Ada get in touch when she was settled. Then she made a request: "Please do not tell anyone of our departure for at least three weeks—and then, only if anyone should ask. Please promise me that. All of you." Every head nodded yes, and with final hugs all around, Genie took her leave, quickly heading to her next destination.

She inhaled deeply and knocked at Adelaide and William's door. She knew they were at home as it was suppertime. What she did not know was how they would receive her.

William cautiously opened the door barely wide enough to see who stood on the porch. He stared, then glared at her. "It is suppertime, as you very well know, Eugenia."

"Yes, I do know that, William, which is why I chose this time to come to say good-bye—because I knew you both would be here."

She was waiting for him to invite her in. He did not. "I thought you'd already said your good-byes," he said coldly, and began to close the door.

"Is that Eugenia I hear, William? Genie, is that you?" Adelaide pushed William aside and took his place at the barely opened door. "I can't find your sewing kit, Genie," she said with exasperation. "I've looked everywhere. Where is it?"

Genie looked at her in total disbelief and some confusion. "Why are you looking for *my* sewing kit, and why would you imagine I would leave it behind?"

"Because you will no longer have need of it and I do. I don't have all those specialty needles and scissors that you have."

Genie was rendered speechless for a moment, during which anger rose within her, and when she could talk, she summoned words designed to inflict pain. "Even if you possessed all those specialty needles and scissors, Adelaide, you would not know how to use them."

William shoved his wife aside, swung the door open wide, and glared at her. "So you finally reveal your true self, Eugenia Oliver, smug in your fancy education and able to show off skills only you have. You must be so proud of yourself."

"As you must be, William, having learned so well the ways of your master, how to diminish and demean others while keeping yourself secure on your pedestal. Your wonderful mother, however, would be appalled and ashamed." And she turned and walked away, making certain her emotions were under control, at least outwardly, before she knocked on Arthur's door.

"Miss Eugenie!" he exclaimed when he opened his door, flinging it wide open and welcoming. His smile wavering, he asked, "Is you all right? You look to be . . . not all right."

The old man, too wise in the ways of the world, was not fooled by someone he knew so well.

"No, Arthur, I'm not all right. I have just left William and Adelaide . . ." She let the sentence trail off, unable to give words to what she was feeling. But she didn't need words. Arthur knew exactly what words to use.

"They act like they been took over by some other folks. It's still William and Adelaide's bodies, but it is some other somebodies livin' inside of 'em and doin' the talkin' for 'em."

"Have they mistreated you as well?" Genie asked, keeping

151

her voice calm.

He chuckled. "Oh yeah, they have. When I told 'em you give me your house, they got some kinda mad. You shoulda seen and heard 'em! Told me I was tryin' to be above myself. Like I didn't know they was sayin' somebody like me don't deserve to live in a real house." Genie took the old man's hands in hers—strong, work-worn, calloused and rough hands that held hers so gently—her small hands almost invisible in his large ones.

"I have come to tell you that you can move in tonight if you'd like to, Arthur. Pack all your belongings and get yourself moved so that you wake up in the morning in your new home. I have also come to tell you good-bye, and that I will miss you. And to say, Arthur, how proud I am to know you and call you my good and dear friend—"

"I cain't move tonight, or any time, Miss Eugenie, 'less I can send for Absalom and Richard to help me." The sadness and defeat in the old man's voice frightened her.

"Why do you need help, Arthur? Though if you really need Absalom and Richard to help you, I will go immediately to get them—"

"I don't have the hoss and cart no more. William sold 'em."

A rage she had not known she possessed rose swiftly within Genie. She had never been so angry—not even as a slave, not even when betrayal by a trusted confidant almost resulted in the capture of Harriet Tubman. The mistreatment of this gentle old man for no reason other than jealousy and spite infuriated her, and her first impulse was to return and confront them. Tamping down her anger until it cooled and her thinking became more rational and orderly, Genie knew that confronting William and Adelaide about their mistreatment of Arthur most likely would cause them to mistreat him further. How could she have so seriously misjudged these two people and believed them to be honorable and generous and kind and decent?

She hugged Arthur quickly and walked away. Red-hot

rage and cool, rational thought shape-shifted within her. Genie needed to find a way to help Arthur. She altered her gait, walking more slowly. It was dark now and though she was armed, she was alone, and no one knew where she was. She envisioned the route to Abby's, pictured the shortcuts and alleyways. It would not do for her to be taken on her last night in Philadelphia, most likely costing everyone else the opportunity to escape. For that is exactly what they were doing— escaping. Violence over the election of Abraham Lincoln had erupted throughout the country, fueled by the belief of the slaveholders that they were soon to be deprived of what they believed was their God-given right to own other human beings, though it also was their belief that Blacks were less than human, which justified their behavior.

The rage and fury she felt over the Tillmans' treatment of Arthur rose within her again, even more swiftly and powerfully than it had just a few moments earlier. She had never before experienced such a feeling—and why had she not? She was born a slave and, by herself and on her own as a child, she had escaped that evil. What she had felt then, and what she continued to feel over the years, was relief and gratitude. That is what the majority of her people, as far as she could tell, felt: relief at their perceived safety in a city like Philadelphia where so many free Blacks lived, and thankfulness for it. What was increasingly clear, and what should be clear to all of them, was the fact of their complete and total vulnerability, their complete and total lack of safety. And they could not save themselves from the danger, nor could they prevent it, for every such action designed to protect themselves from violence was a violation of every law and doctrine put in place to govern them, and violations would result in their immediate destruction. Their only recourse was to leave. So Genie and those dearest to her, Maggie and Jack and Elizabeth and Eli, were going to Canada in the company of other dear ones: Ezra and Ada and Abby and Donnie. Genie and Maggie and Jack and the children were escaping, while the others were merely traveling. The fact of their presence served to mitigate the rage within her, for their co-travelers would guard and protect the escapees, with their lives if necessary. These thoughts and revelations calmed her, and Genie continued on her hurried walk. The relief among the assembled when she walked into Abby's front parlor was palpable, as was the concern.

"Eugenia, what took you so long? And whatever is the matter?" asked Maggie, who knew her best and could read the expression on her face as if it were inscribed there. The words spilled from Genie's mouth, her anger and upset stunning her friends. She told them everything. A shocked silence prevailed.

"What can we do?" Abby finally asked. "We must do something. We cannot allow that good and decent man to be mistreated, especially since he cannot protect himself."

Jack snorted. "He most certainly could protect himself if he chose—he has the upper body strength of two men half his age—but then he most likely would beat William half to death. That old man is as strong as I am. His legs don't work."

"But what do we do? What can we do?" Ezra asked again. "When we leave, he will be at the mercy of the Tillmans."

"Tomorrow, after we've delivered our crates of cargo to Captain Addams, I will take care of getting Arthur and his things moved," Jack said. What he didn't say was that he intended to visit William Tillman as well, and he had no expectation that his anger would have diminished.

With that settled, Genie extended the good wishes of everyone at Joe Joseph's for their safe travels and their promises to write—everyone except William and Adelaide, that is, who treated the departure of people they once considered friends as if it were of no importance.

Maggie had prepared a light supper and they all ate. Ada took Genie aside and presented her with a package. Puzzled, Genie opened it to find a writing box containing the pen that Ada said she should keep, and there also was a second pen, two

154

bottles of ink—one blue, one black—and a sheaf of heavy writing paper. In addition, the box held books: Phyllis Wheatley's poetry, Mr. Shakespeare's Sonnets, and two books authored by Charles Dickens—some of *The Pickwick Papers* and *A Christmas Carol*. She hugged Ada, and wept.

Ezra lit a fire in the grate in the parlor and told them how and why Montague Wright in all likelihood would not be living a happily ever after life in the former home of Abigail Read, and when he told them why the cheering and laughing went on for quite a while.

"But he must be allowed to move in," Ada said, growing serious, her scrupulous eye ever on the bottom line, "until all is legal. He must be allowed to sign the contract and pay for his new home and move into it before . . ." pausing and smiling, "it is requisitioned by the United States Army. And Ezra, you must count that money before he signs, every single coin—and coins only, remember, no bank notes—because Montague Wright is a . . . a . . ."

"Rogue and a despicable little man," Ezra said.

"And those are his good qualities," Abby said dryly.

"I do wish he had known it was Arthur's horse liniment and Eli's application of it that ultimately healed Ezra, and nothing that he did," Maggie said.

"I wish so too," Eli, who had been almost asleep, said. "Me and Arthur and Ma Maggie were your best doctors, not him."

"That you were," Ezra agreed. "I would not have healed so well and so quickly without you, and that is the truth."

They were quiet and at ease in each other's company. Their thoughts were on the new homes they soon would create: the home of Margaret and Jack Juniper and their two children; the home of Ada and Ezra MacKaye, who would marry as soon as both were in Toronto; the home of Eugenia Oliver and Abigail Read, who yearned for the opportunity to create a home together. "I think . . . no, I firmly and strongly believe that we all will be together in Toronto by Christmas," Maggie said, "and we will be sharing a roasted and stuffed goose and figgy pudding."

"And treacle tart," Abby added.

"I pray that you are correct," Ezra said solemnly, sounding almost prayerful.

"I think we all join you in that," Maggie said, "including Henry."

"Who is Henry?" Genie asked.

"I am Henry," said the man they all knew as Hezekiah English, who had been so quiet they'd thought he was asleep. Standing up, he said, "I gave myself the name of the slave boat captain when I came here because I did not have a name in this place. And I gave myself the name English because all the people I saw who told me what to say and do were English people." He looked at each face looking back at him, coming to rest on the Junipers. "Then I learned different people and I did no more want that name. I asked Mrs. Margaret the name of her papa and she said he was called Henry Weems, and I said I would like to have that name, and she said yes, and now I am Henry Weems, but I am not the papa of Mrs. Margaret."

"Congratulations, Mr. Weems!" a laughing Genie said, standing and applauding. As one who had named herself after escaping slavery, she well knew the value and power of claiming a name for oneself. Ezra, Ada, and Donnie all shook his hand, and Henry beamed.

"I still do wish it was possible to reach the Toronto place with no need to travel on the water," Henry said solemnly.

"As do I, Henry," Abby said, and added, "welcome to the family."

CHAPTER FIFTEEN

On a frigid late November dawn the passenger cabin of *The River Dancer* was spotless, but Captain Addams paced nervously, awaiting the arrival of the families of Jack Juniper and Ezra MacKaye. Their cargo crates, already loaded and strapped down, occupied less space than predicted, a welcome change from what most often was the underestimation of what was to be shipped, Montague Wright being the most recent culprit.

He had claimed to have "two or three smallish crates" to ship from Toronto to Philadelphia, and that they were "not at all very heavy." In fact, there were five outrageously heavy crates, and Wright brushed aside all attempts to chastise him for his misrepresentations. And then he had attempted to avoid payment, the scoundrel.

The sight of the day's passengers banished all thoughts of the vile doctor. Of course, the Captain recognized Juniper and MacKaye, who were accompanied by four of the most beautiful women he'd ever seen. As they drew closer and came beneath the dockside lights that impression was heightened.

"Good morning, Captain," Jack Juniper greeted him. "May I present my wife, Margaret, my children, Elizabeth and Eli, and my sister-in-law, Eugenia." As the women and children greeted him, Addams thought the two Black women even more lovely up close, and the little girl certainly would challenge the women in the beauty department, for she was a most beautiful child, just as the boy looked destined to become a likeness of his strong, handsome father.

"Captain," Ezra MacKaye said, extending his hand, "it seems that you've chosen a fine day for a sail."

"I agree, Mr. MacKaye, and welcome aboard to all of you."

Ezra introduced Ada Lawrence—his betrothed—and her cousin, Abigail Read. The only trait the cousins shared was beauty for one was fair-haired while the other possessed a smoldering darkness that most likely had caused many hearts to race.

When Ezra introduced Donald Bruce, Addams readily and fully understood why these men were sending a bodyguard with their families. Bruce was pleasant and congenial, with a firm handshake and a ready smile and enough of Scotland left in his voice to mark him as a relatively recent arrival. Addams watched Bruce as he cast his eyes over his charges, making certain he knew exactly where each stood and how close they were to each other. It would be necessary to first kill Donald Bruce before any harm could come to any of these people. A closer look at the sturdy Scotsman suggested that would be no easy task.

Behind them all came a four-wheel cart pushed by one of the dockhands and piled high with the belongings of the passengers. "Shall I show you to your cabin?" Addams asked and led the way.

He watched the women as they looked all around, opening and inspecting the built-in cabinets. Then the four women looked at each other and nodded their acceptance and approval. The children shouted their excitement. They bounced from bed to bed, claiming first one, then another, until their mother— Margaret was her name, Addams remembered—asked them to please stop. Which they did. Immediately. Donald Bruce examined the three windows in the cabin, reassuring himself that no entry could be gained from outside. Then he examined the door, making certain that when locked from the inside, it could not be opened from the outside. Only then was the cart wheeled in and the belongings of the passengers unloaded. Jack and Ezra looked at their women and children, the pain of having to release them etched in their faces, but staying was not a viable option, especially for Genie, Margaret, Elizabeth, and Eli. The pro-slavery, anti-Black sentiment was as fervent in some parts of Philadelphia as it was in some Southern city or state. Yes, they had to leave, and the sooner the better.

"I'd like to cast off as soon as possible," Captain Addams said. "There's a bit of a wind, and if we can begin the journey with sails up that will allow us to make good time on our first day." He saluted and left them to their good-byes.

The women were stoic and brave, most likely already having shed their tears. It was Eli who, when the reality of the situation struck home for him, wept. He flung himself into Jack's arms, crying that he didn't want to go to Toronto if his papa wasn't going, too. When Jack got him quiet, he explained, as he and Margaret had done several times, that when they reached Canada, Captain Addams would return for the men, who had to wait because there was no room for them in the cabin. "Look around you, Son. Where would Ezra and Henry and I fit in this tiny space with all of you? Look around and tell me."

Eli looked around the cabin. "You and Uncle Ezra and Mr. Henry are too big to fit with all of us. But you promise you will come soon?"

"I promise you, my boy," Jack said, hugging him tightly.

"I promise, too," Ezra said, with a hug of his own. The boy was as dear to him as the son he hoped to have.

And over the boy's head both men exchanged looks with their women that were promises, too. They would be with them as soon as humanly possible. Then they took their leave before they wept like Eli.

Donnie, who had opened and then closed and locked the door behind Jack and Ezra, remained standing beside it while the women saw to the making of beds and the stowing of their belongings. They were strangely silent. Even Eli and Elizabeth were quiet and reflective.

"Which bed do you wish to claim, Donnie?" Maggie asked.

"This one, Mrs. Maggie," Donnie said, pointing to the one closest to the door where he stood. Then he indicated the three across the cabin and asked that Maggie, Abby, and Ada occupy those three, and that Genie and the children occupy the two closest to him—Genie in one and the children sharing one.

"I want my own bed," Elizabeth insisted. "I don't want to share with Eli."

"Will you share with me?" Genie asked, judging correctly that the looks on the faces of Maggie and Eli indicated a storm brewing inside the cabin even if fair weather reigned outside. "Yes, Auntie Genie," Elizabeth agreed, and before Eli could comment, knocking at the door claimed their attention.

"Who knocks?" Donnie called out.

"First Mate Edward Jones," came the reply, and Donnie opened the door to admit a tall, thin, ginger-haired man with skin as weathered and leathered as that of Captain Addams.

"Good morning to you, sir," Donnie said.

Jones saluted them and said, "Captain Addams sends his regards and asks that you join him to witness our departure from Philadelphia if you are so inclined."

The children, their spat forgotten, hopped up and down hugging each other, and all the women, except Abby, displayed equal excitement, minus the hopping from foot to foot. "All is calm above, is it not, Mr. Jones?" Maggie asked the first mate.

"Yes, ma'am. It is a beautiful morning, if a bit chilly," he said.

Maggie put an arm around Abby. "It will be fine, but if you're not comfortable on the deck, I'll come back here with you."

"As will I," Genie added.

"And I," Ada said.

Eli and Elizabeth, still wiggling like a basket of puppies,

kept their eyes on First Mate Jones. They loved Abigail Read but to join Captain Addams on the deck as their boat sailed out of Philadelphia was a once in a lifetime opportunity, one they didn't want to miss.

"Lead the way, Mr. Jones," a relieved Donnie Bruce said, grateful that he'd not had to insist that they all remain below, because he could not have permitted them to be separated.

The boat lived up to her name for she did seem to dance her way up the Delaware, so light and easy was her motion. Only the rapid, constantly changing scenery on the river's banks was proof of how fast they were moving. The *Dancer's* two sails flapped and billowed in what obviously was a stronger wind than Donnie had initially believed.

Their recent dispute consigned to the past, Elizabeth and Eli stood beside Captain Addams, their smiles as bright as the morning sun. Even Abby, the color returning to her face, smiled happily as the wind blew her black hair all about. She remained in the tight embrace of Genie on one side and Maggie on the other, with Ada standing close behind her. Though not being a man of the sea—or in this case, the river—Donnie imagined that if they continued northward at this pace, they could easily reach Canada in the predicted five or six days, if not sooner. He knew enough to know that water speed was measured in knots, but what was it in kilometers? If he got the chance, he'd ask Captain Addams. Or maybe he would ask Mrs. Maggie who, after all, had been married to a man of the sea for many years.

His eyes sought the captain in the bow, and even from this distance he could see Eli and Elizabeth shivering with cold as they scurried away from Captain Addams, across the deck to their mother, attaching themselves to her, seeking the warmth of her embrace.

"Is everyone sufficiently frozen?" Maggie asked. "Shall we go below decks and warm ourselves?"

Everyone agreed, and with thanks and a cheer to their captain they hurried down the narrow passageway to the even narrower steps and down to their cabin. Donnie led the way so he could be the first to enter. He opened the door and stopped short. So did the happy, excited chatter behind him.

Was there a problem? He relaxed his tense shoulders and stepped aside so they all could see what he saw. The table and chairs were out of the cabinets and set up for a meal, the table covered with a cloth, seven heavy plates, and cutlery stacked on top. A second, smaller table that hadn't been there before bore a large metal teapot, steam emanating from the spout. Seven heavy mugs, and bowls of milk and sugar awaited as well. Suddenly every one of them realized the presence of sharp hunger pangs.

"I'll pour the tea," Genie said.

"And I'll set the table," Ada said.

"And I'll sit down and be ready to eat when the food arrives," Abby said, laughing. Moments later, without asking who knocked, Donnie opened the door to admit the steward with their breakfast.

"A very good mornin' to you all," he said cheerfully, Ireland as full and rich in his voice as Scotland was in Donnie's. "I hope you'll find everything to your likin'. I'm Finn and you can find me in the galley if you're wantin' anything more."

A chorus of "Thank you, Finn" followed him out of the door. The warning glares of Maggie, Abby and Genie followed Donnie to the door, which he locked, and when he turned and saw the glares directed at him, he pasted his most innocent look on his face and asked, "What is it?"

"Don't you dare say it, Donald Bruce!" Abby admonished.

"Say what?" he asked innocently.

"Bleedin' Irishman!" Maggie, Genie and Abby said in unison, and Ada laughed so hard the breath caught in her chest and Genie had to clap her hard on the back to restore normal breathing.

Breakfast was boiled eggs, bacon, buttered toast with pots of jam, and bowls of dried fruit—apples, apricots, raisins, and currants. There was a lot of everything, which was good because they all ate like Eli, who seemed not to be taking breaths between bites.

"Eli," Abby admonished, startling him. "Breathe." And everyone laughed again, even Eli.

Genie was happier and more relaxed than she'd ever been. Though she felt Abby's fear of being on the water, she did not share it, and both she and Maggie would do all in their power to soothe and comfort Abby and keep her mind otherwise occupied.

When they'd all eaten their fill and Finn had cleared away the plates, leaving only the teapot and bowls of dried fruit, Maggie spoke.

"Jack paid a visit to William Tillman—"

"Oh, dear," Genie said, the trepidation in her voice signaling that she could well imagine the outcome.

"Indeed," Maggie replied succinctly, ... the end result being that Jack eventually got the money from the sale of the horse and cart. "At first, William insisted that he had bought the cart and horse, claiming not to recall Genie paying him for them.

"Jack said he only had to hit him once before he refunded Genie's money. Jack gave the money to Arthur; then he and Henry moved Arthur into the Back Street house." Maggie paused in her narration. It was clear that she had more to say but seemed reluctant to do so.

"What is it, Maggie?" Genie asked gently, expecting Maggie to say that Jack, not satisfied with a single blow, had given William the good thrashing that he deserved. She regretted having this feeling about a man she had once considered a good and dear friend.

She looked from Elizabeth to Eli, hesitated, then decided that they should hear what she had to say. "It seems that William

163

did not pay Arthur—had never paid him—for his work at the forge—"

"What?" Genie was on her feet, her genial mood having evaporated like smoke, along with whatever good feelings she had remaining for William. Her fury was etched in her face, her body taut, and though her mouth opened and closed, no words came out. Abby took her hand and squeezed, speaking for them both with the question: "Was Jack able to extract an explanation for this behavior?"

"It seems that Mr. Tillman felt the room that Arthur lived in at the rear of the forge rent-free was considered sufficient payment," Maggie replied sadly.

"I hope Mr. Jack gave the scoundrel a good thumping!" Donnie snarled, fists curled at his sides as if imagining doing the deed himself.

"He might well have inflicted a deeper pain," Maggie replied with a satisfied smirk. "I am happy to report that Arthur no longer works for William Tillman. The money he got from Jack for the sale of the cart and horse is the most he's ever had, and the man has worked every day of his life since he was six years old, so he now will spend his days sitting on the front porch of his house, entertaining guests. And Jack said that Arthur told him he had many friends that William didn't permit him to spend time with because they interfered with his work."

As if summoned, Finn arrived with another big kettle of tea and a basket of cake slices. The six passengers greeted him with smiles and Donnie thanked him warmly, making him wish that all of *The River Dancer's* passengers were as pleasant. The feeling was especially true after Donnie followed him into the narrow passage and pressed several coins into his hand. Finn didn't know what to make of it.

He turned it over and over in his mind: a Scotsman and four Colored people, one of them sounding like the Queen herself and the other Colored woman like somebody from France. Finn would not have believed it possible had he not experienced it himself. And he'd heard one of the below-decks crew say they were rich people—so rich that the cargo hold was locked. No one was allowed to enter. Rich Colored people and a bleedin' Scotsman handing out tips. "Saints preserve us," he muttered in imitation of his mam.

Ada had news to share as well: Retrieving several sheets of paper full of diagrams, along with several maps, she informed them that her sister and brother had identified potential homes for them, as well as locations for Jack's boot-making shop and the building that would house Abby and Genie's business and Ada's office. They passed the maps and diagrams among themselves, studying them, almost memorizing them, noting how close the homes were to each other. They would be neighbors! The two largest houses—the ones to be occupied by the Junipers and the MacKayes—fronted different streets but shared a back alleyway and most certainly could share the large carriage house and stable that adjoined one of the houses.

"I'll claim that as my home if there's no objection," Donnie said with a wide grin, pointing to the carriage house. "Do ye think they might have been kind enough to leave us a carriage?"

"A very good question, Donnie," Ada said, "but knowing my brother as I do, if there was a carriage he most certainly would have said so. We probably will have to buy our own, and the horse to pull it. Maybe we'll find ourselves another Gerald."

Abby experienced a pang of sadness at the mention of Gerald's name, but brightened significantly at the mention of the house Ada's sister had identified for her and Genie. It was on the same street as Ada and Ezra's house, but six or seven houses away. It was smaller than the MacKaye and Juniper houses— two stories instead of three—but with high ceilings and wide rooms and a solarium at the back of the house overlooking a garden "that currently is in deplorable condition, but which has tremendous potential."

"Will your brother and sister be neighbors as well?"

"No, thank goodness. They live nearer my parents, out in the countryside," Ada replied, "but I told them that we—all of us—wanted to live in the city, that it was necessary to be near our businesses and near to each other." She paused and sighed. "I love my family and they are full of good intentions, but they interfere far too much, and have far too many opinions about things they know little about."

Joy, happiness, and excitement overflowed, capturing even Abby, who completely forgot that she was on a boat sailing up the Delaware River. She focused only on the fact that she soon would share a home and a business with Genie in a place where Genie could walk freely and be a whole person and a citizen.

"And . . ." Ada said excitedly, drawing the word out dramatically, "when we arrive there will be people on hand to select staff—cooks, housekeepers, ladies' maids, even gardeners and groundskeepers, and . . ." She stopped talking, turned a deep shade of red, and almost whispered, "nursemaids."

There was a moment of stunned silence as the meaning of the word conveyed its unspoken message. Maggie hurried to embrace her. "I most certainly will welcome tiny Ezras and Adas, but does the large Ezra know that nursemaids are on the list of household help to be interviewed?"

"He is the reason I will be interviewing nursemaids," Ada said with her cackle of a laugh, adding that her husband-to-be wanted to—and here she blushed deeply again—begin the process immediately. "To quote the man, he wants a son exactly like Eli and a daughter exactly like Elizabeth, and he wants them immediately."

Though they did not understand the finer points of the conversation, Elizabeth and Eli grasped enough to understand that they somehow factored into Ada and Ezra's plans to have a son and a daughter who would be like them, and that pleased them greatly. It greatly amused their mother. "He does understand, does he not," she said with a chuckle, "how long it takes one to arrive? And that they begin life as tiny little things that require an almost unspeakable amount of attention and care?"

Now Ada was laughing, and Maggie, Genie and Abby joined in, all bestowing hugs of congratulations on the one-of-these-days mother-to-be and assuring her that she and Ezra most certainly would be wonderful parents. "As long as you and Jack will be available if I need help," Ada said.

"You know that we will," Maggie replied.

"Genie and I will host the wedding supper," Abby said with excitement. "How soon do you think you and your sister can organize a wedding?"

"It may well be necessary for us to wed at the city registrar's office instead of our family parish church."

After a moment of stunned silence Maggie asked, "Does that mean the nursemaids—"

"No!" Ada shouted. "Dear heavens no. I am worrying and frightening all of you for no good reason and I am sorry." She inhaled, sighed, and shook her head sadly. "Ezra belongs to the Kirk, the Church of Scotland, and my father will not permit me to marry outside the Church of England. So, if we wish to be wed with immediacy—and we do—it will be in the office of the Toronto City Registrar."

Donnie Bruce stood up and cleared his throat. All eyes, full of surprise, were on him. He looked at Ada. "You may tell the vicar or priest or whatever he is to clean up his fine robes and get ready to put on a first-class wedding because Mr. Ezra MacKaye is a member in good standing of the Church of England. He was studying and taking lessons at that big church down by the water—"

"Christ Church?" Abby asked.

Donnie nodded. "That's the one. He wanted to surprise you, but I see how upset it makes you to think that you canna get married the way you want. And I most certainly want to see some wee bairn calling the fearsome Ezra MacKaye Papa sooner rather than later."

Genie recalled the frigid night she and Eli had met Ezra behind Christ Church—how many years ago? It seemed a lifetime. She had arranged the meeting because Ezra needed information that Eli had, but Eli thought the tall, white man was a slave catcher and initially refused to speak with him. Would Ezra remember? Genie was certain that he would. Perhaps that fateful meeting was why he chose Christ Church as the place to take his religious instruction. She looked over at Eli who seemed to be dozing and doubted that the place or its name would hold any significance for him today. She disliked reminding him of painful events in his past. She met Abby's questioning gaze and nodded.

Abby took up the street diagram again and found the location of the house she would share with Genie. "The wedding supper celebrating the nuptials of Ada Frances Lawrence and Ezra—" She stopped and frowned. "What is his middle name?"

"Duncan," Ada and Donnie replied in unison.

"—and Ezra Duncan MacKaye will be held at 531 Hurston Avenue, Toronto, Canada."

CHAPTER SIXTEEN

Montague Wright was throwing a temper tantrum. There was no other word for it. Ezra had heard of them though he'd never seen one. Back home in Scotland, before he'd left for America at the age of eighteen, he'd heard the women in his large, extended family—his grandmothers and mother and aunts and sisters—complain about two little cousins, siblings, who were notorious for the power and frequency of their temper tantrums. They were the children of some member of his extended family, though the tantrums of the little ones made them famous throughout the family. He could remember the family's discussions perfectly. "I certainly would never allow such behavior in my house!"

"Where do they learn it?"

"No matter where—a good slap will quickly put a stop to it."

And here was Montague Wright, a grown man, ranting and raving because the Bösendorfer piano was gone from Abigail Read's parlor. He paraded up and down the room, waving his arms about. He stamped his feet. Then he accused Ezra of having stolen the instrument. That's when Ezra slapped him. Blessed silence descended. Wright touched the side of his face gently. Already, a raised red mark in the shape of Ezra's hand appeared and if it wasn't already painful, it soon would be.

"Mistress Lawrence provided you with a document listing

every item that would remain in this house. Every item that you would, in fact, be purchasing. Did you read it, Dr. Wright?"

"Of course I read it," he snapped, still touching the stinging red welt on his face.

"Then why are you looking for a piano that you very well know is not here?"

"I thought she might have left it," he said wistfully. "I remember it well, its highly polished beauty and the richness of its sound."

Ezra studied him. He knew the man was a dilettante, but he had not thought that he was mentally deficient. "Whyever would you think that? What would lead you to believe that Mistress Read would abandon such an instrument?" He also knew that Wright had been inside Abby's home exactly once, and he could not imagine that she had allowed him to touch her piano.

"Because such instruments are exceedingly costly to ship across the Atlantic to London, where she could readily and easily purchase another," he said, his focus on the side of his face replaced by his usual offhand manner of dealing with matters. Ezra sighed internally. Abby's piano now resided in a place of honor in the parlor of Mrs. Florence Mallory, five houses away. Not that Montague Wright would ever see the inside of that lady's residence. "Dr. Wright, shall we conclude our business so that you may take full possession of your new residence?" And so that I can be well rid of you, Ezra thought.

Wright emitted a little squeal and clapped his hands excitedly. "Oh yes! But first I'd like to take a tour, from top to bottom!" He ran up the grand staircase, hands caressing the highly polished banisters. He gazed worshipfully up at the chandelier on the third-floor landing, then entered and inspected each of the suites. He opened the door to the back hallway leading up to the servants' quarters, looked around but did not enter, and returned to the landing where he performed a pirouette before dancing down the stairs to the second floor. Before following him down,

Ezra gently closed the door to the suite that had been Ada's.

"This, I believe, is Mistress Abigail's suite?" Wright said, entering it. Ezra did not respond; the man very well knew that it was, and Ezra did not follow him in. Wright took his time walking and looking all around, touching things as if they still belonged to Abby. But Abby and Genie had taken the things they cared about and had left everything else to Montague Wright to do with as he wished. "Oh how I would love to see what she purchases to replace these magnificent things left behind."

Once again, Ezra did not respond. It was not necessary. He followed the silly little man back down to the first floor where, with a now purposeful stride, he paced about Ezra's former suite, before hurrying into the kitchen for a thorough exploration. "I am so very pleased with how clean and orderly everything is," Wright said.

"How, then, will you leave your residence when you move into this one, Dr. Wright, if not clean and orderly?" The man blushed furiously and the welt of Ezra's handprint on his cheek showed in stark relief—a nonverbal but shouted response. Ezra almost wished he could see how Wright would leave his current residence, almost as much as he wished he could witness the arrival of Colonel James Pitcairn to this one.

Ezra sat at the dining table and withdrew from his case two copies of the contract Wright would sign, making the Read mansion his own. "I assume you have your own writing implement, Dr. Wright? A special one to mark such a special occasion?"

Ezra withdrew a pen and bottle of ink from his case, pretending not to notice Wright's discomfiture at realizing he should have brought his own case. "Er, em, I regret I have not brought pen and ink—"

"No matter," Ezra said lightly as he pushed the contract across the table to Wright. He offered the pen. "And may I see your payment, Dr. Wright? Before you sign."

Wright halted the motion of his hand, pen in midair, before he'd made a single mark on the contract. "I beg your pardon?"

"You do realize that Mistress Read already has signed this contract and that your signature makes it binding? Accordingly, I have been advised by Mistress Lawrence not to permit your signature without proof of payment." Ezra kept his voice neutral, apparently to no avail.

"Mistress Lawrence," he spat. "She is a—"

"A what, Dr. Wright?" Ezra said quietly, his voice no longer neutral but icy and more than a little threatening.

Whatever Wright heard in Ezra's voice unnerved him. Gathering a modicum of common sense, along with his wits, rather than answering, Wright withdrew a pouch from his inner pocket and placed it on the table. "This should satisfy your Mistress Lawrence," he said with a feeble attempt at nonchalance.

"Please empty the contents onto the table," Ezra said.

"Surely you don't intend to count it," Wright exclaimed.

"I surely do," Ezra replied. Separating the coins, gold from silver, he began to count. And with an exasperated sigh, Wright withdrew another pouch, which he slid across the table. It was not as full. Ezra stopped counting and gave Wright a long, steady, steely stare. Then he took up the contract and folded it.

"Here. What do you think you're doing?"

Without answering, Ezra emptied the contents of the second pouch onto the table—more silver and gold coins and perhaps a dozen bank notes. "You know the terms of the contract: payment is to be made in pound sterling and gold eagle coins only. No bank notes—"

"No notes drawn on New York or Philadelphia banks," Wright said, stopping just shy of shouting. "These notes are drawn on the Bank of Canada and the Bank of England. Legal tender where Mistress Read is going!"

Ezra didn't ask how Wright thought he knew where Abby

was going. He asked instead, "Where did you come by these notes?"

"Not that it's any of your concern," Wright huffed, "but I obtained them from a business associate who travels extensively. He mistakenly retained these notes from his travels and, with no immediate plans for further travel to either country, he was pleased to exchange them for New York and Philadelphia notes."

A decision he'll soon come to regret, Ezra thought to himself, as he began counting Montague Wright's money. It was all there, for which Ezra was grateful, though he could not and would not overlook the fact of the man's attempt to cheat Abby. He returned all the money to the bags and returned the contract for signature, which, when it was blotted, he folded and returned to his case with the money. Then and only then did he give Wright the contract signed and dated by Abigail Read, and by Ada Frances Lawrence as her agent. He stood up, donned his coat, hat and scarf, and turned toward the door.

"I hope you will enjoy your new home, Dr. Wright."

Ezra walked out the front door of the Read mansion for the final time. In a carriage parked down the block a door opened, and Colonel Pitcairn stepped out, as did two soldiers who flanked him. They walked with purpose toward the front door of Montague Wright's home as the door opened and Wright stepped out onto the porch. Then he waved his arms, beckoning to someone from a carriage parked in the opposite direction. Pitcairn and his men halted and, instinctively, took cover behind a privet hedge. Ezra knew Montague Wright well enough to know that the man's total focus would be on whomever he was signaling and not on who might be hidden in the bushes, so he stood and watched. And laughed.

Ezra then hurried to Pitcairn and his soldiers hiding in the bushes, saying, "In those crates are the Smith and Wesson revolvers I told you about, and the man overseeing their delivery to Montague Wright is the Philadelphia police chief."

As much as he'd like to witness Pitcairn take possession of Wright's home and the weapons, Ezra had had his fill of the silly man and intended never to see him again. In fact, in all honesty, he had no desire to spend further time with Pitcairn, either. Though he was the opposite in every way from Wright, he was single-minded and humorless and therefore, to Ezra, not very interesting. The man would do his job and, if he was correct, the United States would be at war with itself in the relatively near future. The outcome of that war would decide which man was a traitor, Wright or Pitcairin. Ezra MacKaye would read about it in the Canadian newspapers. At this moment, however, he wished to spend his time with people he genuinely liked.

He would go first to Arthur and take him to dine at Joe Joseph's. Then he would spend the remainder of the evening, and perhaps the night, at Jack Juniper's. He had no clients to see—that work was finished. His crates were packed and ready to be shipped. They were in his office, waiting to be transported to Captain Addams's boat, and that day could not arrive fast enough.

Henry Weems, the former Hezekiah English, also thought to dine at Joe Joseph's establishment. Jack did not wish to accompany him. Jack did not wish to do anything or go anywhere. His every thought was of his wife and children; his only desire to be with them.

So Henry set out alone. He knew the way, via the main roads as well as the side streets and alleyways. He also thought about how his new life would be in Toronto, and though he had no concrete ideas or plans, just the thought that a simple journey like the one he was making now would not require strategies for avoiding men who wished to capture and sell him was sufficient to sustain him.

He didn't see the men until it was too late. Four of them walked quickly toward him, armed with ropes and sticks. He turned quickly into an alley and began to run. The men shouted at him. He looked around to see two of them. When he looked forward again, the other two were coming toward him. Henry increased his speed and careened into a narrow alleyway—not much wider than a footpath— behind buildings he recognized. He now knew where he was. He stopped running, stopped breathing. Two of his pursuers, cursing him loudly, passed him right by, close enough to touch him, and when they'd disappeared into the darkness, Henry emerged and ran back to the main road.

"There he is!" and suddenly all four men were in pursuit. Henry was fast but, despite the cold, many people were out. Though the crowd hampered his pursuers, he, too, was slowed.

Knocking people out of the way, hitting and shoving, they soon were upon him. "I never saw nobody with arms and legs so long!" one of them said, grabbing one of Henry's long arms and twisting it. Two other men threw themselves down to the ground and grabbed Henry's legs, pulling hard and throwing him to the ground. But he continued to kick and flail, waving his arms and pumping his legs, his movement fueled by fear and anger in equal measures.

"Goddammit, hold him still!"

"I cain't get a good holt on him! Keep still, you nigger you!"

"Owww! The sonofabitch hit me in the face!"

"Then hit him back but make him be still!"

Blows rained down upon Henry. He was hit on the head and face and back and stomach, and on both legs and arms, with sticks and bats and some kind of club. The pain was excruciating.

"Don't break nothin' on him! We cain't sell him if he's broke."

"Evil white devils!" Henry roared. "Evil white devils!" he said again, and then again, and then again. "You will not make money from my body, Evil White Devils!" The men stopped hitting him and stood staring down at him. "Evil white devils," Henry said again, but he could not see them because of the blood filling his eyes.

"Tie him up—"

Henry kicked and lashed out, chanting the words of his homeland, the only words he remembered from that place and the language of his people, and he chanted them over and over and over, in a rhythm, as if accompanied by a drum. He did not know, or remember, what the words meant, and perhaps he'd never known. He knew only that his mother repeated the words on that horrific journey across the Atlantic to America, that she repeated the words until she died.

"What the hell—"

"That's some African nigger talk, that ain't no American nigger talk, and there ain't no tellin' what he's sayin'!"

"Evil white devils," Henry said, clearly and plainly, before resuming the chant in his native tongue.

Suddenly there came a loud, mournful wailing from the crowd that had gathered, and a voice began to repeat the words that Henry was chanting, in the same language, and as if directed by a choirmaster, they took turns, Henry and an invisible face in the crowd, alternating the chant.

Henry, then what sounded to be a woman, then Henry again. Those around them listened in respectful silence. They did not understand the words and so could not join in repeating them, but they understood that the voices and the unknown language belonged to those born across the water. They felt the shared deep pain.

Suddenly someone in the crowd yelled, "Evil white devils!" and quickly it became a chant:

EVIL WHITE DEVILS!
EVIL WHITE DEVILS!
EVIL WHITE DEVILS!

Henry could not see the people but it was enough to hear their voices, and they fueled his resolve not to be captured alive.

"Shut up, you niggers!" one of the would-be slave catchers screamed.

"You will make no money from my body, evil white devils!" Henry hollered as he struggled mightily against the ropes that bound him. Then he broke free and, as if propelled by an internal engine, he ran, long legs and arms pumping like pistons.

"I never seen a nigger run that fast!" one of the cops exclaimed.

Then the woman, Henry's chorus mate, ran, and she could have been Henry's sister with her long, thin limbs. She ran in the opposite direction, as fast as Henry had run.

"Stop them!" the leader yelled.

The men fired their weapons, some at Henry, some at the woman—and within seconds both long-limbed sprinters were on the ground, dead.

But voices in the crowd still lived.

EVIL WHITE DEVILS!

The chant continued over and over, followed by a lone voice chanting in some other African language no one else seemed to know, chanting that became keening. Wailing in grief for a language slave owners had decreed, many, many years ago, could never be spoken. People known to have come from the same place on the same ships were separated to stop all communication and kill the languages and the memories. But the words were spoken by those who knew them and by those who remembered them, spoken quietly and privately, until there were but a few remaining who remembered.

"Shut up, you niggers! Shut them up!" One African word was one too many. "Shut up, damn you!" The leader, frustrated, angry, frightened, aimed his gun and fired several times into the crowd. Then people were screaming and running away, which was not his intention.

"I command you to stop running! By order of the Philadelphia Police Department I command you to stop running!" A command obeyed by no one. In seconds only three members of the crowd remained, prone on the ground, two of them dead. The one who still lived began chanting:

EVIL WHITE DEVILS!
EVIL WHITE DEVILS!
EVIL WHITE DEVILS!

Until a bullet stopped him.

Then, only seven people remained in the once bustling commercial area, and three of them lay dead on the cold ground. The four slave catchers looked on in disgust. All that work and they would have earned not a farthing to show for it.

"What the hell are we gonna do with them?" one of the gunmen said pointing to the dead bodies of two men and one woman.

"I'll send the animal removal people to pick 'em up when I get back to the station house. You boys go on home."

"I never seen a nigger run as fast as those long-legged ones," one of them said.

"I never heard one talk like that," another said, "like they wasn't no way scared of us, and they all 'spozed to be scared of us. Ain't they?"

No, they were not. The cop knew that only too well. Not only were many of them not afraid, many of them—like the dead ones before him—were angry, and the hot anger inside them burned whatever fear they might have had to the ground. "That's why we got to keep 'em in chains. We cain't let 'em walk around, going where they want, doing what they want, when they want." But chains, while they could perhaps contain fear, could not contain anger, and that was too frightening a thought to utter out loud. The angry and unafraid and newly self-named

178

Henry Weens lay in a pool of his own blood in the middle of a Philadelphia street. There were two more like him—angry, unafraid, and dead, lying in pools of their own blood, waiting to be collected by those who collected the corpses of dead animals. And then what would happen to them? Would they be buried or burned or tossed onto a garbage pile? The people who loved them and would miss them would never know what happened to them. But perhaps they would know they died angry and unafraid, and that no slave catchers made money from their African bodies.

Ezra MacKaye enjoyed the walk from Joe Joseph's restaurant to Jack Juniper's home despite the frigid air. With no clients, and therefore no business concerns, his mind was free to dwell on that which was most important to him now—the life he would create with Ada Lawrence in Toronto.

Despite the pleasant nature of his thoughts, however, he still was who he was: former soldier, former Pinkerton's Agent, current Private Inquiry Agent, and in all those iterations of himself, the seeing, hearing, understanding of events was crucial. What he now saw was the greater than usual number of police about, but they did not seem to be tense or agitated, as if on guard for trouble.

Perhaps that was because there were no Black people walking about, not a single one, and that was unusual, too. In fact, he hadn't seen a Black person since he left Arthur at home in the Back Street. When he walked down Thatcher Lane, toward Eighth Avenue, he saw Adelaide Tillman, and he knew that she saw him, but she averted her gaze, crossed the street, and almost ran down the block to her house. Without a doubt Arthur was well away from them, thanks to Eugenia and Jack. And though Eighth Avenue was home almost exclusively to Black businesses, none seemed to be open. Miss Adelaide's Hat and Dress Shop certainly wasn't. Yes, it was a cold winter night in late November, but there was no snow and ice to make walking treacherous, so where was everyone?

Not only was Ezra the only person walking, but he was also the only white person walking in what was a largely Black area. Suppose one of the coppers wanted an explanation for his presence? He had just come from dining in a Black-owned eating establishment and now he was en route to visit his Black friend with a bag full of fried chicken and roasted potatoes. He recalled the back way Jack took to his home, via alleys and side streets, and he quickly left the main road to follow that route, which he knew well. Even though the police seemed not to be in pursuit of anyone, Ezra did not wish to attract their attention, though he had attracted the attention of several dogs and cats intrigued by the scent of the fried chicken and roasted potatoes in the bags he carried.

Knowing how bold and fearless street animals were, Ezra raised the bags up to his chest and stuffed them inside his coat, wrapped in his scarf. He should've done it sooner. The warmth at his throat was as welcome as the scent of the food, though as he'd just eaten, he should not be indulging thoughts of the food. It was for Jack.

A man who entered the side street and walked toward him from the opposite direction stopped and stood staring at Ezra. He was not tall but even at a distance Ezra could see that he was powerfully built. Ezra slowed his gait but did not stop. He needed to pass by the man in order to turn into the side street.

"'Evening, sir," the man said in a low voice as Ezra approached.

"Good evening to you, sir," Ezra replied, quietly as well as cautiously. The man did not look to pose a threat, but Ezra would be prepared if he was proved wrong.

"You are Jack Juniper's friend, are you not?"

Ezra was taken by surprise and sought a quick recovery. "Yes, I am. Ezra MacKaye is my name," he said, offering his hand.

Taking and shaking Ezra's hand, the man said, "I am Thomas Hill. I live in this house but given the events of earlier this evening I'm entering from the back door rather than the front."

Ezra's stomach knotted. "What events were those, Mr. Hill, if I may ask?"

Hill peered at him. "Have you not seen Jack then?"

Ezra grabbed the gate to Thomas Hill's back garden to steady himself. "Has something happened to Jack?" His voice was a croak.

"Oh, I do apologize! No, as far as I know Jack is well. It is Henry, and it is very likely that Jack doesn't know what happened to him."

"And what has happened to Henry?"

"He is dead, Mr. MacKaye, killed by the police less than one hour ago, right out there almost in front of my house."

Ezra dropped the bag of food and Hill quickly scooped it up just ahead of an angry snarl from a dog Ezra hadn't known was there. "I am sorry to be the one to deliver such hard news."

"Please tell me what happened," Ezra asked, and Hill told him. All of it. As he listened Ezra pictured Henry, the self-named Hezekiah English who chose to become Henry Weems. The sad, shy, awkward man who became a self-assured, calm, competent man thanks to Maggie and Jack Juniper. Jack would be pained, without a doubt, but Maggie would be distraught. Not only was she teaching and helping Henry, but she had become his friend, caring about him. The emotion from that woman had transformed the African. Ezra was grateful it would not fall to him to tell her, though he soon found telling Jack proved difficult enough.

"But he was going to Joe Joseph's. That's what he said when he left. He promised to go directly there, Ezra, and Henry well knew the danger of straying into the wrong part of town," Jack said.

"He was not in the wrong part of town," Ezra said, telling his friend, word for word, what Thomas Hill had related, including every word that Henry had spoken. Except for the African-language chant.

Jack sat on a bench near the door and was silent for a long time and Ezra knew he was thinking of and remembering Henry Weems. "Deep within, I confess I am not surprised. He always said he'd never be a slave, and his hatred of slave catchers was powerful. He died honorably, and for that I am most grateful." Jack was quiet again, thoughtful. "I wonder if he made it to Joseph's—"

"He did not, Jack," Ezra said gently. "I was there with Arthur, and Henry did not come while we were there, nor had he been there before we arrived."

Jack's shoulders slumped in acceptance of the awful truth. "I wish we could leave this place tomorrow. I cannot bear to be here much longer without Margaret. How did she accept being without me all those years when I was at sea?"

"Women are better and stronger than we are, Jack, you know that. They do what must be done and endure what must be endured."

"Aye, that they do," Jack said with a mixture of pride and sadness.

"I realize I'm a poor substitute for Henry, but could you put up with me living here until it is time for us to leave?"

Jack clapped him on the shoulder so hard Ezra feared dislocation. "I welcome you, my friend, especially since you come with the gift of food," and he deftly opened the bag of chicken and potatoes. He hurried to the stove and lit the fire under the kettle, put tea in the pot, and put the bowl of sugar on the table. He retrieved the jug of milk from the window ledge where it was frozen and placed it on the stove to thaw, finally taking two plates from the cabinet and placing them on the table. Ezra welcomed the preparations as if he had not recently eaten, and he was relatively certain Jack had not. A sudden thought all but paralyzed him: Jack, alone in his empty home, had been waiting for Henry to bring him dinner. His heart broke.

CHAPTER SEVENTEEN

*T*he *River Dancer*, her crew, and passengers enjoyed two swift-moving days and calm if cold nights on their river voyage. They were able to employ the sails on the better part of those two days, which, the captain was pleased to tell them, meant that they would reach their destination ahead of schedule. He also informed them that they would tie up that evening on the banks of a town that had a market where he liked to restock. He and all but one of the crew would go ashore after dinner, and he explained that after he paid for the provisions he would return to the boat. "I'll not be away for more than an hour." The other crew members, he said, would follow with the cart-loads of provisions. Finn served their dinner as usual that evening, then cleared away the empty plates. He left a pot of hot tea and a basket of cake slices, bid them good night, and left.

"There's a chance we might arrive early—" Maggie began, and suddenly everyone was talking at once, their excitement unleashed and running rampant. Everyone was up and taking turns dancing in circles with the children. Then Donnie began a Scottish jig and everyone moved aside and gave him the floor—clapping in time with his fast-moving feet.

"Oh Donnie!" Ada exclaimed. "Can Ezra do that?"

Donnie collapsed onto his berth and wiped his face with a

large handkerchief. Then he gave Ada a sly look. "Let's us put him to the test, Mistress Lawrence," he said.

"But what do you think, Donnie? Can he?"

"I'm certain that he learned how—"

"We must put him to the test then, Donnie." Ada was as excited as Elizabeth and Eli and she was dancing about the cabin, a child holding each of her hands. "And I want to learn it, too."

"Me, too," Eli said. He released Ada's hand and began hopping about, stamping his feet and making an oddly rhythmic pattern, and everybody clapped in time with his feet.

"You're a natural Scotsman, laddie!" Donnie enthused.

"Don't let his papa hear you say that," Maggie said darkly.

"Oh that's right. The man is a bleedin' Liverpudlian."

Eli's feet stopped. "A liver what?" He looked at Maggie, then at Abby.

"It's what people from Liverpool are called," Maggie said, stifling a laugh. "You know that your papa is from Liverpool. He told you that, did he not?"

Eli nodded. "That's where ships from all over everywhere come. Papa said the Port of Liverpool is the biggest in the world. But what's a Liverpuddle? He didn't tell me about that."

"Then you must ask him—" Maggie began.

"When we get to Toronto!" Elizabeth shouted, dancing a jig of her own.

"Why don't we have some tea and cake?" Genie said, immediately restoring calm, and opening a conversation, one they'd had many times, about what they all would do once they were in Toronto, and they were full of thoughts and ideas and plans and imaginings: What would Toronto be like?

"Not like Philadelphia," Abby said into a moment of silence, and received a loud round of applause.

Then Donnie abruptly stood up and went to the cabin door. He opened it, looked into the passage, then listened. "Lock the

185

door behind me," he said to Genie, but she grabbed his arm before he could exit. She recognized the look that foretold danger when she saw it.

"What is it, Donnie? Is there a problem?"

"The captain said he'd return in an hour. It's been ninety minutes. I'm going to be certain that he is all right."

"But you don't know where you're going," Genie said, stepping into the passageway.

"You and Eli arm yourselves, and keep a close eye on the windows and the water." And he was quickly gone, and Genie quickly locked the door.

"What is it, Genie?" Maggie asked.

"Donnie is worried about something," and she told them what he said. All of them well understood danger when they heard it described and they followed instructions. In addition to the guns, Genie had managed to find and hide several thick pieces of wood, and she gave one to Maggie, Ada, and Abby. She didn't need to tell them what to do. Eli raised the first alarm almost immediately.

"I see something." He had kept his face pressed to one of the windows since Donnie left and though it was near dark, if Eli said he saw something, then he did. "Somebody swimming from the back of the boat to the side—" He lurched backward because there suddenly was a face at the window and fists pounding, then rocks pounding. Eli recovered and raised his pistol so the man at the window could see it. Shocked and frightened, the man stopped his futile assault on the window and sank into the river.

Genie hurriedly unlocked the door and, pistol in hand, ran out. Just as quickly, Ada relocked it. Genie hurried down the back passageway. If one would-be robber entered the water from the rear of the boat, another most likely would follow. She also assumed robbery would be the reason men would plunge into the icy Delaware River. Denizens of the river, from the dock in

Philadelphia to every hamlet and village along the way, would know that Captain Addams and *The River Dancer* transported a cargo of wealth. She stopped mid-stride at the sound of nearby pounding. The locked cargo hold where their belongings were stored! She sprinted along the passageway and down the stairs to the lower deck. Two men faced the locked door. One swung at the padlock with a hammer, missing the target more often than he hit it, while the other urged in a drunken sing-song chant, "Hurry up, hurry up, hurry up."

"Put the hammer on the floor," she said quietly, but he didn't. Instead, he raised it, aimed it in her direction, and took a step toward her. She raised her pistol and shot once, eliminating the hammer and most of the hand that held it. He didn't immediately realize what happened but his friend did.

"Oh Jaysus, Paddy, yer hand yer hand yer hand!" And he began a drunken, lurching run in Genie's direction but she knew that he was not aiming for her—he wanted the door behind her—so she stepped aside and allowed him to lurch past her. He fell twice ascending the steep stairs, and she heard his heavy, hobnailed boots traverse the deck until she no longer heard him. Then she followed him up the stairs, along the deck to the ramp and off the boat, where she saw him making better progress than she expected.

She pursed her lips and emitted a long, shrill whistle, and smiled sadly as she recalled Adelaide referencing the fact that she whistled as proof that Genie behaved more like a man than a woman. She shook Adelaide out of her mind as she heard Donnie's answering whistle. Twice. He was in trouble. She took off at a run in the direction the whistle came from and found herself in a small copse of trees on the riverbank about a hundred yards from the bow of *The River Dancer*. She whistled again, softly, as she approached the copse, and Donnie emerged half carrying, half dragging Captain Addams. She hurried forward and, supporting the captain's other side, they quickly got him to his boat. Getting him aboard was a struggle because he was dead weight but they managed. Then they answered all of his questions—at least the ones they could answer. He opened a drawer at his console and withdrew a bottle of whiskey. He pulled out the cork and took a gulp. Then he doused a cloth, which also came from the drawer at his console, with a large amount of whiskey and placed it to the back of his head where matted blood was visible.

"Hellfire and damnation!" he yelled, jumping to his feet and swaying. Donnie caught and steadied him. He took another gulp of whiskey. "I do truly apologize to you—"

"You owe us no apology, Captain Addams," Genie said.

"Most certainly I do because almost certainly someone in my employ is responsible for what has happened this night."

"Did you see who hit you?" Donnie asked, and Addams shook his head, immediately regretting it. "I haven't seen any of your crew since we tied up here." Donnie looked at Genie and she shook her head.

"I didn't recognize either of the two trying to get into the cargo hold," she said. Addams turned white and swayed again. "I said trying," Genie repeated. "Your padlock held, Captain."

"Oh thank heaven!" he whispered, and it really sounded like a prayer. "Do you know if the provisions were delivered?"

Donnie shrugged and looked at Genie. "I don't think so, Captain," she replied.

He cursed. "I've paid for those supplies so I'd better go see to it that they're delivered."

"I'll go," Donnie said.

"You don't know these men here—" Addams began, but Donnie withdrew two pistols from his pockets, bared his teeth, and headed for the door.

"Will you first let Eli and the others know that you're all right, Donnie?" Genie asked, and he smiled a real smile and nodded. Before he could leave, though, Finn appeared, and he

188

was frightened. Not without cause, because Addams tore into him with what little strength he had left in him after his ordeal, and it wasn't much, which was the only reason Finn still stood upright.

"I swear to you, Captain, that I did not do any of those things. I told not a single soul about the people or cargo on this ship—"

"Then how would anyone know to try to rob us? You must have said something."

"Only that they were the nicest passengers we had ever carried, Captain, and they are!" And when Addams gave a brief nod, Finn continued, saying he told some family members and several friends how the passengers were the only Blacks he'd ever been close to and how it was clear that they were educated and rich, how even the little children were smart and they obeyed their mam. He looked at Genie and said, "I beg your pardon, Miss, I mean you no disrespect." She nodded and he continued. "I court a woman in the town and as soon as we were free, me and two of the crew ran as fast as we could to meet the women—"

"You're all courting the same woman?" Addams asked, looking askance.

Finn reddened. "No sir, Captain. They're courting friends of the woman I'm courting."

"Send them to me when they return, and you go with Mr. Bruce to get the provisions and get them loaded. We will get underway immediately. I don't want to be here when a would-be thief not only has no prize to show for his night's work, but he's minus a hand." And he had to work hard to prevent a smile at Genie.

And they did, but it was slow going without the lights of a pilot boat to follow in the inky darkness. Addams kept the engines on low, and *The River Dancer* crawled her way along that night, but by keeping to the middle of the river and keeping a close eye on the bank, he made certain that no danger followed or waited ahead. Even when the following dawn broke and the sails were raised, Addams kept to the middle of the river and did not tie up for the night until lights of a distant town were visible. And with a guard posted on the deck that night, for the first time since the trouble he felt relaxed enough to sleep in his cabin. His passengers, in their cabin, felt relaxed enough to finally discuss the events that shook all of them to the core. They had let themselves believe that once away from Philadelphia they would be safe. They tried to convince themselves that the reason they were imperiled was different—that it was their perceived wealth that endangered them and not their color. After all, in Philadelphia only Abby would be considered wealthy. Not even Ada, despite her very substantial fortune, would be considered wealthy. But deep within, the thing that worried each of them most was the fact that if harm had come to them, they would have no way to inform Jack Juniper and Ezra MacKaye. More than worry, that reality caused them deep pain. Over and over they told each other how happy they would be when finally they were in Toronto. When they were home.

Late on the second night following the trouble the boat began a gentle rocking, as if it were keeping time with the pocket watch Captain Addams had mounted on his desk. Of course it wasn't. The watch served no purpose except to be a permanent display of his wife's affection for him. However, Addams frequently allowed himself to imagine the day when ocean- and river-going vessels would possess instruments to measure longitude and latitude, wind speed and direction, and even the depth of the water.

For now, however, experienced and knowledgeable captains like Addams left the bow and ventured outside, into the dark and cold, to learn what the rocking of the boat might mean. In this case—nothing at the moment. But soon there would be more wind. Strong wind. He hoped it would not occur before first light. He wanted the crew to be as rested as possible because they all would be tested by what might come.

When Finn brought their breakfast the following morning, the boat was no longer gently rocking, though Captain Addams had gotten his wish that the weather would not change before first light.

"The sails are up again, isn't that right, Finn?" Eli asked excitedly.

"Right you are, young Eli," the steward said, standing with his legs spread wide, one foot in front of the other, to maintain his balance. He served a dry breakfast—baskets of toast with pots of butter and jam, several kinds of dried fruit, copious amounts of bacon—but no eggs or juice or milk for the tea. "Captain Addams fears the winds will become stronger and we don't want liquid to spill over you," Finn explained with apology. "We know ye must have your tea, but please keep the pot on the table here, well away from yourselves, in case it should spill."

He gave the table a last look and took a wide-legged walk to the cabin door. Leaving, he said, "I'll return to you when it is possible."

"Can we go above and see—" Elizabeth began before a chorus of loud "Nos" silenced her.

"If we have sails up all of today, we may well reach home by tomorrow," Ada said, trying to sound more excited than worried, while Genie and Maggie settled for merely looking worried, because Abby looked terrified. Only Genie's arms wrapped tightly around her prevented her from hyperventilating. Maggie knew that Abby would not eat so she fed herself quickly, made certain that Eli and Elizabeth had full plates, then moved across the cabin to change places with Genie so she could eat and have a cup of tea.

"I'll go up top and have a chat with Mr. Addams," Donnie said, opening the door. Genie immediately locked it behind him, then tried to convince Abby to eat half a piece of dry toast.

"No," Abby whispered, shaking her head.

"Half a cup of tea with copious amounts of honey?" But Abby shook her head no before Genie completed the question.

"You must, my dear," Maggie said gently, "even if only a few sips. You must not become dehydrated."

"What's dehy . . . what was that word, Mama?" Eli asked, sounding and looking concerned. Anything that affected Abby or Genie negatively worried him, even to the point that he stopped eating.

Maggie repeated the word, explaining what it meant, and why it was necessary to avoid the condition. He looked at Abby, resting in his mother's arms, her eyes tightly shut, her breathing labored, her face drained of all color, her hands tightly balled fists. Genie had explained to Eli and Elizabeth why Abby did not like boats and water, why she feared them, but they had never seen that fear, and were frightened by it. Genie saw their fear and hurried to comfort and reassure them.

"You know that your mother and I will take the best possible care of Abby, don't you?" Genie asked gently, an arm around each of them. They burrowed into her, and she now could feel their fear. "You know there is nothing to be afraid of, don't you?" she asked. They were silent for a few long seconds.

"But Abby is afraid," Eli finally said.

"And Abby knows so many things. She would not be frightened if there was nothing to fear," Elizabeth said, sounding quite mature yet fearful.

Maggie and Jack definitely had their hands full with these two, Genie thought. Then she had another, more sobering thought: how wise to get them out of Philadelphia and America. These children would never be servants, nor have to pretend to be stupid. What could they hope for if they remained in America to be but three-fifths of a person and never a citizen? Perhaps in Toronto they could become—whatever was possible. Otherwise, this would be a wasted journey.

A knock at the door brought Ada to her feet, ear to the door. She lifted the handle, and Donnie bustled in on a wave of frigid air. "Winter has arrived up top!" he proclaimed with a dramatic shiver, hoping the blast of cold winter air he brought in with him would be sufficient to quell any other concerns.

Genie released Eli and Elizabeth and, imitating Finn's wide-legged gait, hastened to pour a cup of tea for Donnie, who gratefully wrapped his hands around it, sighing as they began to warm. He looked all around as was his custom, ensuring that all was as it should be. What he really wanted to see, however, was Abigail, and what he saw answered the question: how much should he tell them?

"Are we in a storm, Donnie? Is that why there is so much wind?" Ada asked, giving him the opportunity to formulate a suitable response.

"There is a severe storm passing by us," he replied. "However, Captain Addams referred to it as an advantageous situation. He will engage the propellers—you'll hear them soon and feel the rumble beneath us—and we will speed forward. When we sail out of the storm and you feel us slow down," here Donnie paused dramatically, waiting to be certain he had everyone's attention, including Abby's, "we will be in Canadian waters, and Captain Addams says we will reach our destination before the end of the day."

"Oh, what good news!" Maggie called out, with Genie and Ada chiming in. The children clapped and cheered, and Abby managed a wan smile. Then *The River Dancer* shuddered as the propellers started up and the craft lurched forward with a powerful side to-side rocking motion that lasted several seconds before smoothing. Then they were moving forward more rapidly than ever before and Donnie knew they were in the place Captain Addams told him about, where several bodies of water converged. He knew that he could not speak those words, but he did not need to, for Abby cried out and moaned as if the water beneath her was the dreaded Atlantic. Donnie made certain their cabin door was locked just as the forceful rocking, side-to-side motion resumed, almost knocking him off his feet. He gestured to the children to join their mother in their bunk, which they did without hesitation or argument, and Ada returned to hers when he looked her way.

Abby buried her face in her hands, unable to control the flood of tears that had threatened to break free for the last hour. Genie held her tightly, letting her weep. The last dry cloth fell to the floor. Genie freed one arm and reached down for it just as *The River Dancer* lurched violently, throwing her off the bunk and to the floor. She landed hard on her back and couldn't prevent a painful cry as her head hit the cabin floor with a loud thump. Abby cried out again and tried to reach for Genie but the constant rolling of the craft made that impossible. Grateful that it did—it wouldn't do for both Genie and Abby to be injured—Donnie reached forward and let the boat throw him to the floor beside Genie. He reached in vain for something to hold onto and instead found hands holding him—one of Maggie's and one of Ada's as he reached to grab Genie by the arm. He pulled her to him and held her to keep her from rolling around on the floor. Abby was calling for her, trying to sound much braver than she felt.

Then the boat ceased its most violent rocking and shaking, and Maggie lowered herself to the floor. Keeping her back firmly against her bunk, she pulled Genie to her and began to quickly examine the back of her head. There was a small lump that probably would get a bit larger, but there was no blood, a good sign. Genie whimpered when Maggie touched the lump but after a quick glance at Abby locked her lips and squeezed her eyes shut. Ada carefully made her way to Abby's bunk and sat with her. The children joined them, and they all sat quietly and as calmly as possible until, after what felt like hours, the boat was sailing smoothly.

"Everyone, we are now sailing on Lake Ontario towards Toronto," Ada said, to sighs of relief rather than cheers until they were certain there would be no more rough water. Once certain that the water was calmer, they gradually calmed themselves and began to speak aloud the words that until now had been only thoughts, hopes, wishes, and dreams about what life might be like in Toronto. Each of the four women harbored a strong, almost palpable, idea of what her initial thoughts and feelings would be upon arriving in Toronto: Ada expected to feel a sense of joy at finally coming home after so many years away, while Abby hoped and prayed the new place would feel like home to her because Philadelphia and America certainly never did, and she didn't remember if London ever had.

Maggie shared these feelings—she and Abby had discussed them—but more than anything she wanted Toronto to be a safe place for her children to grow and thrive. She did not want them to live confined, claustrophobic lives. She did not want them to bear the burden of other peoples' limitations and shortcomings. For their part, Eli and Elizabeth embraced what was about to happen as did children everywhere and always: with excitement.

And Genie wanted to never again have to think of herself as a runaway slave, and to live in dread and fear that someone could or would learn this deeply buried but never forgotten secret she harbored. Tears filled Maggie's eyes and she nodded. Her husband had expressed the same feeling when he agreed to move to Toronto without hesitation. To think it possible that the two people dearest to her could finally live without fear made her as happy as knowing that her two children could grow up to be—whatever they were capable of being. Those things were sufficient for Margaret Juniper to embrace Toronto as home. "And I can be a citizen."

CHAPTER EIGHTEEN

Ezra and Jack grew tired of waiting, but they could do little else except share the stories of their coming of age, Jack in coastal Maryland, Ezra in Edinburgh, Scotland.

"After what you have endured, Jack, I marvel that you are able to be a kind and gentle and loving man to your wife and children, and a good and dear friend—to Genie and Arthur and to me. And how good you were to Henry, too," Ezra said. They were sitting in the dark in the kitchen of Jack's home, the only light provided by the fire in the stove, which they constantly fed because the night was cold.

"What would you have me be, Ezra? A beast like those who brutalized me? An angry and bitter man? If I were those things, I would never have earned the love and respect of a woman like Margaret."

"And she is indeed a very special woman, Jack."

Jack tilted back in his chair and closed his eyes, thinking about and envisioning his Margaret. Ezra quietly observed him. He doubted he would ever fully know this man even after twenty or thirty years of friendship. Jack opened his eyes and returned his chair to its proper position on its four legs. "All that is past, Ezra, is past. I am still here and present, and I claim to be a better man than those who brutalized me."

"You'll get no argument from me."

"How and why did you come to leave Scotland for Philadelphia?" Jack asked,

"I left Scotland when I was eighteen because it was clear that the only way I could earn a respectable living there was by working the land or herding sheep, activities pursued by generations of my relatives. But I had no interest in the land. Or in sheep," the Scotsman said drily, adding that doing nothing would have been frowned upon.

"What did hold your interest, Ezra?" Jack asked.

"America and everything on offer here—and there was so very much." Ezra told his friend about the things he had heard and seen upon his arrival in New York—such a great, fine city, and nothing like it in Scotland. "In London, perhaps, but—" He shrugged and the look on his face was that of the eighteen-year-old boy longing to get away from home. The problem, Ezra said, was that farming was the only job he knew. He didn't have the education or the skill to do jobs that paid decently. "I also didn't have a relative already employed in a shop or a business who could put in a good word for me—which the Irish and the Italians and the Jews and the Greeks did have."

His next stop was Chicago and, Ezra said, it was much more welcoming to the newly arrived Scotsman, the burr in his voice so thick that only a kinsman could understand him. "I cleaned hotels and restaurants and even train cars for almost two years. Then the rooming house where I lived was destroyed by fire. And because we had nowhere else to go, two friends and I joined the Army, which turned out to be a blessing. In addition to food, shelter and clothing, I learned all there was to know about munitions, which impressed my commanding officer, Major James Pinkerton."

"The same Pinkerton who's responsible for your move to Chicago?" Jack asked.

"The very same," Ezra replied, "and when he left the army and joined the Pinkerton Detective Agency I followed him, got hired, and here I am."

Jack laughed and said, "I think perhaps you omitted a few details, Mr. MacKaye, but it is clear that the Pinkerton's Agency provided you with a good start in your life in America."

"It seems Pinkerton's is prepared to provide me with a good start in my new life in Canada as well," Ezra said, explaining that when he had visited his office the previous day to settle his accounts with his landlady, he found a letter from Col. Pitcairn. Ezra pulled it from his pocket and offered it to Jack, who unfolded and read it.

"Pitcairn has this kind of influence?" Jack asked, more shocked than surprised, for, according to the letter, he had arranged for Ezra to become a supervisory officer with the Toronto Constabulary, or a regional superintendent with the Ontario Office of the Pinkerton Detective Agency. Both positions were available and awaiting Ezra's arrival in Toronto.

"I confess my surprise," Ezra said. "I assumed that Pitcairn was angry with me for rebuffing his offer to return to the military, but it now seems he was more than a little grateful for my assistance in dealing with Montague Wright and his illegal bank notes and Smith and Wesson revolvers." Ezra had wondered, he told Jack, how he would earn a living as a private inquiry agent in a city where he was unknown and where he knew no one. And though his wife-to-be would have more than enough income for their comfort, he would never be the kind of man who lived off the work of a woman.

"Have you decided which job you will do?" Jack asked.

"It was an easy decision, my friend. It will be a return to Pinkerton's for me. I've already telegraphed the director with my thanks and my acceptance. Besides, given what I've seen of police behavior in New York, Chicago, and Philadelphia, that is not a job I would want."

Jack breathed a huge sigh of relief and said, "I cannot tell you how pleased I am to hear you say that."

"Stop your infernal pounding on that door and your bloody shouting!" Mrs. McDougall hollered, moving quickly for a woman of her girth. She powered up the stairs and down the hallway of her building to confront Montague Wright before he knew what was upon him. "Can you not read the sign affixed to the door? 'Fully Furnished Office to Let with Immediate Availability,' is what it says—"

"I can read the sign!" Wright snapped.

"Then why are you pounding on the door like an eejit and calling for a man you must know is not within?" Mrs. McDougall peered over her rimless spectacles and down at Wright. "If Mr. MacKaye were within, he would have admitted you if for no other reason than to stop your insane bellowing."

Ezra MacKaye had leased space from her for more than six years. Not only was he her favorite tenant, but he was also a good and decent man. How, then, could he possibly know this sniveling wreck of a man?

"I need to speak with him urgently. He has done me a great wrong, and I must confront him. He must make things right—"

"Then speak with him in Canada, which is where he has gone, and leave my building immediately."

Wright looked from the sign on the office door to the landlady and back to the sign. Ezra MacKaye had gone to Canada. He had ruined the life of Dr. Montague Wright and gone to Canada. What was Wright to do? What could he do? His perfectly ordered world was rapidly unraveling and it was all because of Ezra MacKaye. Not only was his Society Hill mansion not his, but it somehow now belonged to the United States Government, which, according to Colonel Pit-something, viewed him as a traitor. And to make matters worse, as if that were possible, his sister had arrived on his doorstep with a dozen suitcases and boxes demanding to be admitted. She now had nowhere to live since her own brother had sold her Maryland estate house out from under her, she said, accusation heavy in her shrill voice. Well of course he had sold it. He needed the money from the sale to purchase Abigail Read's mansion. He had not considered for a single minute where his demented sister would live, but certainly not with him. This was all Ezra MacKaye's fault, damn the man!

"You will leave my building or I will have you removed," Mrs. McDougall said, and what he heard in her voice, and what he saw in the eyes of the two very large men who had joined her in the hallway, caused his shoulders to droop. Very near tears he turned away from the door that no longer gave access to Ezra MacKaye and stumbled down the hallway to the stairs. The horrible man was going to live in Canada while he, Dr. Montague Wright, now was a prisoner in his beautiful mansion with his awful sister for a cellmate.

Jack and Ezra shared a meal every day with Arthur, and today would be their final one. They came to tell him, knowing and expecting it to be a wrenching encounter. They were loath to leave the old man here alone but he had refused their invitations and suggestions, offered more than once, to join them. "Y'all don't need to be worryin' yourselves with a crippled old man," he told them every time they suggested he join them, so they stopped asking. They went first to Joe and Aurelia's to get the fried chicken backs and roasted potatoes that Arthur loved, and to say good-bye to those good people and their staff, whom they had come to know and like as much as they liked Joe and Aurelia.

"Aurelia must've known you were coming, Ezra," Joe said, "'cause she made the chicken fricassee you like so much, so find someplace to sit."

Ezra asked Joe Joseph for permission to hug his wife, then asked Aurelia Joseph for permission to hug her. He and Jack followed Joe to a table near the kitchen even though other tables were available, and they saw why once they were seated: William and Adelaide Tillman were on the opposite side of the restaurant. They both glared their dislike at Jack and Ezra, who ignored it as they exchanged greetings and pleasantries with nearby diners.

"I wish Arthur wouldn't stay here with these awful people," Ezra said. "Why won't he go with us, Jack?"

Jack sighed. He, too, wished Arthur would join them in Toronto where Eugenia and Margaret and the children would welcome him like family, and treat him as such. He would never forgive William Tillman for his treatment of Arthur Green. "Probably because he's afraid. It will be a difficult journey for us, Ezra, and we're younger and our legs are strong."

"And Arthur is stronger than both of us, Jack. You know he is."

"The man ran to freedom once in his life, Ezra. Maybe he thinks that's enough."

"But you didn't, and Genie didn't."

"We're not all the same, Ezra," Jack said quietly and patiently. "I'll run as long and as often as I must to ensure my safety and my freedom and that of my family, and I think Eugenia feels the same." He smiled at some thought that crossed his mind but he didn't speak to it, and then Aurelia was there with their plates of food, steam and mouth-watering scents rising from them. She placed them on the table as Absalom appeared with their glasses—water for Jack and lemonade for Ezra. And both men were silent until their plates were scraped clean and Absalom was back to collect them.

"We won't have to wash these," he said with a wide grin. "Just maybe rinse 'em a bit." Then he leaned across the table and, keeping his voice low, said, "The Tillmans don't like it that Miss

Aurelia serves your food herself. She don't do that for nobody else 'cept the rev'rend from the AME church."

"Aurelia and Joe are good people and we will miss them," Jack said.

"They said—the Tillmans did—that Miss Eugenie—"

Jack raised his hand to halt the flow of words from the boy's mouth. "I will not hear any evil or stupid words from those people about one of the best women I know, my wife being the other one." He looked hard at Absalom. "And you should know better."

The boy ducked his head and nodded. Then he inhaled deeply. "Will you tell Eli we said to take care of hisself and we miss him, me and Richard do? And we miss Miss Eugenie, too."

Then Aurelia was at the table with the bag containing Arthur's food, and it was time to leave Joe Joseph's Family Dining for the last time. "Do you think there will be an establishment with food like this in Toronto?" Ezra asked in a plaintive tone, and Jack laughed.

"In Toronto, Ezra, you will have your own home with your own wife and your own cook and you will be able to eat food like this every day—that is if your wife tells the cook to prepare it every day." And Jack couldn't stop himself from laughing— at the look on Ezra's face, at the memory of Margaret's face when Ezra implored her to make chicken fricassee yet again, at what he imagined the look Ada's face would wear when her new husband requested the same dish every day.

The night had turned cold and they walked briskly to Arthur's. He opened the door before they knocked, and they knew it would be warm before they entered because they smelled the rich scent of the applewood pipe tobacco that Arthur smoked and which he sprinkled on the hearth fire, so as it rose from the chimney it gave the cold night air a homey scent. They would miss this old man.

"Who's the lucky lady?" Jack asked, entering what had once

been his home, thanks to Genie Oliver's generosity.

"You didn't make yourself this pretty for the likes of us," Ezra said, giving Arthur the bag containing his dinner, glad to feel some remnants of warmth.

"What are y'all on about?" Arthur growled, looking confused, annoyance very near the surface and ready to erupt as was always the case with him.

"The close shave and the side part in the haircut," Jack said, warming his hands at the hearth and watching Arthur as he did so. "You didn't do all that for us ugly men. That's the kind of thing you do for a pretty woman."

"Or when you 'bout to move to Canada," Arthur said softly, watching his friends for their reaction, hoping they still were willing to take him. He held his breath, watching their stunned faces and their wide smiles.

"You changed your mind!" Jack, pumping his hand, executed a little hop-skip. "Eugenia will be so happy, Arthur."

"All the women will be," Ezra said, pumping the hand released by Jack. "We're happy and we're not women."

"Good thing, too," Arthur growled, "ugly as you are. Now, when do we leave?"

"Tomorrow morning early," Jack answered, watching Arthur for a reaction.

"Then I got to find somebody to live in this house quick-like."

Almost immediately Jack was on his feet, running for the door. "How about young Josie and Robert?" And he was gone without waiting for the answer that he knew was coming.

"You best go with him, Ezra—"

"He's faster on his own. He knows all the side streets and alleyways—and all the dogs and cats that live in them," Ezra replied.

Nodding at the truth of Ezra's words, Arthur said, "I don't want to be a burden on y'all, but I do want to go with you. I want to be with the people I care 'bout and who care 'bout me."

Ezra, assuring Arthur he would not be a burden, described an arduous journey requiring four modes of transportation, the most challenging of which would be getting across the river to New York—

"I thought the women-folks was going all the way to Canada in a boat on the river."

Ezra, nodding, said, "Pinkerton's found a faster way but one that would be too rough and too difficult for women and children, and, truth be told, too dangerous."

"Dangerous for us?"

Ezra gave an evil grin, one Arthur hadn't seen before and was glad he hadn't. "Dangerous for any man getting in the way of us getting to Toronto and our women."

The following morning the three men were in a boat owned by Pinkerton's and operated by a former officer of the British navy and a Pinkerton's agent of long standing, Harrison by name though it was unclear whether that was a first or surname because he refused to answer the question when asked. He saluted Ezra in recognition of his status as a superior, then ignored all of them as he focused on getting the boat, a sturdy though disreputable-looking craft, across the river to New York harbor. Sufficient time for Jack to provide all of the details for the third or perhaps fourth time of his return visit the previous evening to the Josephs with Arthur's offer of his home to Josie and Robert, their joy at hearing the news, and general merriment that ensued. Joe and Aurelia had closed the restaurant early so that everyone could help Josie and Robert gather their belongings and load them into the horse cart for Richard and Absalom to deliver to their new home—where Arthur and Ezra greeted them and helped unload the cart before sending Richard and Absalom on their way. Or attempting to, for they refused to leave, insisting instead on transporting Arthur, Ezra and Jack back to Jack's. While in truth the three men appreciated being able to ride instead of having to walk, having no way to know whether the two boys were able to return home safely was deeply worrying, though Arthur was more philosophical about it.

"Don't forget them boys was livin' on the streets when Miss Eugenie saved 'em and took 'em to the restaurant for the Josephs to hire. They prob'ly know better than anybody 'cept Miss Eugenie herself how to go safe."

Jack nodded and touched his friend's shoulder, acknowledging the truth of his words. And acknowledging another truth as, for the first time, he said, "I was thinking the only people I cared about were safe in Toronto, forgetting that I do care about some other people." And because there was no more to be said, the three men did not speak again until they were safely on the ground at the harbor of New York looking askew at the coach that was their first transport to their final destination of Rochester, N.Y.

"That rattletrap don't look like it could get us outta sight of the river, never mind to Rochester. Wherever that may be," Arthur growled. "And them is the sorriest-lookin' hosses I ever did see."

Ezra and Jack shared Arthur's opinion of the coach but did not speak it aloud, and since neither man possessed Arthur's expertise in matters of horseflesh, they had no comment on that matter either. Ezra, however, was greatly annoyed that the coach driver seemed not to be at hand, which could only mean that he was not employed by Pinkerton's but merely hired for a job. That, then, would explain Arthur's assessment of the coach and horses.

"How far is this Rochester?" Arthur asked.

"About . . . four hundred—" Ezra began.

"Great God almighty!" Arthur exclaimed. "I feel my lumbago

actin' up already and we ain't even got in the coach. And them hosses look to be starvin' so unless the driver brings some feed, they'll drop dead along the road."

Ezra walked forward for a closer look at the coach and horses as Jack walked in the other direction, toward the town. "I hope I'm mistaken, Ezra, but if I'm not, our wayward coachman approaches, drunk as a lord, and in no condition to transport us anywhere."

Ezra and Arthur walked over to Jack and looked where he pointed. The man saw them and staggered slightly faster toward them. "Hey, get away from that wagon! Go on now, get away."

He was upon them now, smelling as foul as he looked. "I am Pinkerton Superintendent Ezra MacKaye, and if you are the person hired to transport us on the first leg of our journey to Rochester—"

"Nobody said nothin' to me about haulin' no niggers and I ain't doin' it." Already unsteady on his feet, the drunk's anger further imbalanced him and he stumbled and fell. He reached up to Ezra, looking for and expecting assistance regaining his feet, but Ezra turned away just as Harrison, the morning's ferryman, approached.

"Is there some difficulty here, Superintendent?" he asked.

Pointing to the coach Ezra said disdainfully, "That is supposed to be our conveyance to our next stop, to Rochester. My colleague, Mr. Green, informs me that neither coach nor horses are up to the task. And," disgust replacing disdain, "we can all see that the coachman is not."

The coachman, managing to regain his feet, staggered toward them and addressed the ferryman. "I know you. You drive the boat what brung them over here. Tell 'em I don't haul no niggers—"

"You shut your ignorant mouth or I'll shut it for you," Harrison snarled, and turning to Ezra, looked about to pose a question before Ezra spoke his own.

"Is there a place where we can hire a coach and driver on short notice?"

"There is, but it likely will be costly."

"No matter," Ezra snapped. "We must reach Rochester in time to board the boat taking us across the lake to Toronto."

"You still got to pay me even if you don't go nowhere, and I still got to pay Meechum—"

"Meechum." Harrison snorted. "That place is a dump, probably in worse shape than this wagon, and he won't accept your colleagues either."

"You mean niggers—"

Harrison punched the wagon driver, whose name they still didn't know. Walking away, with Jack, Arthur and Ezra following, he led them down a gravel path to a barn. He opened the door, waving them in and calling for "Wrangler." Almost immediately a tall, bald, skinny man—to call him thin would be exaggerating—entered from what Arthur could see was a tack room and bid them good morning. Looking at Harrison he said, "Aren't these passengers from your morning crossing? I thought they were in a hurry to be on their way."

Explaining succinctly though thoroughly why his passengers were still present, Harrison finished by asking Wrangler whether he could supply a coach, driver, and horses for the three men to travel to their next destination.

"The coach and horses are no problem, but I don't have a driver available."

"I can drive the coach if you can send somebody to bring it back," Arthur said.

"Then I think we can do business, gentlemen. I can drive the coach back when I bring saddle horses to you."

"You got a way to get them saddle hosses back home?" Arthur asked, and Wrangler gave him a long, speculative look, followed by a wide smile.

"You love horses, don't you, sir?"

"Better'n most people 'cept these two gentlemen and their families. I lived and worked with 'em all my life, and I never had a hoss lie to me or cheat me or steal from me. If I do right by the hoss, that big, beautiful animal will do right by me."

"Then let's go to the telegraph office so I can let Charlie Smith know to expect guests some time tonight. Do you want three rooms if he has them available?"

"We do," Ezra replied

"And I assume that payment will not be a problem?" Wrangler asked.

"You may so assume, sir," Ezra replied.

And while they had time on their hands Harrison showed them where to eat. Before returning to his boat, he asked Ezra if there was an opening in the Toronto Pinkerton office and if so, whether he could be considered for employment, and Ezra told him the truth: that he was new to the job and didn't know what awaited him, but if he could hire he certainly would give preferential treatment to Harrison. Then he frowned and admitted that he didn't know exactly where his office was, never having been there. Explaining with a smile that he knew exactly where Pinkerton's office was because Toronto was his home city, Harrison left in a hurry, explaining that he was expected back in Philadelphia to pick up a passenger and wishing them a safe journey to Rochester.

One look at the coach and the pair of horses hitched to it satisfied Arthur that the journey would be swift and safe, and after Wrangler showed him the three saddle horses that he would deliver the following morning to the inn where they'd be staying overnight Arthur had no further worries about their safe and timely arrival in Rochester. Wherever that was. Like most who lived in the place called America he had no concept of its vastness though as Wrangler explained the origin of his unusual name, he was able to learn a bit. For instance, according to Wrangler, thousands if not millions of horses roamed the open spaces of the West. There were no towns or cities and not many people because there were no trains to transport them. Stagecoach was the only mode of travel, and not only was the journey long and arduous, it was dangerous, because the people who already lived there—the Indians—did not want white people invading their land, which Arthur could readily understand. But the young and adventurous Wrangler had wanted, needed, to see for himself, and what he saw awed and excited and terrified him: horses more beautiful than any he had ever seen, who ran faster than he could imagine possible, and who refused to be tamed even when one could be caught. He had lost his hand when such a horse threw him and ran away. Wrangler's hand was entangled in the rope that still attached man to horse, the powerful beast running faster than the wind, never slowing or tiring, until Wrangler's hand detached at the wrist. He lost his foot to an Indian who had captured him and grew angry when Wrangler kept running away, thinking that cutting off the white man's foot would stop him from running. It never stopped half a dozen slaves whom Arthur knew personally so perhaps the white man was no different since no man wanted to be a slave. And when Arthur asked how he now was at home in New York, the tall, skinny man said that a slave, running away from the family bringing him West to farm the land, had made the arduous, dangerous journey with him back to the East. And the slave who helped him? Arthur asked. Already in Canada, a place called Halifax in a place called Nova Scotia.

The closer they got to Rochester, the colder it got. The final leg of the journey, bringing with it the knowledge that their next night would be spent in a hotel in Rochester was almost warming, until the arrival of their final conveyance: a two-person trap pulled by a single large dray horse. They'd spent the previous night in a horse stall covered by hay and horse blankets and while not freezing, they were definitely looking forward to hot baths and warm beds.

"Y'all go on and send somebody back for me," Arthur told Ezra and Jack. "Sleeping on the ground in a stall is not new to me. Y'all go, but hurry back if you don't mind." And leaving all the remaining food with Arthur, they left, urging the trap driver to hurry, to be as fast as the big horse would go. Watching them until they were a distant blur on the horizon and settling himself on a bed of straw beneath all of the horse blankets, Arthur dozed until nightfall when he left the comfort of the stall and went outside to the cook pit, a deep hole in the ground, stones pounded into the dirt to preserve the heat, and embers still glowing red. Adding sticks and straw to get a blaze going for heat, he ate the remainder of the roasted potatoes and fried chicken backs supplied by the cook of the house where they rented the owner's barn for what was supposed to be one night. Ezra's offering to pay for a second night met with little resistance. Arthur, eating until full and drinking delicious cold water from a nearby stream running too swiftly to freeze, and feeling ready and able to sleep, banked the fire and, retaining all possible warmth, buried himself beneath the horse blankets and straw and slept.

However, sleeping deeply was not something people who knew about living in fear did so Arthur came fully awake at the sound of whispering voices close by. Who could it be? Who would it be? Who knew he was here and how would anyone know? Only the owner of the house knew and only he could or would tell someone. But why? He'd been paid . . . unless that's why. He had his money and therefore had nothing to lose. Holding a pistol in each hand, Arthur crept out. Circling around to come up behind the whispering men, he shot the three of them dead, dragging their bodies to the creek where they'd most likely freeze and therefore not begin to stink and alert animals or people to their presence. Returning to the fire pit he once again added twigs and bark and leaves to entice the flames to grow hot, and hurrying inside to remove two of the smaller stall doors from their hinges he carried them outside and laid them beside the fire pit thankful that no horses were inside to be endangered. Placing layers of straw on each of the doors he lit them until they burned away, then more straw until it, too, burned, then more straw over and over until the doors themselves were alight. Secreting himself on the far side of the shed, away from the house where the owner lived, he waited for what he was expecting and it wasn't long before half a dozen men ran into the clearing, calling three names, names of men who would never again answer. Arthur ran toward them preaching and chanting, flaming doors hiding him, terrifying and paralyzing them and lighting the night:

"God's big Seraphim is the biggest of all th' angels and they got wings of fire! They burn right through evil and ugly and set everything on fire! Everything in their path they burn and vanish! God hisself gonna meet these Big Angels in the sky and give 'em wings to cover they faces and wings to fly away! Big fiery wings and they'll vanish you and burn you alive if you get in they way! That's what God said! And this big Seraphim angel is comin' at you to vanish you!"

And running toward them waving the fiery stall doors, chasing them until they screamed and disappeared, Arthur returned to the fire pit and placed the doors on the ground, leaving them to burn until they were embers. Collecting his few belongings and his pistols, he moved deep into the forest adjacent to the road, watching the night grow deeper and darker, until its gradual lighting allowed him to be hopeful that Ezra or Jack would return soon.

Rumbling coach wheels and two pairs of fast-trotting horse hooves were a welcoming sound until, coming to a sudden halt, the frightened calling of his name brought him from hiding.

"Arthur! Arthur Green! Where are you, man?" Jack called loudly, willing himself not to sound panicked.

"What's burning, Arthur? Where are you? Please answer!" Ezra, sounding fearful, called out.

"Maybe he can't answer," Jack said in a near whisper. "Lord help me, I must tell Margaret that I come to her without Henry. However will I tell Eugenia that I've lost Arthur?"

"You ain't lost me, Jack Juniper. I'm right here freezing to death, but I'd rather be riding to Rochester. Wherever that is."

"Then let us go, Arthur Green, so that we can go home to Toronto—"

"Draw your weapons, and be ready to fire!" Emerging from the forest and brandishing a pistol in each hand, Arthur was fearful looking, making Jack and Ezra glad he was on their side.

"Who the hell are they?" A furious Ezra MacKaye, pistols raised, striding forward, was halted by the fearful-looking Arthur, telling him to get the coach and horses to safety back down the road until the fighting was finished. "Who are they?" Ezra demanded again, watching Jack hurrying to tell the coach driver to get to safety.

"They belong to the man what owns the place. This makes their third visit but the only one in daylight."

"Then let's make certain they don't return." A growling, angry Jack Juniper was indeed a frightening sight if their would-be attackers were watching. But if they were, they either didn't understand or they missed what their would-be prey were doing by moving into a three-pronged attack-and-defend position, guaranteeing their success no matter what. It was a brief but bloody encounter. No more shouting, yelling, screaming, or cursing by the attackers since most of them were dead, and the rustling sounds of retreat were the signals that Jack, Ezra and Arthur needed. Running to the waiting coach, they were aboard and underway, Arthur falling asleep almost as soon as his butt met the coach seat after having heard every word of Jack's promises of a bath and shave with really hot water when they reached the hotel.

"You know this is not an accident or a coincidence, Ezra."

"Yes, I do," Ezra growled in equal parts anger and worry, because he could not afford to overlook the possibility—the likelihood—that someone within his organization had deliberately sabotaged their journey, placing them in danger.

"And Ezra—"

"You don't need to say it, Jack." They would be with their families in Toronto before the end of this day, and there would be hell to pay if harm came to any of them.

CHAPTER NINETEEN

As *The River Dancer* sailed smoothly into the Port of Toronto, the passengers could see that this was not the busy, bustling Port of Liverpool or even the Port of Philadelphia. It was much smaller with much less activity. It was a beautiful day—bright and sunny, though cold, and with little left of the strong winds that had caused such difficulty on the final day of their journey

They had lost track of Captain Addams when they disembarked but now saw him, just as the totally unexpected sound of thundering horses' hooves bore five horseback riders at breakneck speed in their direction. Only Donnie Bruce knew who the riders were, and he could hardly believe his eyes. "Pinkertons," he whispered. Then he practically shouted, "Ezra has sent us Pinkertons. Can you believe it?!" He could hardly believe it himself, for he didn't know how it could be possible.

The five horsemen halted and dismounted and tipped their hats. "Which one of you lovely ladies is Mrs. Ada MacKaye?"

Ada stifled a laugh and stepped forward. "I am ... ah ... I'm Mrs. MacKaye," she said, adding, "and yes, Donnie, it seems that Ezra has indeed sent us Pinkertons. But how, sir, did you know when to arrive when we ourselves did not know when we would arrive?"

The apparent leader of the Pinkertons, who identified

himself as Detective Avery Scott, explained that Superintendent MacKaye had provided a range of possible dates for their arrival. They had checked into a hotel and hired a watcher to alert them when *The River Dancer* docked. At that moment Captain Addams appeared and was introduced to Pinkerton Detective Scott.

"I have secured transportation for your crates, which are being unloaded from the hold and which then will be loaded onto the carts for delivery to your homes." He looked at Detective Scott. "I hope that is satisfactory."

"Most assuredly so, Captain," Scott replied, and followed the seaman to where the crates from Philadelphia were being carefully and securely loaded onto three wagons. Since the majority of the crates were destined for the Oliver Read business, they all were placed on a single wagon. Then, Addams further explained, since the Juniper and MacKaye families lived in close proximity to each other, their crates would share a wagon, while the Oliver/Read residential crates would have a separate wagon to convey their belongings to their home. "Is that acceptable to everyone?" Addams asked, and when he received nods of assurance, he excused himself to see to the process. Scott immediately signaled to two of his men and sent them to see to things, and then held a quiet conversation with the captain, paying him for transporting the passengers and their belongings from Philadelphia to Toronto as quickly as possible. Then he turned his attention to the new arrivals:

"Superintendent MacKaye sent special instructions for handling the crates going to the Oliver Read business, including orders that the business be guarded around the clock once the crates are inside." He turned to Ada and said, "I believe you have the key to the premises, Mrs. MacKaye?"

Ada looked at Genie and Abby, who removed a chain from around her neck and gave it to Ada, who gave it to Scott. He held it up to show that two keys dangled from it. He gave it to one of the detectives and two of them mounted their horses and rode off to take charge of the crates that would become the entity Oliver Read. He pointed to one of the detectives and assigned him to the Juniper Family, and the other to the Oliver/Read residence. He himself would be responsible for the MacKaye residence. And the Pinkertons left the group of women and children to go do their jobs.

The women looked at each other. Genie spoke first. "Did I understand him correctly? He did say Superintendent MacKaye, did he not?"

"That is indeed what he said but I assure you, my friends, that I am as surprised and as uninformed as you are," Ada said, her gray eyes sparkling. Being uninformed seemed to suit her.

"Superintendent MacKaye," Maggie said, savoring the sound the words made, as well as the apparent power they conveyed.

"I think we should follow the Pinkertons and ride to our homes on the carts with our belongings," Genie said, shivering.

"Me, too. I just realized how cold I am," Abby said.

"Yes, let's go home," Ada agreed, sharing happy and excited looks with each of her friends. Then she looked for Donnie but didn't see him. "Where's Donnie?"

It was Eli who spied him. "He's over there with Ezra's Pinkertons man talking to Captain Addams," and they all hurried to where they were huddled close together to ward off the cold air blowing in from the water.

Donnie was giving Addams a leather pouch. "Ezra and Jack asked that I deliver this to you upon our arrival, with their thanks, Captain. I will be very happy to tell them you honored your promise to keep us safe and to deliver us not just on time, but, by my calculations, at least three days early."

Then they dispersed to become passengers again, this time on the wagons bearing their belongings to their new homes. And for the first time since they found themselves back on terra firma, Elizabeth and Eli began chattering nonstop and hopping from foot to foot and being generally annoying. They bounced up and down in the wagon, and when they reached home they ran from room to room; ran up and down the steps; and ran out the scullery door, across the mews, and into Donnie's carriage house, and then into Ada's house where they ran up and down the stairs. And when they exited her house and started back across the mews, they saw their mother in the scullery door of their house, waiting for them. She was not happy. But before she could act on her displeasure, nearly a dozen people, most of them women, half of them Colored, entered the mews from the main street, and they were running. They waited for an older woman to catch up, and to come and stand in front of them. She was a bit breathless but introduced herself as Mrs. Jenson. She was, she said, hired by Mrs. Alice Miller—

"That's my sister!" Ada exclaimed, hurrying to shake hands with Mrs. Jenson, and to receive the explanation that the newly arrived were to choose household staff from the newly assembled before them, with special attention paid to Sarah and Lucille.

"One of you has children?" Mrs. Jenson asked, and when Margaret nodded, she called out, "Sarah has experience in families with children and she is an excellent cook." And a young woman in her late twenties stepped toward Margaret and smiled. As she directed her gaze at Eli and Elizabeth, they hid behind Margaret.

Mrs. Jenson assigned a nursemaid-nanny to Ada, a woman in her forties who could help set up the nursery until "such time as it is needed." And then she quickly assigned a lady's maid and a parlor maid to Abby—to Genie's astonishment—along with a gardener. Then additional staff was quickly chosen—cooks, housekeepers, and laundresses. Then Mrs. Jenson laid out the rules. Only the nursemaid-nanny lived in and stayed overnight; everyone was paid on Saturday and had Sunday off. Any dissatisfaction with staff should be reported to Mrs. Jenson immediately. Each house was stocked with basic provisions sufficient for two evenings' meals and two mornings' breakfasts, and a supply of wood and coal. She welcomed them to Toronto, thanked them, and left the way they entered the mews. The two women and one man who remained followed Mrs. Jenson.

Getting acquainted with their new staff was a baptism by fire for Toronto's new residents because they now had to receive and decide on the placement of their belongings, and the advice and assistance supplied by the new staff proved that correct choices were made. The houses soon began to look and feel like homes, especially as parlor grates and kitchen stoves were lit and warmth began to creep into the long dormant rooms.

An exhausted Maggie found herself still annoyed with her children. "Come in here immediately," she said. "Go with Miss Sarah upstairs for your baths, and obey her every direction. Do you both understand me?"

"Yes, Mama," they said meekly and in unison, and hurried upstairs. Before she followed them Sarah suggested that she roast a chicken with carrots and potatoes and serve it with bread and butter. Then Maggie realized that she was as hungry as she was exhausted.

"That sounds wonderful, Sarah, thank you. And if the children give you any trouble—"

"I think they're too tired to cause trouble, Mrs. Juniper," Sarah said with a smile, and followed Elizabeth and Eli upstairs.

Abby and Genie did their own version of bouncing up and down and running up and down the stairs and in and out of rooms. They could not imitate Elizabeth and Eli because their staff was present and observing them, so Abby accepted Eloise's—her new maid's—invitation to bathe, while Genie offered to help open and unpack the crates, though she left it to Ruth and Alice, the housemaid and the parlor maid, to decide where to put things.

The only thing she wanted to find immediately was Ada's gift of the writing box, and once she had it in her hands, she felt a bit guilty for not being more helpful to Ruth and Alice with the unpacking and placement of the household belongings. She thought that Abby really should be doing the unpacking of the crates because, after all, she had lived all her life with multiple sets of dishes, linens, silver, and glassware. Though if she were being totally honest with herself, Genie had to admit it was exciting to have choices, just as it was exciting to have multiple rooms to sit in, though she could sit in none of them until she, too, had bathed and donned clean clothes.

As grateful as she was to be forever out of Philadelphia, she was overjoyed to be off that boat. Bless Captain Addams for making it a faster than expected journey. She sat on the floor in the kitchen, embossed-leather writing box in her lap, marveling at its contents. Not only did she now have pens and two colors of ink—blue and black—she had books. Her own books! Ada had written her name in them, so Genie would always know they belonged to her—to *Eugenia Oliver*.

Ada delighted in her new home—briefly. Oh how she wanted Ezra to be here to share in the joy of their arrival. Like her friends, she explored, walking from room to room and up and down the stairs, then out the scullery door to look across the alleyway to see the Junipers' house, and next door to see Donnie's carriage house. He was standing on the porch above when she looked up and she waved at him, then hurried inside so he wouldn't see her wiping away tears.

"Mrs. MacKaye," Lenora, her maid, called out when she entered the house. "Are you ready to bathe? The water is hot."

"Of course," she said, following her upstairs.

Donnie had followed Lenora to the scullery door, where he knocked and entered. He had already introduced himself to the staff and explained his relationship to all the families, including the fact that he had made the journey to Toronto with them. Now he said, "I think your mistress is in need of a bit of uplift. She's missing Mr. MacKaye."

"Yes, Mr. Donnie, I agree. Do you have a suggestion?"

A nodding Donnie instructed her to brew a strong pot of Earl Grey tea, and he emphasized strong. Heat milk to almost scalding and pour it into the strongly brewed tea, then add lots of honey. And serve it in a large cup, not a small teacup. "A *large* cup!" he emphasized and suggested that if there was no large cup then a bowl would suffice.

"A bowl?" the cook asked, her eyes widening. "Are you quite certain about that, Mr. Donnie?"

He gave her a wink and a bow. "I am, madam, I assure you, and I would never give you faulty information on a matter of such importance." And as if to prove the point he sat at the kitchen table, struggling to keep his eyes open. He had shaved and bathed but he had not slept, and he was exhausted, but the several Pinkerton guards notwithstanding, these people were in his charge and he would not close his eyes until they closed theirs.

He jerked awake as the cook, standing over him and clearing her throat, showed him a tray with a two-handled soup bowl on it. He could smell the distinctive aroma of Earl Grey and the mixture of hot milk and honey. "Excellent, madam," he said, and followed her to the stairs. She ascended while he waited below, and in several seconds he heard Ada's voice.

"Donnie Bruce! Is that you down there?" she called out.

"Yes, your majesty, it is I!"

"Bless you, Donnie. And thank you."

He bowed though she couldn't see it. Then he bowed to the cook and headed toward the scullery door. Before exiting, he suggested that she see if Mrs. MacKaye was ready for more tea and heard her calling for Ada's maid as he exited the scullery door.

"Mrs. Juniper. Mrs. Juniper . . ."

Maggie forced herself into wakefulness to find a woman looking down at her, a woman she did not know . . . ah! A woman she met several hours ago whose name she did not recall. She looked quickly around the unfamiliar surroundings: She was in her house, her home, in Toronto, and the young woman looking down at her with a worried expression was her lady's maid. Doris, was it? "Your bath is ready, Mrs. Juniper," she said.

Maggie stood up quickly. "The children—"

"They are bathed and dressed in their nightclothes, and they are at the dining table eating their supper. Cook is with them."

Maggie sighed. "I do hope a bath will help me think more clearly," she said as she followed Sadie—that was her name—up the stairs. She took her time because she needed to ponder the fact that three women now did the things for her children that as recently as yesterday she did alone. Cared for the children and their father, and never feeling undue stress or strain. Or perhaps she always did, but because there was no other way, she gave it no thought. Now, at the end of this day, exhaustion claiming every one of her senses, if she'd had to bathe, dress, and feed the children, she certainly would have done it, but she was truly thankful that those tasks now belonged to others. She was also more pleased than she ever could have imagined that the task of bathing and dressing herself now would be assisted by others, for she doubted that at this moment she had the strength required to heat enough water to fill a bathtub, or sufficient fortitude to remain awake long enough to bathe herself.

"Sadie, is there a school nearby where my children can attend? And where is a good place to buy clothes for them and my husband?"

"Colored children cain't go to the public school in the city,

221

but the school for Colored children is near to where the best market is. I can write it down for you."

"That is just as well," Maggie replied. "I much prefer that we have our own school."

The following morning, after they all were rested and restored, the good friends wasted no time gathering to see each other. They met in the alleyway behind the MacKaye and Juniper homes after sending Donnie in the carriage to collect Genie and Abby. It was as joyous a gathering as if they had been apart for weeks or months instead of mere hours. They hugged and laughed—and wept—briefly and visited each other's homes with the same joy and excitement each woman had experienced upon entering her own new home for the first time.

Despite the chill, scullery doors remained open, and the scent of fresh baked bread emanated from both homes, as did the welcome smells of bacon and sausages, coffee, and freshly brewed tea. Something containing generous helpings of cinnamon and nutmeg wafted from the Juniper kitchen, and they all went from kitchen to kitchen sampling whatever was cooking, gratefully joined by the Pinkerton guards who were invited to share.

"So very kind of your husband to provide security for us," Abby said with a sly grin and a hug for her former housemate.

"You are referring to my husband, the secret Pinkerton superintendent?"

"He was no doubt waiting to be able to tell you in person—"

"Mrs. MacKaye!" Ada's housekeeper rushed toward her looking alarmed. "There are people pounding on the front door, and a man, an old man, keeps trying to pull the door open."

Ada muttered something under her breath, then thanked the woman.

"Do you wish me to let them in?"

"No, I'm coming," Ada, already en route to the scullery door, changed direction. She looked angry.

"Ada?" Abby asked, following. "What is it, Ada?"

"My family, no doubt," she said, sounding considerably less than welcoming, hurrying toward the sound of loud pounding on the front door, audible as soon as they entered the kitchen. She rushed through the house to the front door, flinging it open with some force, light gray eyes darkening and blazing angrily at the four people on the porch.

"Where have you been?" the older man, her father, demanded.

"Why are you pounding on the door like a demonic burglar?" Ada demanded, her own anger barely contained. She wanted to pound something, too: her father!

Two women, one older than the other but both obviously related to Ada, pushed their way inside and began a thorough investigation, as if it were their occupation to do so, looking within the crates, even lifting some items out and showing them to each other.

"We didn't know where you were," the younger man, her brother, said in an accusatory tone.

"I was outside with my friends, where you will join me," Ada said, taking a handful of linens away from her mother and sister and returning them to the crate. "All of you, come this way. Now," and she pointed toward the kitchen.

"You will not speak to your mother and me like that!" Ada's father roared. "We will sit right here in this living room until—"

"You will do what I ask of you, or you will leave my home." Ada was trembling with rage, and her voice shook as well. Abby walked to her and put an arm around her waist, pulling her close.

"And who are you?" Ada's father snarled.

"I am Abigail Read, Ada's good friend, and her distress causes me distress," Abby said, sounding every bit the British aristocrat that, in truth, she was, and which had the desired effect on the Lawrence family. As a unit, the four of them crossed the parlor and dining room to the kitchen where Ada stopped them.

"Before you go outside, there is freshly baked bread, freshly brewed coffee and tea, and very large amounts of bacon and sausage," Ada said, adding that she thought they should be hungry since they had arrived so early and most likely without having breakfasted.

Her family looked at her, aghast. "Are you suggesting that we take food outside to eat?" her mother asked, practically choking on the words.

"Then please go out if you don't wish to eat," Ada said calmly, and held the door open for them as they filed out looking terrified.

The festive air prevailed, just as Ada and Abby had left it a few moments ago. Genie noticed that Abby was holding on to Ada but since neither woman seemed to be in distress, she continued her conversation with Maggie. Neither of them looked away from Ada and Abby for more than a few seconds, especially given the hostile glances the Lawrence family was directing at the gathered crowd.

"Come, let me introduce you to everyone," Ada said, walking over to her family.

"We will be leaving now, Ada," her mother declared, giving a final disapproving glare at the gathering before turning to return to the house.

"I assume you'll be joining us for church and Sunday dinner as usual," her father said, and it was a statement and not a question.

"I'm not certain that I will," Ada said. "I have work to do at Oliver Read, in addition to the task of bringing order to my own home."

"Speaking of which, wherever did you get those magnificent linens I saw in those crates in your house?" The inquiry came from her sister, Ellen.

"What linens? I didn't see any linens," Ada's mother said.

"You will see everything when there is organization and order within these walls," Ada replied, and was about to say more when she saw her maid hurrying toward her with a paper on a tray.

"Please excuse me, Mrs. MacKaye, but one of the Pinkerton men just delivered this telegraph message from Superintendent MacKaye."

"I'll take that!" and Ada's father grabbed the telegraph message from the tray.

"You most certainly will not," Ada replied so coldly that it startled and shocked her father, and he loosened his grip on Ezra's message enough that Ada was able to snatch the paper from his grasp. Her father's behavior left her momentarily speechless, but when she found speech, it came with fury. "Now leave my home, all of you. I either didn't remember or I didn't realize how truly rude and overbearing you are."

"She called you missus," Ada's mother cried out. "Ada, what is the meaning of that? Have you married and neglected to tell us? Answer me."

Ada could not respond. She hurried to the front door and held it open until her family had departed. Then she slammed and locked the door and opened Ezra's message. And wept. Ezra would arrive very soon—via a combination of ferry, train, horseback, coach, and, finally, boat across Lake Ontario from Rochester to Toronto. Employing all of those means of transport, Ezra said, will take less than half the time they had spent on *The River Dancer*. She hurried outside to find Maggie, who also wept when she read the message. Jack would be here soon.

Genie and Abby hurried over to Maggie and Ada. Why were they both weeping?

"What wonderful news!" Genie exclaimed after reading the message, embracing both Maggie and Ada. She knew how fortunate she was that she and Abby had arrived at their new home together. If she had been required to wait for Abby to arrive, that would have been more torturous than the journey itself.

"I wish Ezra had been in Pinkerton's and planned our travel,"

Abby said wistfully. "I gladly would have endured multiple modes of transportation in lieu of being confined in the bottom of a boat, rocking back and forth and up and down for a week, feeling as if my insides would detach from the rest of me."

Genie gave her a raised eyebrow and said, "With the greatest of sympathy for your poor insides, four women, two children, and a bodyguard going from ferry to train to horseback to coach to boat—not even Pinkerton's could organize that for a smooth or speedy operation." And she laughed as she attempted to imagine it, saying that it was a journey specifically designed for the likes of Jack Juniper and Ezra MacKaye. Not only could they both manage the challenge, but they also most likely would enjoy it.

"Is a coach the same as a carriage?" Abby asked.

"No," her friends answered in unison.

Genie locked arms with Abby. "None of that has any importance now, my dear. We are safely in Toronto, within easy reach of our friends."

"And that is more wonderful than words can say." Maggie grabbed Ada's hands, trying to find words for the feelings they all shared, the strongest ones being their relief at no longer having to cross the city of Philadelphia to see each other, a journey that had become more dangerous every day. "However did you manage all this wonderful housing, keeping us close together, from such a great distance?"

"To be perfectly honest, it helped that all of you had the funds to purchase the properties. My sister then searched for a suitable neighborhood near downtown and managed—"

"The sister who was just here?" Maggie queried, surprised. "Ellen, is it?"

Ada nodded sadly, the recent encounter with her sister a vivid and painful picture in her memory. Her parents must not have known of Ellie's involvement . . . nor had her husband, for that matter. "I fear that my long absence left her at the mercy of our parents, who have become monstrous. It is the only word I can think of to describe their behavior. And I'm very much afraid that Ellie's husband is every bit as overbearing as my father, and my brother is of no assistance."

With a most irreverent grin, Genie said, "I would so like to be hiding in the cupboard when they meet Ezra for the first time." Each woman took a moment to visualize the scene—thinking of the Ezra they knew so well, meeting for the first time the unpleasant family of the woman he loved so deeply—and even the least charitable of them felt a tiny pang of sympathy for the Lawrence family.

"Perhaps one day we will be able to tell your sister how much we appreciate her good work," Abby said.

"In the meantime," Maggie interjected, I must rescue Donnie from my children and then hope that he has sufficient remaining strength to take us to a place Sadie told me about where I can purchase clothes for them." She looked at Ada. "Unless you have need of him?"

Ada shook her head, then asked if Maggie wished her assistance.

"No, thank you," Maggie said, "but I would appreciate Genie's company. I think we should learn as soon as possible whether our presence is accepted here in Toronto."

Maggie knew that Genie must have had the same thought, but judging from the expressions worn by Ada and Abby, they had not, and it took a moment for them to understand the reference.

After being reassured by both Genie and Maggie that they were comfortable traveling alone, Abby and Ada returned to their respective houses to begin the work of making them homes. Genie and Maggie approached the shopping expedition as an adventure. They would see and learn about this city they now called home in perhaps the best possible way: via a carriage ride along the streets of the city, from their residential neighborhood to a shopping district. Following

Sadie's suggestions of the best establishments to visit for their purchases, they left it to Donnie to secure directions from the Pinkerton's agents who were their guards until Ezra arrived and who seemed more than happy to be of assistance. And as Elizabeth and Eli were as eager as the adult women to see the sights of Toronto, they rode up top with Donnie, which provided Genie and their mother the opportunity to discuss their thoughts and feelings openly.

The two women were united in their belief that leaving Philadelphia and America was the right thing to do. The carriage ride to locate the school for the children, and the market where they could purchase both food and clothing, was an adventure, and an enjoyable one, but they did miss the comfort and familiarity of having a part of town that was their own, "even though it was becoming more dangerous by the day," Genie said.

"I know that we could not remain there," Maggie said, "and certainly it was no place to raise children. And I feared every day for Jack and Henry alone in the shop."

"If we no longer have to live in fear, coming here will be worth the journey," Genie said.

Maggie nodded. "I agree. So, if there's a school for the children, and a place to purchase food and clothing—" She stopped talking as a thought presented itself. "Do you know that I have not owned a new article of clothing since the death of Abby's mother?"

"And I have not since the death of Carrie Tillman," Genie said, and they were quiet for several moments, listening to the clip-clop of the horse hooves and the chatter of the children. The carriage slowed and the window slid open for Donnie to ask if they wanted to visit the school first or the market, and both responded, "school." They became aware that almost all the people on the street—whether walking or riding in or driving carts or riding the horse-drawn streetcar—were Colored, and the whites walking among them did not appear threatening, and the Colored did not appear fearful. They were not hurrying or rushing . . . except for a few children running and chasing each other as they laughed. But the sound was joyous and happy, not fearful.

"Perhaps it will be better," Genie said, studying the passing scene. Toronto, it seemed, was a much smaller city than Philadelphia but it appeared clean and orderly.

"It appears to be so," Maggie said, sounding something more than merely hopeful. Though people were plentiful, the streets and walks were passable, not clogged and crowded as were those in Philadelphia. Toronto was not a small country town, but neither was it a crowded, bustling, or dangerous city like Philadelphia or New York or Chicago.

They were still observing and assessing all they saw when the carriage slowed to a stop. They heard Donnie and the children jump down, and the carriage doors opened. Genie and Maggie were helped down by Elizabeth on one side and Eli on the other, the children's assistance pleasing both women more than they could say.

"Are we going to church?" Elizabeth asked, puzzled, as the carriage was stopped in front of The North Star First AME Church according to a large and beautifully lettered sign in the front yard.

Maggie was about to reply in the negative when she noticed a smaller, equally attractive sign beside the larger one, which read:

PLEASE ENTER SCHOOL
THROUGH REAR DOOR OF THE CHURCH

They walked around the graceful stone church to the back door where another sign affixed to the door read:

HARRIET TUBMAN SCHOOL
FOR FREE COLORED CHILDREN

"Are we going to school here?" Eli asked excitedly.

"Please say yes, Mama," Elizabeth said, squeezing Maggie's hand.

"We are visiting to learn what is possible," Maggie replied, "and while we are here you two will sit quietly and behave yourselves, am I clear?"

"Yes, Mama," they said in unison, as a small, round woman emerged from a door in the hallway.

"I'm not acquainted with these well-behaved young people, but I would very much like to be," she said, and introduced herself as Lucille Carter, the wife of the Rev. Andrew Carter, church pastor.

Maggie and Genie introduced themselves as newly arrived residents to Toronto anxious to locate a school for Eli and Elizabeth Juniper. Mrs. Carter led them across the hall to another door, which she opened to reveal a large classroom—a large empty classroom—with desks and tables and chairs and bookshelves full of books and a blackboard running along the front of the room. High windows along one wall provided ample light, if not much warmth. It was frigid in the room, though both Maggie and Genie were glad to see two potbellied stoves in opposite corners of the room.

"Mrs. Juniper and Mistress Oliver, may I ask where you've come from, and how long you have been in Toronto?"

"Philadelphia," Maggie answered, adding that they arrived two days ago.

"And did Eli and Elizabeth attend school in Philadelphia?"

"They did," Maggie said, "and I'd like for them to return to school as soon as possible. I can keep their minds and memories sharp for the short term, but there is no substitute for the formal classroom on a daily basis."

Genie added, "I am so very pleased to see a school named for Mrs. Tubman, and may I ask why it is not in session?" It was, after all, midmorning on a weekday.

Mrs. Carter's shoulders drooped, and her hands worried a much-wrinkled handkerchief in her lap. "Unfortunately, we are without a teacher. We have been without a teacher for the past two months."

Maggie and Genie's shoulders drooped too. "Is there another school for Colored children?" Maggie asked. She simply could not accept that her children would not be educated.

"There was one in the next district, but that teacher left as well: The two teachers—ours, a woman who had been here for almost two years, and the one in the next District, a man— wed each other and moved to Nova Scotia." She paused and, giving Maggie a shrewd look, said, "I realize that we have just been introduced but," she hesitated a moment, "would you be interested in being the teacher in this school, Mrs. Juniper?"

Maggie and Genie were so shocked they could not speak. "I am not a teacher," Maggie finally managed to say.

"But you are an educated woman, Mrs. Juniper. That much is apparent, as is your dedication to the well-being of your children, and I can easily imagine that you—and Mistress Oliver—extend the belief in education to and for all Colored children."

"We do indeed," Maggie replied, and reiterated that she was not a teacher.

"Maggie, I think you might consider this," Genie said. "And you most certainly are a teacher—so easily and naturally do you share your knowledge."

Maggie thought deeply for a long moment, searching for a reason to refuse. She could not find one. In truth, with three women to take care of her home, there would be precious little for her to do there, and the daily involvement in the education of Eli and Elizabeth would be a gift. And the opportunity to reopen a school for Colored children was no small matter. "My husband will be here in a few days and I must discuss this with him, but I cannot imagine that he will object."

231

Mrs. Carter asked for the full names and the address of the Junipers, and her eyebrows arched upward at the address Maggie wrote beneath "Mr. and Mrs. Jack Juniper." Then Maggie and Genie, thanking Mrs. Carter for her time, took their leave, unable to stifle their excitement.

Eli and Elizabeth demanded to know whether they would be attending the school that was named for Mrs. Tubman and cheered at the affirmative response. They were not told that their mother would be their teacher in case their father had an objection. Then they rejoined Donnie on the carriage's bench and chattered like magpies all the way to the market. Maggie and Genie were quiet and thoughtful until Maggie said, "We will need another carriage."

"Indeed," Genie said, "since we both will have employment awaiting us every morning, as will Jack Juniper."

The North Toronto General Store was a wonderful establishment; anything worth having was sold within its cavernous space. Maggie and Genie bought clothes, including socks and underwear, for the children and for themselves, and Maggie bought clothes for Jack, with socks and underwear for him as well. They sent the children to wait in the carriage with the many parcels and went to the rear of the market where the food was sold, and where they remained for a very long time, ultimately requiring a porter with a cart to bring all the parcels to the carriage.

Genie and Abby's cook was rendered speechless at the bags of food Eli and Donnie carried in, and Abby was rendered speechless at the parcels of clothes Genie carried upstairs to their bedroom. "Surely you cannot need all of these skirts and dresses."

"What I like most about them, my dear, is that I have not been required to do the alterations. I can purchase a garment and wear it immediately. In fact, I think I'll wear one of them right now." And she proceeded to do just that as she told an excited Abby all about the visit to the Harriet Tubman school with Maggie . . . and of course Abby wanted to go to Maggie immediately. "She will be a magnificent teacher. The children will be fortunate to have her—all of them."

"That is exactly what I said," Genie said.

Sadie's mouth hung open as Donnie and Eli brought in bag after bag after bag of food, and they marveled more as Eli and Elizabeth hurried upstairs with their purchases, eager to try on every newly purchased article of clothing, including the socks and underwear.

"I realize that this is quite a lot of food," Maggie said, "but I want to be certain that the three of you eat whenever the residents of this house eat. Is that understood?"

They nodded, the three of them too overcome with emotion to speak. They had never been permitted to eat the same food the homeowners ate. They could have the leftovers from a previous meal, but if there were no leftovers the cook made gruel for the staff.

Genie and Abby went first to Ada's, who also wanted to hurry immediately to Maggie, but they forestalled her long enough to tell her about the North Toronto Market and all the food they had bought. "Since Ezra will be home soon, we should take you shopping—but first you must make certain that your cook is familiar with the preparation of chicken fricassee."

They crossed the alleyway and knocked on the scullery door at Maggie's. The look they received from the cook was somewhat less than welcoming.

"Would you rather that we entered via the front door?" Abby asked politely. "We do realize that you are otherwise occupied—"

"Auntie Abby, is that you?" Elizabeth called out. "Mama, Auntie Abby is here."

"Where?" Maggie asked, materializing behind her daughter in the scullery door. "Why are you standing outside?"

"I think perhaps we would do better to make use of the front doors," Genie said, even as they entered the scullery door, with apologies to the cook, who was still struggling to find places in which to store all the newly arrived food.

"My goodness, look at all this food," Ada said. "Yes, you most definitely must take me shopping there before Ezra arrives."

They all followed Maggie into the parlor with the promise of tea to follow and the suggestion that Elizabeth and Eli busy themselves in their schoolroom. When the women were alone, they beamed at Maggie and showered her with congratulatory words. "Jack will be so very proud," Genie enthused.

"I am still getting used to the idea," Maggie said, a hint of the pride and excitement she felt creeping into her voice.

They discussed the need for a second carriage, which they agreed should be purchased as soon as possible, especially since they all would be leaving home in the mornings to go to work— Ada, Abby and Genie to the same location; Jack to the same general area; and Maggie toward North Toronto.

"Where does the Pinkerton's superintendent have his offices?" Genie asked, and they all looked at Ada, who gave a grand shrug.

"You must remember that I learned of Superintendent MacKaye's appointment at the same time you all did, though I fully expect that one who occupies such an exalted position will have a carriage and driver at his disposal," Ada opined with a sniff, which immediately turned to a guffaw when Genie said he'd probably choose to ride to work on horseback.

Ada sobered and said it was very likely that she and Ezra would wed immediately at the registrar's office, with a church wedding possible at a later date. Her sadness at her family's behavior weighed heavily upon her even as she took pleasure in the happiness all around her, and Ezra MacKaye was a large part of that happiness, especially for her. She wanted him to be able to live in their house as her husband immediately, and she would not wait for her parents to agree or approve.

"After all his study at Christ Church to be welcomed into the bosom of the Church of England, do you think Ezra will want to be married at the clerk's office?" Abby asked.

"If he hesitates, I'll ask Jack to have a chat with him," Ada replied, her face the picture of innocence, and the laughter rang out. These wonderful friends. They could and did enable her to put aside the pain and anger her family caused, because these friends now were her family. "By the way, Maggie, how much is the school paying you to be its teacher?"

Maggie's look of dumbfounded consternation brought more and longer laughter, especially when Ada insisted that she had accepted a job as teacher, not a position as a volunteer, and she looked at Genie for confirmation.

Elizabeth and Eli clambered downstairs at the sound of the laughter to learn what had prompted it. Since the source of the hilarity could not be shared with them, Maggie decided to share the news of her job—and she emphasized the word—telling the children not to get too excited until after their father agreed to her having a job. She again emphasized the word.

"Of course he will agree, Mama," Elizabeth said, sounding reasonable and wise beyond her years.

"Yes, Mama, he will," Eli said. "And you'll be the best teacher that school ever had."

Late that afternoon, as the dinner hour approached, Maggie and Jane, the housekeeper, emptied the last of the crates of Juniper household belongings shipped from Philadelphia. She did not know yet where every item would be shelved, but Maggie was greatly relieved not to have to see the large, wooden crate occupying space in the parlor—or the dining room or the upstairs hallway. Jane went out the front door to the main road to look for someone who would take a message to Mr. Edward Jones that his services were needed. Jones drove a horse cart, like the one Genie had in Philadelphia, but the rear of his was filled with tools of varying kinds, including a grinding stone for knife sharpening.

Genie and Abby had been first to empty a moving crate and they asked their housekeeper, Helen, how to dispose of it.

"You do not dispose of it," Helen said, appalled at the thought. "You get Mr. Jones to cut it up into pieces that will fit in the kitchen stove or the fireplace. This is good wood and it will make good heat."

So Maggie and Jane carried the crate, first the top and then the bottom, through to the back porch where they left it for Mr. Jones. Maggie also left money with Mary, the cook, to pay him for his work. At Mary's suggestion, some of the wood from the first crates to be emptied was used to construct a sturdy box to hold the cut-up pieces of kindling—most convenient for easy access to wood for the kitchen stove and the fireplaces. Thus, Mr. Jones had become something of a regular in their homes, their regular handyman.

He was older—he reminded Genie of Arthur—and he was soft-spoken and quite handy with every kind of tool. He also was in great demand throughout the neighborhood. It was Genie who first spoke the words out loud: "We most definitely are no longer in Philadelphia, for Mr. Edward Jones would not survive a day there. He would be grabbed and shackled and sold into slavery almost immediately."

"But he is almost an old man," Ada protested. "I thought the slave catchers were most often after young, physically fit men and women."

"But Mr. Jones is skilled," Genie said. "He would be capable of making money for his master if hired out and he therefore would be considered valuable."

And they all, once again, told themselves how grateful they were to be out of Philadelphia. Genie wanted additional proof, so she took herself for a walk in her neighborhood, a reprise, of sorts, from her daily behavior in Philadelphia where she walked to work and often to other destinations when it was not possible or necessary to take the horse and cart. She wanted to see how she was received where she lived, and she asked Abby to please not accompany her. What she experienced pleased and relieved her. Almost everyone she encountered spoke a greeting—a good morning or good day—which often was accompanied by a smile. Those who did not speak nodded a greeting, a touch of the hat in the case of a man. Only two people completely ignored her and Genie did not take offense. After all, not everyone was obligated to speak. The most important occurrence, or lack of occurrence, was that no one attempted to capture her. She was not yet prepared to let her guard down completely, but it was clear that Toronto was not Philadelphia. She hurried home and helped Abby unpack with renewed energy.

Maggie folded the last of the tablecloths and napkins and cleared a drawer in the cabinet for them when a knock sounded at the front door. Jane's look was questioning, and Maggie shook her head. She was expecting no one, and she returned her attention to the task at hand.

"A messenger just delivered this, Mrs. Juniper," Jane said, extending an envelope.

Maggie took it. It was addressed to Mr. and Mrs. Jack Juniper and bore the name and address of The North Star First AME Church. Maggie opened the envelope, read the enclosed message quickly, and smiled. Then she laughed gently to herself: The letter from the Rev. Andrew Carter expressed gratitude that she had accepted the job of teacher at the Harriet Tubman School, and he hoped the salary would be acceptable. And he was, Rev. Carter said, very pleased to be able to report that classes would resume on Monday, 3 December 1860.

Since she had never held a job, Maggie had no idea what would constitute an acceptable salary, but Ada and Genie would know, and she would share this letter with them tomorrow when they returned from Ada's shopping trip. Rev. Carter's letter made her job real, and Maggie now confronted the realization that the children most likely would need more clothes, as would she: a dress for every day of the week, beginning on Monday, 3 December.

CHAPTER TWENTY

As previously agreed upon, Genie accompanied Ada on her shopping expedition to the North Toronto Market the following morning, but Ada found her excitement dampened by her cook's reaction to the influx of so much food. Genie quickly volunteered her cook's assistance, and sent for Maggie's cook to help as well, since both had recently had the experience of having to handle so much food at one time, and Ada gratefully and quickly joined her friends at Genie and Abby's to await the arrival of Abby's new piano.

Because their cook was at Ada's, Genie and Abby prepared and served tea, adding slices of two kinds of cake to the tray. Then they all read and reread Rev. Carter's letter to Maggie. Ada deemed the salary to be quite acceptable, "though not overly generous, as is to be expected from a man of the cloth." Then she added in a most serious tone of voice that Maggie not ever, not even once, permit anyone to expect "that you will arrive early and remain late on school days, that you will provide anything other than instruction for the students, or that you will, no matter the reason given, be available on Saturday and/or Sunday."

Maggie was shocked speechless at Ada's admonitions, as were the others. "Why do you give these warnings, Ada? Do you know something about the Carters that we do not?"

Ada gave a gentle smile. "I know nothing of these people—

except that they almost certainly are good and decent people, and that they readily recognized you as such, Maggie, which you most assuredly are. But you must not permit your goodness to be taken advantage of, even for sound reasons, and good people like the Carters will have good reasons for needing you."

"But how can she—how will she—decline requests to be helpful?" Abby asked, then added, "without seeming to be rude."

"She can say, very politely, that she has other obligations in addition to her teaching that she cannot ignore, and there would be no lack of truth in that statement," Ada offered, adding that a husband and two children certainly constituted obligations.

Maggie nodded her agreement, for in truth, she did not wish to do more than teach.

"Based on my experience with Adelaide, who was a most faithful member of the AME Church in Philadelphia, you might well expect, Maggie, to be queried about your membership in the church—" Genie began.

"To which she can honestly reply that she is Church of England," Abby said.

"And I am," Maggie added. Then her brow furrowed. "Though I honestly cannot recall the last time I crossed the threshold of such."

"I can," Abby said. "It was when Elizabeth was baptized."

"When was I baptized?" Eli asked. "And what does that mean, baptized?"

They had forgotten that the children were present so quiet were they, perhaps because they had managed to eat almost all of the cake. The arrival of Abby's piano saved them from the need to answer that question as Eli's total focus now was on how a piano would enter the parlor through the front door of the house. Abby knew exactly how it would happen since this was not her first piano, but the others were as excited as Eli to wonder and watch. Abby was excited as well because though she did not regret giving her previous piano to Florence Mallory when she left Philadelphia, she did miss having the instrument. She enjoyed playing it as much as she enjoyed its presence.

There were six men. The first thing two of them did was remove the front door, through which blew a strong blast of cold late November air. Genie hurried to light the fire that already was laid in the hearth, and she added a significant number of kindling sticks so the fire would quickly blaze hot.

The piano, encased in a wooden box, was on a wide, flat, wheeled cart, being rolled slowly toward the front door. Many of Genie and Abby's neighbors ventured outside to watch the unusual occurrence. No doubt a piano was not delivered on a regular basis.

The men removed the box and wrapped the piano in thick blankets and quilts and then, three of them on each side, lifted the instrument very slowly and carefully, one step at a time, until it was on the front porch. Then, ever so gently, they laid it on its side and, an inch at a time, angled it so that the legs entered first and then the body and then the other legs.

When the men stood the piano up, Abby showed them where to place it, and they removed the blankets and quilts. The beautiful, gleaming piano looked as if it had been born in that place. Abby's friends in the house applauded as did her neighbors gathered on the porch. Then they went home, and the friends helped restore the room's furniture to the proper places while the remaining delivery man began his true work: the tuning of the piano. When he finished and left, Abby took his place on the bench and fingered the keys, at first slowly, and then more rapidly. She began to play something strong and powerful Maggie recognized from their youth. She was trying to recall the title when Abby suddenly stopped playing. "We will schedule the concert for later. I promised Ada that we will take time today to visit the locations of our businesses."

Excitement was high in the carriage. As usual, the children were up top with Donnie, both proclaiming that they indeed were not too cold and did not need to be inside the carriage.

"I think they must be freezing," Ada said, "but are wise enough to understand that we wish to be able to converse freely and their presence makes that impossible."

Maggie gave Ada a look of wide-eyed disbelief. "Ezra may find them to be little gems and miracles of nature, but I urge you not to make the same mistake," their mother said drily, adding the prediction that Ezra would abandon the notion when he had his own.

When the carriage turned the corner onto Queen Street Abby and Genie gasped and reflexively grabbed each other. Their store was the second from the corner and the lettering on the glass front, in Royal Signage typeface and in royal red and gold paint, read in foot-tall letters: "Oliver Read" and beneath that, in smaller type:

PURVEYORS OF THE FINEST LINEN,
CRYSTAL, CHINA, PORCELAIN, SILVER,
RUGS, OBJETS D'ART
ADMISSION BY APPOINTMENT ONLY

Abby and Genie stood in front of the window bearing their names and holding tightly to each other. Until this moment, Oliver Read had been an idea conceived of by Ada Lawrence. True, they knew her to be a shrewd, even brilliant, businesswoman. They trusted her. But standing here, on Queen Street in Toronto, Canada, gazing at the business that bore their names—they were overwhelmed. And they were a bit weak and wobbly in the knees. Good thing that Maggie stood close behind them, an arm tightly around each of them.

"This is most impressive," Maggie said, and for once Eli and Elizabeth had nothing to say. They stood gazing at the storefront, wide-eyed, slack-jawed, and for once speechless.

Because Maggie was holding them upright, Genie and Abby

were able to extend their arms to Ada, to embrace her. They were as speechless as the children, but they held her tightly for a long moment before she suggested that they return to the carriage and ride around the corner to the alleyway behind the building. The Pinkertons on duty unlocked and opened the back door to admit them. The first room at the rear of the building was quite large. All of the crates were here, and this would be a storage area at some point, Ada explained. The next room boasted newly laid wood flooring upon which was laid a large Persian rug, which Abby recognized as having come from Ada's Philadelphia office. Additionally, newly painted and papered walls, beautiful light fixtures, a ceiling fan, and beneath it, in the exact middle of the room, a beautiful though fully functional oak desk. This, make no mistake, was Ada's office.

"Once my crates are unpacked and my cabinets are in place, I will be able to make certain that those who wish to take possession of items from Oliver Read can afford to do so," Ada told them. "And then I will receive their payment and arrange delivery of their purchases."

Genie and Abby exchanged a look. "Can we afford her?" Genie asked, not in the least bit facetiously.

"If it happens that we cannot, we will have the front window repainted to read, *The Ada Lawrence MacKaye Collection*," Abby said, producing an admirable imitation of one of Ada's signature cackle-laughs.

From Ada's office a short hallway led them into the Oliver Read showroom where workmen were building custom glass-fronted, waist-high display cabinets, and taller, glass-fronted curio cabinets. A large claw-footed table stood in one corner of the room for the display of rugs. Genie and Abby knew they eventually would need to purchase additional rugs but given their expense, they could easily wait until they sold what they had. As it was, they were in awe of what was being created in their names and, truthfully, though more than a little intimidated, both women were as excited as children.

"Shall we take a short journey to see where Mr. Juniper will work his magic?" Ada asked, and a short carriage ride took them five streets east and one north. She had Donnie halt the carriage in front of an empty storefront, the front glass clean and shining and ready to be lettered. "Do you think Jack knows what he wants—"

Maggie emitted a most unladylike snort. "I seriously doubt he has given it a moment's thought, but I think one look at the Oliver Read window will spur his brain into action."

An hour later they returned to Genie and Abby's home where Abby returned to the piano, and almost immediately a pot of tea and plate of cakes materialized. But before the parlor maid could pour the tea the housekeeper literally ran into the room.

"Mistress Read, Mistress Oliver, I'm so sorry to disturb you, but one of those Pinkerton men is at the scullery door and he says that Mrs. Juniper and Mrs. MacKaye gotta come quick 'cause their men are here!"

Eli immediately grasped the meaning of the woman's excited words. "Papa's here!" he shrieked and ran through the house, to the kitchen, and out the scullery door, Elizabeth close on his heels. As understanding sank in, Ada and Maggie were up and running almost as fast as the children. Genie and Abby were close on their heels, every bit as excited as the others to finally welcome the remaining members of their family to their new homes.

Ada leapt into Ezra's arms at a run. He caught her and swung her around before enveloping her in a tight embrace. Maggie would have welcomed her husband in similar fashion, but first Jack had to return his children to the ground. Then he swept his wife into his arms, whispering over and over the promise never to be separated from her again.

When he put her down, she looked all around. "Jack, where

is Henry?" And at the look on his face she knew that there would be no Henry. His absence pained her, but she wondered how much she truly wanted to know what happened to him.

Then she heard Genie cry out: "Arthur, Arthur, is that really you?" And she ran to the old man who lifted and swung her from side to side as if she were a child. "You changed your mind about coming to Toronto. I am so glad, Arthur."

"It didn't seem to make no sense to stay in Philadelphia without y'all," he said. "Even as much as I loved my house what you give to me, it was always gon' be empty if I didn't have no friends to visit. So I told Jack and Ezra I wanted to come. If it was all right."

A welcoming crowd gathered before them, bestowing more hugs on Arthur than he'd had in his life. Then the sudden realization that there was no Henry shocked and saddened his family. And when Jack and Ezra explained the reason for Henry's absence, many tears were shed. There was no Henry but there was Arthur. A balance struck, Maggie thought, though she knew she would miss Henry deeply, and for a long time.

Abby sought out the Pinkerton man who looked to be in charge and he acknowledged that he was Superintendent MacKaye's adjutant, Fletcher Campbell. She looked him in the eye and said, "I have a critical task for you, Mr. Campbell, and I am most serious: You must go immediately to the City Registrar and you must procure the documentation necessary to have Ada Lawrence and Ezra MacKaye legally married today."

Campbell was totally confused. "I thought they were married." He looked toward Ezra and Ada who remained locked in an embrace.

"Ezra no doubt said as much in order to make the necessary arrangement for our safe passage, but they are not married, Mr. Campbell, and unless you want your superintendent to spend the night in the guest room in my home instead of in that house with his wife—"

Campbell paled. "I will go to the registrar immediately. But ma'am, those documents will require information about the principals—"

"Donnie Bruce and I will go with you to supply that information."

"Then let us go," Campbell said, already heading toward the carriage on the street in front of the house. Abby ran to tell Donnie to follow Campbell and after quickly hugging Jack, she pulled Maggie away to tell her what was happening and for her to make certain that Ada and Ezra would be prepared to wed at some point this very day.

Genie watched Abby rush from person to person, knowing that something important was afoot but unable to imagine what. Then Abby explained, making certain that Genie knew that Ezra's adjutant was complicit. She welcomed Arthur again and said she was looking forward to getting to know him because Genie loved him so much. Then she was gone.

Arthur watched Abby hurry away, then turned his steady gaze on Genie and chuckled. "Adelaide Tilllman is one big fool, that's for sure. Kept on saying she didn't know why you always had to go visit 'that Abigail woman.' That's what she called her. I'm glad you didn't pay her no mind, and I know Miss Abigail is, too." Then he laughed out loud. "But no wonder Adelaide didn't like her. That Miss Abigail is one pretty lady. And the two of y'all together is too much pretty for Adelaide to handle."

Genie reeled from the shock of Arthur's immediate insight into her connection to Abby and turned her focus on other conversations happening around them, especially between Jack and Ezra. Their passionate greeting of their women was unmistakable but neither man had entered his new home, and after greeting Eli and Eizabeth they ignored them, intensely engrossed in conversation. They came toward her quickly.

"Did you tell Genie?" Ezra demanded of Arthur.

"He's told me nothing having anything to do with you,"

she replied, her steady gaze meeting his, reminding him of the first time they met, almost exactly three years previously. She was dressed as a man and, hand holding the Deringer pistol in her pocket, she had walked forward to meet him despite the warning that he was a slave catcher. Her gaze then, as now, was unwavering. Ezra relaxed, smiled, and told her everything. She listened. Then she said, "There hasn't been a Pinkerton here in two days, except the two who arrived this morning to meet you."

"There were to be two on duty here until I arrived." Ezra controlled his anger and looked for the two Genie said had just arrived. "Well, where are they?"

"At the city registrar's office—"

"At the—" Ezra exploded. "What the bloody hell is at the bloody registrar's office that has anything to do with me?"

"Your marriage license, my friend," Jack said calmly, and they all would have laughed at the wild-eyed look Ezra gave him had they not understood the gravity of the situation.

Ezra calmed down and said, "I do not have time to get married."

"You cannot live in that house with that woman—Mistress Ada Lawrence—if you are not married to her," Jack said, and Ezra deflated. All resistance left him, replaced by two thoughts that propelled him forward: He would marry Ada, and he would find the Pinkerton traitor.

Ezra gave them a gentle smile. "Which house is mine?" he asked, and when they pointed, he asked the same of Genie, then of Jack. But before he could ask, Arthur pointed behind him.

"If Mr. Donnie will have me, I'll live here in the stable with the hosses."

"I'm sure Donnie will welcome you," Ezra said, and took himself home to dress. But after a few long-legged strides, he turned back and called out to Jack: "Will you stand with me, Jack Juniper?"

"I'd be honored to do so," Jack replied.

"Then you should go get dressed, and I will do the same," Genie said.

"And I'm gon' meet the hosses," Arthur said, "but I wanna see you people all prettied up before you go." And they all hurried toward their respective homes.

Jack looked at the clothes Margaret had bought him and saw the first suit he had ever owned. And there were three of them. And shirts and ties and socks and underwear. And there stood Margaret in a beautiful new dress in colors of deep red and blue and green with streaks of gold throughout. Her hair was piled atop her head and held in place with combs he'd never seen. "You are the most beautiful woman in the world, Margaret Juniper."

She smiled and thanked him and told him to get dressed and to please find his son and get him dressed. He stood still in front of the closet. Then he turned to face her, looking as confused as he felt.

"Whatever is the matter, Jack?" She gave him a worried look.

"I don't know what to wear, Margaret." He gave her a helpless look.

"A closet full of clothes and you don't know what to wear? Jack, really."

"I've never had a closet full of clothes, Margaret, and I've never had a suit, to say nothing of three. I've never worn a suit, or a tie. How do I know what to wear?"

She hurriedly crossed the room to hold him and to apologize. She had been so excited to be able to purchase clothes for him that she had never considered his lack of familiarity with them. She took his hand and led him to the closet where the three suits hung: black, brown, and dark blue. She lifted the blue one out and held it against her dress: "If you wear this one, Jack, we will complement each other."

"That would make me both happy and proud, Margaret, to complement you," he said, as she left him to finish dressing. And glad for the early morning shave and haircut at the Rochester hotel, he donned the dark blue suit and a white shirt and spent several minutes studying his reflection in the mirror, not quite believing he was looking at himself. He would ask Ezra for help with the tie, but because of his profession he had a beautiful pair of new boots to wear with his suit. He went in search of Margaret.

"Oh my!" she exclaimed at the sight of him, and for a moment he didn't understand why. Then he remembered his reflection in the mirror and bowed to her.

"Thank you," he whispered, embracing her tightly.

"Please find Eli and bring him to be bathed and dressed."

Eli was secreted in the potting shed in the far corner of the garden behind Genie and Abby's house. He came here to practice his spelling and counting because he had not kept up with Elizabeth. His parents' disappointment in him would be difficult enough to bear without the added weight of his mother being his teacher as well. He committed himself to improving his skills by the time school commenced on December 3.

Strange men's voices speaking too loudly and too closely so startled Eli that he dropped his writing pad in the dirt, barely grabbing it up and forcing himself into a space behind a row of shelves at the rear of the shed before two men entered. Two men he'd never seen before. When they turned to face the overgrown garden, he was certain they would not see him. But who were they, and why were they in Auntie Genie and Auntie Abby's garden shed? Even in the cold of winter they didn't belong in the shed.

"Being here will almost be like a vacation after chasing

robbers for a month."

"Chasing niggers before they cross the border won't feel like no vacation."

"We don't have to chase 'em though—we just shoot 'em and leave 'em where they fall."

"Are you sure 'bout that, Jimmy? You know for certain that's what they want us to do?"

"That's what Angus said. Once he got rid of that MacKaye fella, we'd be free to do like we would if we was back in Richmond or Atlanta."

"That's where we oughta be, 'stead of up here in damn Canada. Back in Richmond or Atlanta helping the Confederacy win the damn war!"

"We will be helpin', Earl. Everybody's got a part to play and this is ours. Now let's us walk around and get the lay of the land."

"I still don't like it. Nothin' but rich people—"

"Who got a house full of nigger servants, all of 'em women, and they'll trust us 'cause we're the Pinkertons! Be like pickin' the fruit up off the ground."

"When do we get ourselves a new boss?"

"Next day or two, Angus said, soon as he finds somebody to replace that MacKaye."

They pushed open the shed door and left.

Eli stood frozen in place, almost literally, breathing heavily for several moments. Then, easing slowly from his hiding place he crept to the shed door and cracked it open. The two men were walking toward Ada and Ezra's house. Eli ran up the path in the garden to the scullery door and pounded on it until the cook, whose name he didn't remember, opened it.

"Young Eli! What is the matter, boy?"

"Please get Miss Eugenie. Please! I need her—"

And then she was there, taking him in her arms. "Eli, my dear boy! Whatever is the matter? You're shaking like a leaf. And crying. Eli, are you crying?" She hugged him tighter and told the cook to make him a large cup of hot chocolate. Then she pulled a chair close to the stove and held him until he stopped shaking and sobbing, until he was able to tell her what he had seen and heard in her garden shed. Forgetting the hot chocolate, she grabbed his hand and began to run. Eli's legs had to pump really fast to keep up.

"Miss Eugenie, what's the trouble? Is you all right?" Arthur stood on the stable porch looking down at them.

"I think we have a problem, Arthur. Be armed and ready. I'll come for you."

"What problem, Eugenia?" Jack was upon them and were it not for his distinctive voice Genie would not have known who he was. "And Eli? Is there something wrong with you, son?"

"He's fine, Jack, but we need to get him inside."

Once inside, with Genie's urging and his mother's arms tightly around him, Eli told them what he'd heard the two strangers say inside the shed in Genie and Abby's back garden. He was crying again. Maggie held him closer, and Jack kissed him tenderly, once on each cheek. "I am most proud of you, my son. You have saved your family from great danger."

Genie and Jack left Maggie to further comfort Eli and to get him ready to attend Ada and Ezra's marriage, but not before reassuring her that her son was in no danger and neither were the rest of them. Toronto was not Philadelphia. They wouldn't let it be.

Arthur still stood on the stable porch, and Genie walked toward him. She could see that he was armed. She would, she said, return and tell him everything. In the meantime, he should keep an eye out for two strange white men. The old man's derisive snort was his nonverbal receipt of the warning. Jack waited for her at the scullery door of Ada and Ezra's, and it opened before they could knock.

"Oh Jack, how handsome you look," Ada said. "And Genie— what a beauty you are. That dress is most becoming. I expect

Abby will be suitably impressed."

Deflecting the compliment, Genie studied Ada's dress. She'd never seen anything like it—a wedding dress masquerading as an ordinary off-white dress. Except it was anything but ordinary. She was a seamstress by profession, and she'd never seen anything like it. She said as much to Ada and received a secretive smile in reply. Then Jack was behind her, gaping at Ada.

"Mistress Lawrence, you are a vision."

"Jack Juniper, are you making eyes at my almost-wife—" Ezra's mouth and feet halted in their tracks as he turned the corner and saw Ada. "My dear," he whispered.

"I truly am very sorry, but there is information that must be shared immediately," Genie said, and told them what Eli had seen and heard. Ada's eyes immediately looked across the mews at the shed in Genie's back garden and Genie could almost see her thinking, wondering, until they flashed icy gray anger.

But it was Ezra's face that concerned her: surprise, disbelief, shock, anger, fury, and finally dismay. "Now I am certain that I have been betrayed by one or more of my own."

She was struggling to find words of comfort for him when rapidly approaching coach wheels and horse hooves captured their attention: Abby and Ezra's Adjutant Fletcher Campbell, and all of Genie's strength was required to prevent Ezra from grabbing the man from the coach and throttling him.

"Genie? Ezra?" Abby looked her concern from one to the other. Finally Ezra spoke.

"Mr. Campbell. Who are Angus, Earl, and Jimmy?"

Campbell replied immediately and confidently: "Angus McFadden is the man that you're replacing as regional superintendent. He's the one who sent me here today, and he's the one who assigned me to you. I've never heard of the others you mentioned."

"Where's Mr. McFadden now?"

"Chicago," Campbell said, smiling broadly. "He's to be in

charge of a large part of the United States."

Many years ago, when he began at Pinkerton, Ezra had worked out of the Chicago office. It was large then, and important, and it would be even more so now. So if McFadden was promoted to run that office it wasn't likely that he was guilty of sabotaging Ezra's new job—the one he promoted Ezra to in the first place. "Then who would have sent Earl and Jimmy here?"

Campbell was confused and shaking his head. "Only you could send operatives from our office anywhere, Mr. MacKaye." He paused, took a deep breath, and said, "What has happened to trouble you, sir, if I may ask?"

Ezra explained. Then he told Campbell to take him to the Pinkerton Regional Headquarters immediately, and he strode to the carriage.

"Ezra!" Jack's deep voice rumbled like thunder. "You will take yourself to get married first, and then you can go to your office and straighten things out. But first you will marry Ada Lawrence."

"I will not leave my family and friends unprotected—"

"No one will be unprotected, Ezra," Genie said. "Arthur and I will see to that."

Campbell had no idea who Arthur was, but looking at Genie—this beautiful young woman in a dress of rose and gold whose voice was as steely as she was delicate—he wished he could remain to witness whatever might occur should Earl and Jimmy return.

Ezra looked toward his house where Ada stood in the doorway looking at him, waiting for him. She was beautiful and he wanted to marry her. His friends—his family—stood with him: Genie and Abby and Jack and Donnie, and it was Donnie, whom he'd known most of his life, who took charge.

"Ezra, you and Ada will ride in the carriage driven by Mr. Campbell, and I will drive the Juniper family and Mistress Read in our carriage. Then, afterward, the Pinkertons can go to their headquarters and root out what's rotten there, and I will return Mrs. MacKaye, Mistress Read, and the Junipers here, to our home, absolutely certain that Mr. Green and Mistress Oliver will have things under control."

Genie began immediately by asking everyone to instruct their household staff to lock all the doors and not to open them to anyone, including a Pinkerton, no matter what. "Except to me or Arthur," Genie added. Then she went home to change her clothes and to issue the same instruction to her own household staff. And to calm Abby who was weeping uncontrollably.

Genie held her tightly until she stilled. Then she got a wet cloth and wiped her face, and soaked another with icy water from the pitcher on the window ledge to place over her red, puffy eyes. No one had ever seen Abigail Read in a state other than perfection. She said this to Abby and elicited the smile she hoped for. "I never wanted you to be in danger again, ever." Abby wailed the words but kept the cold towel in place over her eyes.

"I'm not in danger now, Abby," Genie replied calmly, controlling with effort the emotion she felt. It had not occurred to her that her actions and behavior frightened Abby. Worried her, yes, but not frightened her. "And I am so very sorry that I have frightened you."

"Whoever these two men are, Genie, they have been in our backyard. Can you lock the shed?"

"I will ask Mr. Jones to padlock the door first thing tomorrow."

"That's wonderful, my dear, but what about right now, today?"

"Abby, dear, please get dressed, so I can get changed—"

"I want to stay here with you, to help you—"

"Certainly not!" Genie moderated her tone, put an arm around Abby, and said, "Ada needs you. She will be relying on you and Maggie."

"Of course. You're right." She inhaled deeply, smiled widely, and turned the deep blue gaze that always weakened Genie toward her. "Please send my maid to me so I may achieve the perfection I know you expect and appreciate."

Genie, laughing, went to her own room to remove the new dress she'd been so excited about wearing and to don a blouse, vest, and skirt with pockets sufficiently deep to conceal her pistols and long enough to conceal the men's heavy shoes she wore . . . just in case. Then she went to talk to Arthur.

The Magistrate would preside over one group ceremony, not individual marriages, and he was ready to proceed very soon. Adjutant Campbell escorted Maggie and Jack to the head of the line amid considerable grumbling, and they quickly completed the paperwork when the clerk realized that the couple were both British born. "London and Liverpool! Let us get these former subjects of the Queen married in the soon to be independent territory of Canada." And with their signed and sealed certificate of marriage in hand Margaret and Jack Juniper joined all the other couples, most especially Ezra and Ada Lawrence MacKaye, in the ornate chamber of the Magistrate. And ten years after a marriage in a Philadelphia church, they found themselves declared husband and wife.

CHAPTER TWENTY-ONE

"You think they fool enough to come back here so soon?" Arthur's tone of voice was a mixture of skepticism and wishful thinking. He wanted Earl and Jimmy to be fool enough to return to their mews so soon, and Genie thought they might indeed be that foolish.

"If they're somewhere they can see what's happening here, then they saw two carriages leave with half a dozen adults, two children, and both Pinkertons. They have no reason to fear being challenged. So yes, I think it's possible."

"Then how we deal with 'em, Miss Eugenie?"

"You up top, Arthur, where you can see everything. I'll stay on the ground and try to get behind them and drive them toward you. You'd never miss a shot from up there if they were just below you."

"Deed I would not," Arthur growled.

Genie positioned herself on her own back porch. The shed would present a better view of the mews, but it was too risky if the men already considered it safe haven. Besides, being on the porch provided some leaked, much needed warmth from the kitchen for the weather had suddenly turned bitterly cold with the threat of snow hanging in the thick cloud cover.

Arthur alternated between watching from the window

inside the warm room above the stable, and the porch. Most of his body didn't mind the cold, but his damaged legs did: they ached worse than a bad tooth when it was cold and damp, and not even wrapping them in blankets, as they were now, helped. His legs, broken all those years ago by the slave owner, never were allowed to mend and heal properly because he never was allowed to rest them. And just as there was no point in crying over spilt milk, there was no point crying over broke legs, the young Arthur had told himself so often that he soon believed it. Or accepted it. The result was the same as far as the old Arthur was concerned.

Arthur kept his eyes on the porch where Genie was until he saw her stand and raise her right arm, their signal for him to be on alert. Then she sank down and disappeared from his sight. He stepped inside to the warmth but watched the mews from the window, and almost immediately two men came into view, weaving more than walking. Two more drunk fools who most likely would find themselves dead if they were as drunk as they appeared to be, and were therefore either careless, foolish, or both. Did people like these two get drunk because they were about to do evil, or did they do evil because they were drunk? Not that it mattered to Arthur; he'd shoot them, if necessary, regardless.

The two drunks passed Genie's house. She stood up and slowly moved off the porch and into the yard. She dropped to the ground when one of the drunks stumbled and fell. His partner turned back to help him up and they steadied each other, turned away from Genie, and continued toward Arthur, whom they didn't see because they didn't look up. They were focused on the scullery door of the Juniper home. They knocked, waited, and knocked again. And again, harder and louder. They rattled the handle. Then they called out, announcing themselves as Pinkerton's.

"This is the Pinkertons! Open the door!" And when there

was no response, one of them picked up a rock, prepared to break the window, when Arthur called out.

"Put down that rock 'fore I shoot you!"

The startled man dropped the rock, reached into his waistband, and withdrew a pistol, which he aimed at Arthur although his wobbling hand made it unlikely that even if he fired he'd be unlikely to hit his target.

Then the other man withdrew a pistol from his waistband and aimed at Arthur, but Genie fired her weapon first. She shot the pistol out of the man's hand, taking several of his fingers as well—the second time she'd had such a result from a well-placed shot. He stood frozen until, in the few seconds it took for his brain to register the pain of the lost fingers, he began to howl. When the first man understood what had happened, he turned, saw Genie, and started toward her, pistol raised. Before he took the second step Arthur shot his raised foot, and he crumpled and crashed to the ground, howling in unison with his partner in unrealized crime.

Genie went to the scullery door and called out, "This is Genie Oliver and you're safe now. No, don't open the door. I just want you to know that Arthur and I are here and that you're safe. We don't think there will be more trouble, but we'll be watching just in case. Please keep the doors locked until Maggie and Jack and the children return."

Arthur already had the pistols dropped by the two men, and he stood watching them cry. "What're we gon' do with 'em?" he asked.

Genie shrugged. "Everyone will be back soon, and Ezra and Campbell can decide what they want to do with them. We can watch them from up there, where it's warm."

Newly married and happier than he'd ever been in his life,

Ezra MacKaye entered the front door of the Toronto, Ontario, Canada Regional Office of The Pinkerton Agency, and paused to read the writing on the glass:

EZRA D. MacKAYE,
REGIONAL SUPERINTENDENT

He allowed himself a small smile and strode forward toward a large, glassed-in office that bore the same legend on the door. A man was seated in a leather chair behind a large wooden desk, upon which his large feet in their dirty boots rested. Ezra crossed the room in several steps, knocked the man's feet off the desk, and pulled him upright by his shirtfront.

"Who in bloody hell are you?" the man roared.

"I am Regional Superintendent Ezra MacKaye," Ezra said softly. "Who in bloody hell are you?" he roared back, and watched all the color drain from the man's face. That reaction answered at least one question. Whoever the man was he hadn't expected Ezra to survive the journey to Toronto. Ezra turned to Campbell. "Do you know who he is?"

"Never seen him before," Campbell replied, shaking his head.

"Then bind his hands and put him in a cell—"

"You can't do that!" the man yelled, slapping in vain at Campbell's hands and the length of animal skin he held, until Ezra stepped in to assist.

Suddenly there were at least a dozen people in the office, half women, half men, all of them looking with interest as Ezra and Campbell completed the wrist restraints, disgusted with their prisoner.

"Are you MacKaye?" one of the newcomers asked, and when Ezra replied that he was, they clapped and cheered and welcomed him to Toronto. One by one they introduced themselves and told him what they did, and he told each of them that it would be necessary to tell him again tomorrow because he would not remember so much information vying for space in his mind. What he did need to know immediately was who was on the overnight shift, and the six people who stepped forward said they were.

"Are you able to keep him secured and isolated tonight?"

"If he makes a move or a sound, I'll shoot him myself," said a rotund, balding man.

"If you don't mind, I'd rather have him alive so that I can determine who he is," Ezra said. "But he is to speak with no one, is that clear? Now please show me where he will be held."

When he was satisfied that some semblance of order was restored to the regional office and that he was, in fact, the man in charge, Ezra sat in the chair behind the desk and began opening drawers. He hoped to find information and instructions about tasks facing him in the Toronto, Ontario region. Every drawer was empty.

"He took everything out of the drawers," the balding, rotund man said. "But I know what he did with it."

Ezra stood up and the man backed up a step. "May I know your name, sir?"

"Ronald Fraser, sir. Ronnie, everyone calls me." And a surprised grin lit his face as he shook the hand Ezra extended to him. "Would you like for me to retrieve—"

"And I'd like for you to do it quickly, Mr. Fraser," Ezra said, though Fraser was already out the door. Ezra's smile relaxed the others so he asked another question: "Would there be keys to the drawers in the desk?"

Several of his staff—Ezra now thought of them as such—shrugged, but a couple exchanged a glance and left the room. Ezra looked at those who remained. "I apologize for the upset you have endured the last few days, but please consider order restored. Now, who are the telegraph operators?" And when one woman and one man raised their hands, Ezra asked them to please return to their duties. He shook their hands, and they left smiling. He next asked investigators and agents to identify themselves and all but one woman raised their hands.

"I won't remember your names if you tell me now, but I will learn them soon. In the meantime, please be prepared to update me on your cases tomorrow, and unless you have an assignment tonight, you may leave," and he shook their hands as they departed.

"I'm Louise, your secretary and administrative assistant," said the woman who remained. "That man, whoever he is, told me I was fired—"

"If I didn't fire you, Louise, you're not fired, and I'd be pleased to see you tomorrow morning at nine sharp."

"I'll be here, Superintendent MacKaye." Louise shook his hand and left, just as Ronnie Fraser bustled in, dragging a dusty canvas bag.

"I don't know what all is in here but for certain the contents of your desk drawers are some of it." He dragged the bag around the desk and left it at Ezra's feet.

"My thanks to you, Mr. Fraser, and if you're finished for the day, I'd appreciate seeing you at nine in the morning."

"I'll be here with pleasure, Superintendent." Fraser saluted and left.

Fletcher Campbell started to speak when the two who went in search of the desk keys returned, breathless and disheveled, but triumphant as each held a ring of keys that they dropped into Ezra's outstretched hand. He quickly ascertained that two of the keys opened drawers in the desk. He walked to the office door and discovered that two of the keys fit the locks. He'd worry about the other two later. "Does he need a doctor?" Ezra asked.

The two agents shook their heads, and he was certain both were experienced. "He may need a plaster or two but not a doctor," the woman agent said, and her male colleague nodded his agreement.

"Either of you have anything to report tonight?" And when both shook their heads, Ezra shook their hands and told them to report at nine in the morning, and they left.

"Well done, Superintendent," Fletcher Campbell said with awe and admiration. "Mr. McFadden said I'd learn a lot from you. How right he was. You've done a good day's work—"

"Not yet I haven't, Mr. Campbell," Ezra snapped. "I don't know that man's name or who sent him and his cohorts or why, and I need to know those things." Because he has frightened and endangered my family, Ezra thought, especially those who believed themselves safe once away from Philadelphia. He wished he had time to review every piece of paper the interloper had hidden, but he did not because a woman he'd married a few hours ago was waiting for him in his new home.

Ezra pushed the canvas bag under the desk with his foot and prepared to leave when a man rushed into the office. "I heard you were here, but I had to come see for myself!" It took Ezra a moment to recognize the boatman who had rowed him, Jack, and Arthur from Philadelphia to New York. "You didn't change your mind, did you?"

Ezra shook the man's hand, assured him of his welcome, and told him to introduce himself to Fletcher so that Ezra could hear his name because he didn't remember it. Then he said, as an idea lit his brain, "Please take me home, Mr. Campbell, and take Mr. Harrison with you. And the two of you return here with Jimmy and Earl, and lock them in the cell away from the current prisoner—I don't want them talking to each other."

"You want me to bring criminals to jail before I'm officially assigned to this office?" Harrison stuttered, astounded.

"You wanted to work for me in the Toronto office, didn't you? Well, this is your first assignment and it most likely won't be the last, so get used to it, and the sooner the better."

The heavy Christmas snowfall reminded them all of their last Christmas in Philadelphia, which also reminded them why they were in Toronto, because this year they were all together. Last year they were not because it was too dangerous for Colored people to travel across the city for fear of being captured and sold into slavery. This year Christmas dinner was held in the home of Eugenia Oliver and Abigail Read who could not have lived in the same house as equals in Philadelphia, another reason they were grateful to be away from Philadelphia and America. And earlier this very week another reason presented itself as five days ago the first Southern state withdrew from the United States of America, making real a place called the Confederate States of America where slavery would be not only legal but encouraged. Ezra had not yet told his friends and family, had not even told his beloved wife, that there existed within the Pinkerton organization a cadre of men, perhaps even high-ranking ones, dedicated to the cause of furthering slavery in America. Ezra would dedicate himself to identifying them, exposing them, and costing them their jobs. Today, however, he would dedicate himself to enjoying his first Christmas dinner with his new wife, and with the other people dearest to him. And what a Christmas dinner it was.

At Maggie's suggestion, her cook and Ada's presented themselves at Genie and Abby's so that their cook would not bear the responsibility alone of cooking a feast for ten people. Each woman prepared her best dishes, so the dining table groaned under the weight of a huge, stuffed goose and an equally large ham, along with roasted potatoes and yams, and beans and greens, and many kinds of bread. So many pastries and desserts crowded the sideboard that even Eli and Donnie would find themselves sated.

All the housekeepers also were pressed into service once Abby decided which table linens, china, glassware, silverware, and candelabra to use, so the rooms of the house not only were festive but breathtakingly beautiful. So were the diners as everyone donned their finest for the occasion, and that included Arthur and Donnie who were surprised by the gifts of new clothes for Christmas. The two of them strutted and posed and modeled and enjoyed every bit of attention that came their way. And at a second long and beautifully appointed table in the kitchen the staff ate, drank, and made merry, too, after Genie and Abby told them they would see to anything their guests needed that didn't already exist on the table or the sideboard.

There was more merriment after dinner, with Abby on the piano and Ezra on the violin. Maggie and Jack danced, and Eli and Elizabeth made pitiful attempts, but the singing was impressive and there were several quite good voices, including Abby's lady's maid.

Their enjoyment in and of each other increased as the evening progressed. Not one of them ever doubted the wisdom of leaving Philadelphia, but if pressed to be completely honest, perhaps one or two of their number would have admitted to wondering whether safe passage would truly be theirs. They mourned the death of Henry Weems even as they praised his courage at the moment of his death, and they welcomed Arthur Lee Green. He was part of their family. Three cheers were raised for Maggie Juniper who would begin her job as the teacher at the Harriet Tubman School for Free Colored Children in a week, and for Ezra MacKaye, the new superintendent of the Pinkerton Ontario Regional Office. The biggest cheers, however, were raised for Mr. and Mrs. Ezra MacKaye. Long life, true happiness, and many children (not too many, Ada and Ezra said in unison).

"I didn't get a chance to tell you, did I," Genie said much later that night, "how much I finally felt at home here after my walk this morning. Everyone I met smiled and said Happy Christmas. A few even confessed that they sometimes stood on the porch and listened to you play the piano, and they complimented your prowess."

"I wonder if Ezra and I had an audience tonight?" a sleepy Abby said.

"I wouldn't be at all surprised. You were wonderful. And did you know that Maggie and Jack could dance like that? What a magnificent couple they are." Then Genie sobered and added, "I just hope they teach their children how to dance sooner rather than later."

Abby stifled a giggle and said that she and Maggie had learned ballroom dancing as children and that Maggie no doubt taught Jack. "But he really is quite graceful for such a big man."

"This was my best Christmas ever, Abigail, and I thank you for it," Genie said. After a moment, she asked, "Do you think women will ever be able to marry? Each other, I mean?"

Abby snapped fully awake and sat up. "Not as long as men walk the earth."

"Perhaps the time will come when most men will be like Jack and Ezra and Arthur and Donnie. And Eli."

"I'm glad you're so hopeful, Eugenia," Abby said as she drifted back into sleep, "but I won't be holding my breath in anticipation of that day."

ACKNOWLEDGMENTS

To the women of Bywater Books—founder, publisher, editors, copy editors, proofreaders, and cover designer: you expend and extend unwavering time, energy, support, and love to those of us who call the House of Bywater our writing home—thank you! You're simply the best. And to the incomparable women who share this writing home with me—thank you for keeping the lights burning brightly so that I always arrive home safely.

ABOUT THE AUTHOR

Penny Mickelbury is a trailblazing author and an award-winning playwright. She is a two-time Lambda Literary Award finalist, was a writer in residence at Hedgebrook Women Writers Retreat, and is a recipient of the Audre Lorde Estate Grant. Before focusing on literary pursuits, Penny was a pioneering newspaper, radio, and television reporter based primarily in Washington, D.C., wrote journalistic nonfiction and was a frequent contributor to such publications as *Black Issues Book Review*, Africana.com, and the *Washington Blade*. In 2019 she joined the other members of the *Washington Post's* Metro Seven as an inductee into the National Association of Black Journalists Hall of Fame. After an almost 25-year sojourn in Los Angeles, Penny recently returned to her Atlanta hometown.

A NOTE ON THE TYPE

This book is set in Adobe Caslon Pro. William Caslon was an English gunsmith and designer of typefaces. In 1722 he created an extended set of serif typefaces that were based on seventeenth-century Dutch old style designs. Because of their remarkable practicality, Caslon's typefaces met with instant success. These, as well as all of their consecutive revivals, are referred to as Caslon. Among those revivals are two Adobe versions, called Adobe Caslon (1990) and Adobe Caslon Pro, which includes an extended character set.